SOUTHSIDE
RUDY
YID

A Novel

By

MORRY FRANK

SILVERBACK
BOOKS II

First Printing June 1998
Second Printing November 1999

Library of Congress Catalog Card Number 97-66863

ACKNOWLEDGEMENT

Sweet Dreams written by Don Gibson
Used by Permission of Acuff-Rose Music, Inc.
© Copyright 1955, Renewed 1983
All Rights Reserved.

Published by

silberback books

*117 W. Harrison Building
Suite S-199
Chicago, Illinois 60605*

ISBN 0-9640912-0-8

Printed in U.S.A.

SOUTHSIDE
RUDY
YID

*... his dark story from the
rail mill to Lankershim Blvd.*

The following events, characters, and names are either made-up or are used fictitiously. Any resemblance to actual incidents, persons, or names is coincidental.

In this book the author uses Yiddish words and terms that are spelled the way he remembers them being spoken.

MARCH 1984

He came to Chicago with a shirt and a sandwich. At Calumet Rail a desolate mill by the old Pennsylvania tracks they see in him a tongue-tied boy used to hard work so they assign him to the hot side of the rail mill, a place that has gotten a name for malingering.

On the hot side six ton ingots rumble over tracks, being lengthened and shaved to scale. They come to the end of the line shaped like rails but red hot and sloped on the end. Behemoth saws descend cutting off butts up to six feet long. Out on the cast-iron catwalk, workers called buttpullers stand back as sparks fly, then move in with steel tongs. They pince the butt ends on the sloped nose, drag them out over steel slabs to a narrow ramp and shove them off into railcar buggies a few feet below.

A buttpuller works thirty minutes on then gets sixty off. You have to have a grip and be able to work in a hundred and forty degree heat and not wobble. The steel slabs and catwalk are hosed down and your step is to be steady not to slip from the ramp, down onto the cuts below. Getting burned by fire is one thing and by red steel another. The skin splits back to the bone.

CHAPTER 2

The night foreman puts on gloves and goggles and pulls a few butts to show him how. He hands him the tongs and goes back to the office. It isn't much training but you have the makings of a buttpuller or you don't and you find out in the first turn. If rails back up on you or your legs give out, they hand you a long shovel and send you to the slag pits for five dollars an hour. You don't get a second chance and not many ask.

The newhire steps back as rails rumble in, blades rip down and sparks fly out the breezeway. He hurries in over the slabs up the ramp to the line. Wincing from the glow, he hooks onto the cut and pulls it off dragging it out behind him. Onto the narrow bridge, he pushes it off the ramp down into the buggy below.

Overhead in an air-conditioned cubicle a wheelwright named Jasper sits with the saw operator. Watching the newhire turn his face from the rail reminds him years back of a runaway he'd come upon huddled in a railcar in Ft. Wayne's yards. The boy had twisted his head away like that.

He lowers his haunch down a set of rungs, shuffles across the catwalk on a stiff leg and leans back on a ramp rail so that the newhire coming on with the next butt has to swerve it around his feet. He nods to the wheelwright, getting back a stare still on him when he brings out the next cut. This slope-shouldered man with a split lower lip and low slung jaw is there to watch, he wonders, or might be tetched. In Eddyville a man who looked like him and just as big used to pin on a tin badge, get on an old bike and pedal up and down the street all day.

Dragging out the next cut, he loses grip and the butt hooks across a wet slab toward a bench the stampers use. If there, their shins would be barked and burned. The newhire hurries over, hooks onto the butt and pulls backwards, brushing by the

2

wheelwright as sparks fly from the next cut.

Up on a tar paper pavilion across the track, Stamper Eddie plugs in his coffee pot. As the A&P blend brews, he gazes down over the balustrade, shadowed to one side. A vinegary little man, he has been a spy for management for a long time but now that the mill is dying and will close any day, he's become a slacker like the rest. But he will turn on you so railmillers check with him before trying to pull something. Not much is lost on him anyway which is why he looks down on the newhire with the stare of a one-eyed weasel. Jasper limps up the curved ramp to the pavilion and sidles up, his muscular tongue swishing his chew.

The slag is falling good now, the saws cutting at six feet and two hundred pounds. The newhire is losing his grip and pulling backwards with two hands. Jasper nudges Eddie and asks if the rump on the new boy "don't look good for a rippin'?" Eddie a man of damn few words examines the wheelwright's gaze for fakery then says what he used to back in the chow line in the old brownshoe army when the cook fried him up an egg to top his johnnycake. "Bust the eye!"

Eddie picks up and leaves with his pot, and Jasper approaches two black slackers, saying he's going to bunghole the newhire below and if they want to join in to be his guests. To show he means it he unbuttons his trap, pulls out a strong-looking member for a fifty-year-old man and slaps it against a pole. The two slackers eye each other.

Half hidden in a corner near a torn tarp sits Southside Rudy Yid who watches this vulgarity with the narrow gaze of a pool hall loiterer. It is a sly look but how sly can you be if you've been a buttpuller for ten years. Down below the newhire's grip is failing, the strain too much on his young hand. He shoves aside five or six butts cutting the night air through the breezeway and stops at the cooler to gulp water after every pull. With twenty minutes to go he isn't going to make it.

Jasper reappears at the ramp, muscles in his jaws like knots and eyes like stones. The newhire brings the next butt, eyes

3

batting. Jasper grins to himself. He might not even put up a fight. Just tell him to get back behind the scale piles, swab him up with blue glaze and bore up in him where he's moist and tight. He feels himself with a rough hand oblivious of the glare from the red cuts in the buggy below. It casts his face as yellow as his teeth, and the smears on his overalls as though he's come up from the fields with manure on him.

Rudy Yid comes down the catwalk to the ramp, leaning back on a rail opposite Jasper who wonders what he's up to. If he's the newhire's relief he's early and no buttpullers relieve early. As the newhire guides a butt between them his dazzled eyes look to Rudy Yid who makes no move to help, giving Jasper the idea he's there to horn in. Just three feet between them Jasper angers at the proximity. As he feels he has to say something, he has a thought. He doesn't want to go it alone anyway. In the right role two enemies take part better than old kicks just to prove themselves. Jasper's yellowed eyes fall on Rudy Yid.

"Are you a connoisseur?"

Rudy Yid coughs up a gob of phlegm that a touch of steel mill pleurisy makes ready, rolls it round and spits full in Jasper's face.

Jasper staggers, throwing his hands up in fear of his left hook. Snapping slime from lip and chin, he backs away, pointing, "Now I'm gonna sue."

He hops down to the gravel, hobbling to the office. The night foreman takes his report but wants nothing to do with it, leaving it on the desk for Monday morning.

Rudy Yid finishes the newhire's shift, does his own and goes to the canteen for a cold drink. It is two in the morning and the white stone floor has been mopped with disinfectant. Heavy black women behind the counter eye each man walking in on it. He goes to a soda machine. A group of white operators are at a table with lunch pails and coffee. Seeing Rudy Yid one slaps down his mug.

"A man spit on me," he nods, "he better finish the job. *Kill* me, Jack, or I'll keep comin'."

"Believe it" says another slouched with a toothpick. "Two lowest things you can do: spit a man's face and steal his lunch. Joker stole my birthday poke. Ol' lady packed Polish ham on rye, sweet banana peppers, and berries and cream. I hope the cocksucker chokes."

An hour later some of the same stand on the gravel in front of the washhouse trying to get up a crew. Rudy Yid comes out of the breezeway with a short, hundred-pound butt. Yanking up on the nose so it glides, he slings it two-handed over the rail. The butt whirls end over end smacking into the latrine wall, scattering the instigators. Two run off and two run into the latrine and look out the louver.

Rudy Yid hitches up his pants: skulking buffoons and sexual deviates, and the heroes made of them in movies and storybooks: strongbacked plaintalking men hammering steel by the sweat of their brow so the sons of their loins will have it better, as if there was no janitorial work around town that those longhaired uneducated bastards couldn't get.

Five years earlier in 1979, ABC came to the rail mill to shoot a movie about two-fisted steelmen fighting to save their jobs and way of life from an Arab buyout. It starred Emmy winner Edner Bus as chunky old steeler Billy Jinko who could still outwork outdrink and outdream anybody there including union and management.

On the first day they brought Edner Bus to a scale pile and put a big camera on him as a hundred movie hands stood back, some of them very attractive young women. Charley Polite an old hand at scale digging was brought over from the pits to show Edner how. He demonstrated with knees bent, arms in, letting his legs and hips snap up most of the thrust.

According to the newspaper Edner Bus claimed to have been a steelhog in younger days. He looked impatient as though he knew what was being shown. When he got his hands on the shovel he attacked the pile like a lunatic, forgetting to keep his elbows in. Slag flew like birdshot and movie hands ran for cover with clipboards over their heads, yelling "*Stop, stop him!*" He was seized from behind and bore half-crazed toward the director who gasped, "My Gawd, he's aflame — he'll keel!" Two lackeys dove under his haunch breaking his fall on their backs. Struggling free they helped stretch him out flat and cool his head and neck with ice packs. When that didn't bring him to and he kept blabbering, they pulled down his trousers, spread his thick thighs strapped by a blue thong and ensconced an ice pack under his scrotum until his testicles popped out like leather bongo balls. Rolling his eyes Edner let out yips like from a fife then lowed as if in a pasture.

He was back on his feet for lunch which was served for the mill on portable tables with red cloth. Instead of sitting with movie people, Edner pushed back his hardhat and hunkered down with old steelhogs chomping bratwurst and cold sauerkraut, his beady eyes shifting side to side to help pass mustard and pickles. You couldn't tell him from the others. Shunning bread and potato salad, he had seven or eight swollen sausages which burst in his teeth. When one old guy cracked wise that he could still ride hump and his *ol' lady* underneath squeaks like an oil can, Edner's mouth stayed up in a grin as if he enjoyed hell out of the remark.

After lunch the ABC crew filmed in the rail mill office, and the hot side started up. At three o'clock Rudy Yid went to take an early shower after his last turn. Black George the old washhouse attendant sat head bowed and legs crossed as heavy bursts came from a stall. Coming up Rudy Yid peeked around at Edner Bus on a commode, temples strained and neck bulled as his farts pounded like artillery. Black George puffed on a cigarette with a slack jaw, muttering "Mercy, have mercy."

The movie was shown six months later on a Wednesday night in October, and Rudy Yid sat watching as Edner Bus playing Billy Jinko rallies his crew in a last-ditch effort to save the mill, working thirty hours without stop, running a record number of rails and holding off the buyout for six months. That done Billy Jinko and his men burst into a black-tie affair downtown, collar the anglo steel executive who tried to sell them out and dunk his head into a giant punch bowl. Then Billy Jinko hoists the bowl in his arms, lets out a scream and dumps it on his own head while Tommy Varga playing a Hispanic firebrand against Billy Jinko at first now stands by him like a son.

After that Rudy Yid lost all respect for movies and wondered how they got that idea. The real owners were two invalid Jewish brothers who lived alone in a high-rise on Lake Shore Drive, had been losing money for years, were Negro phobic and afraid of even stepping into the mill for fear of being assassinated.

CHAPTER 3

He finishes his second turn at three-thirty but his relief hasn't come. The mill is down, the ingots stopped. He goes to a brick hovel at the end of the catwalk where black buttpullers sit in the night eating fried chicken and throwing the bones on the floor. He pulls open the door and the stink rears his head. There is no light but he makes out five or six.

"Where's Lucket?"

"Lucket's not here, close the door."

He keeps looking.

"He's not here; close the *goddam* door."

He goes up the catwalk and sees Lucket by the washhouse with a broom laborer, one of two who move the dust around.

"*Hey*, get up here. You're late."

Lucket comes around the catwalk singing in contralto. He's stocky with a goatee.

"You're seven minutes late."

"What's it matter? The mill's down."

"It's down, it's going, you gotta be on time."

"I didn't know I was late."

"I just called; you kept talking to that broom pusher."

"Why I gotta jump for you?"

"Because I'm here ten years and you're not here a month. You come late again I'll be waiting for Ozohan in the morning and personally get you fired. It'll be my pleasure. You left some butts here last week I had to clean up."

Lucket's brown lips twitch between his whiskers. "Be like that. Snake me for seven minutes."

"When the old Polacks were here seven seconds was late."

"That's the old world. Those old dudes knew one polka one pull one pair long drawers for fifty years."

"Come late again it'll be your last time."

He heads to the washhouse as Lucket goes into the hovel telling the other blacks he's been confronted. Stepping back out with two of them, he yells "*Punk!*" at the top of his lungs.

In the washhouse Rudy Yid lifts the base of his locker, slipping a hand underneath to the cement. He pulls out a short boning knife rolled up in oilcloth, slipping it into a side pocket of his asbestos jacket.

The mill stays down and he sleeps in the washhouse on a stone bench, sitting up at seven in the morning. A chill in his spine he takes off his shirt to clean up.

He gets back to his room at eight-thirty, sleeps a few Sunday morning hours then gets up at noon and drives to the North Side.

In a park there near the lake, the Chicago Communist League is on one side, a hundred strong including women. Across the grass stand twenty of the Jewish Wall. Both sides await a group of Nazis who are late.

Passing time the communists berate the Jewish Wall as sick Jews. Five Chicago police stand between them. Another ten are up on the sidewalk holding back spectators, many of them getting out of the church across the street. News crews arrive and line up with the communists as Jewish Wall members are pointed out to cameramen and ridiculed. Rudy Yid appeals to Jewish Wall boss Marv Lazzar, a big Jew in a white shirt. "What are we waiting for? Let's get some blood on our hands."

Lazzar smokes a cigarette down to his nails and stomps it out. "They're for another time."

The Nazis come out from behind a library, no more than ten and none alike: lean and squat, peaked and bald, poker faced and jut-jawed. A chubby boy in an emerald shirt looks like an older brother dressed him in a chestbelt and swastikas. On the Nazis' flank two in plaid shirts and cowboy boots look like paid bodyguards.

The Nazi leader in brown brilliantine no sooner steps to the fore when communists hooting like strikers swarm past the police. Three Nazis break and run but the rest are trapped. The Nazi boy is flung down by his chestbelt and kicked and stomped until blood spatters from his nose and mouth.

Rudy Yid steps around Marv Lazzar and calls for the Jewish Wall to follow but none move more than an inch, so he goes himself. Coming up from behind he hits one communist back of the skull sending him lurching long-legged through his friends, then slings in shots from both hands clearing five feet from the Nazi boy who crawls between his legs and grabs on as a squad of Chicago police charge with visors and sticks. Kicking free of the boy's hold he flees. Ahead, near trees, neighborhood vigilantes move to cut him off. Turning he sees a narrow-shouldered policeman running up on stiff legs, a pained pinched face behind the visor. He cuts toward him cocking a fist. The policeman skids to a halt, swinging the club twohanded eyes closed. Coming in on the breeze he slams a forearm up under his visor and tramples him underfoot. In the clear he runs by a crouched snarling cameraman whom he'd bowl over and heel had he an extra minute. He escapes down the street dodging moving vehicles.

After dark on a North Side street bordering Evanston, he stands on a walk between a lean-to and a bowling alley. He is

pale from a light above. His nose to a security screen he asks
Marv Lazzar to take him back. Lazzar's white sleeves are
rolled up. Behind him his stocky redheaded wife and another
Jewish Wall member sit at a table with submarine sandwiches.
"It's not up to me" he says.

He drives back across town in time for the news and gets a
look at himself driving back the communists and then switches
channels and sees himself trample the cop and flee the camera.

That night as the wind shakes the windowsills he decides
not to go to work in the morning. There is a rail mill
expression: If they're waiting for you, skip a day or two.

He gets up early anyway and goes out to find a body-and-
fender man who owes him an eighty dollar refund. At six that
night he walks into Roth's with half the money and gets the
usual at the counter: three slices of brisket, coleslaw, and a
shot of V.O. in a paper cup. Howard Broitman is in a booth by
the wall. The last time he sat with him, Howard ignored him,
joking with employees and reading the police blotter in the
South Side News. Howard comes weeknights from work,
hurries through the blue-plate special cutting small squares of
meat and smelling each one, then wipes the table clean and
rolls up his sleeves for what he likes: kibitzing and coffee.
Looking up he sees Rudy Yid at the counter.

"Hey, you were on the news last night. They showed you
with the Nazis. What happened?"

Rudy Yid goes to a table aside the booth. "What'd you
see?"

"You were getting pounded in a fight and a fat little Nazi
crawled between your legs."

"They say I was a Nazi?" he asks, rolling a sliver of pickle
in a slice of meat.

"That's the idea you'd get. What happened?"

"The communists jumped a Nazi kid so I ran over."

"Where was the JW?"

"Standing there watching."

"Can you blame 'em? Helping a Nazi. How'd that get into your head? What'd Marv Lazzar say?"

"He said they don't want me back."

"Don't want you back!" Howard slavers and wipes his mouth. "Bad as they need help! When they get on the news at night I pull the covers over my head and cringe."

"I don't care what they look like," says Rudy Yid, "but they don't wanna do nothin'. We had the chance, those commie whores calling us sick Jews. I said 'Marv, let's get some blood on our hands,' but he says they're for another time. How many times are there gonna be?"

"Where were the Nazis?"

"Behind the library. You should have seen 'em line up — like somebody ate 'em up and shit 'em out."

"You expect those guys to look like Thor? Worms like that started the Nazis."

"Yea, but you want *somebody* to beat up."

"You know who's here? Neckman."

"Neckman's back?"

"He's stopping in. They're gonna commit old Neckman."

"For what?"

"He's spitting everywhere, turning his food over and calling Neckman's mother a whore."

"He was always like that, wasn't he?"

"Not like this. His mother has a lock on the bedroom and says either he takes a shit or she has a coronary. Neckman says if it's him or her, it's gonna be him."

"What'd he say about Hollywood?"

"I asked him if he was flying with the stars out there and he said all he did was write."

"Write what? You ever see anything with his name on it? The gantze deal about that eight-minute movie. Film student *genius* at Chicago Circle. What was so genius about it?

Neckman, the disbeliever, bouncing down Michigan Avenue on a pogo stick and everybody looking at him like he's crazy. And the simcha at the temple: Jules Neckman off to Hollywood, the next Otto Preminger; the sisterhood's crying and the Rabbi's up there beaming like just think we bar-mitzvahed this shmuck; and the shtarkers in front in Fish Johnson suits all laughing it up. If they wanted a laugh they should have filmed Neckman walking down the street on his toes — the only American guy alive who never wore out a pair of heels."

"He was a toewalker. So were Julie Sobol and Harvey Bornstein."

"Not like Neckman. Neckman pushed off on the last two like a fruit. You ever see him with his shoe off? That foot was perfectly white, unused. Not a rub or a crease but those last two toes were curled and swollen blue, pissed off at somebody. He could have torn off a nose with those two toes."

He has another thought. "At least he didn't come back famous. Can you imagine what he'd be like? The way he used to turn his back and leave you standing there talking into thin air."

"He never did it to me."

"You were his dog; he spared you that."

"He never spared anybody anything. Like he said that night. 'Here we sit in temple to send me off to make movies which will be of my intent to question your faith in any house of God.' "

"If I was the rabbi I'd have kicked his ass. If the old Rebbe was there he'd have caught one upside his fuckin' head. I saw the old Rebbe slap him once. Tall lanky fuck. Starts crying, 'No more, man! No more!' Called the Rebbe *man*."

"You caught one too for laughing."

"He wasn't serious with me. He hated Neckman like rat shit. He hated the whole family. When they ate fish they started with the head."

Howard goes to the counter for more coffee coming back when the Greek who bought the delicatessen from the Roths doesn't have time for him. Rudy Yid finishes the brisket and coleslaw.

"So what's with the shlongs?" asks Howard tapping a sugar packet.

"I got more problems than shlongs. I spit in a wheelwright's face."

"For what?"

"A kid hired on from downstate and this wheelwright goes to the niggers and says he wants to bone him."

"They talk like that. I spent a summer in the wheelmill. It's their way of putting up with the place."

"Were you there?" asks Rudy Yid. "Did you see it? He pulls out a dick like a horse and slaps it against a pole. It scared me to look at it."

"Right there in the mill he wanted to bone him."

"Yea, right there. Who's gonna stop him, those old dicks at the gate? Just get him out back behind the slag piles and rip him off. Then he asks me if I was a connoisseur, like I wanted to join in."

"He's white?" asks Howard.

"Yea he's white."

"I didn't think white guys did that."

"You're very naive. They call 'em sodomites. There was a whole city of 'em once."

A long-limbed character in a long blue coat and cowl comes in. Glowering he turns to inspect the delicatessen case.

"That him?" asks Rudy Yid.

"Yea."

"You'd think he'd come say hello."

A Mexican counter boy scoops chopped liver onto a blue plate, spreads crackers round it like playing cards and puts an olive and raw onion ring on top. On the way over Neckman bites into a cracker with a dab of liver, swirls it in his mouth

13

and stops in front of his old schoolmates.

"*M-m-m.* I get home last night, ten years gone, and who's brawling on TV but Rudy Yid. You with the Nazis now?"

"No, the JW."

Neckman slides into the booth, throwing back his cowl. His black hair is flecked now.

Howard leans over. "The commies are pounding a Nazi fuck, and who runs to help but this shmuck."

"He was eleven or twelve" says Rudy Yid. "They broke his nose."

"What did you care if they broke his whole head?" asks Neckman.

"I'm not standing there while grown men stomp a kid. Especially not those whores, those ingrate traitors."

"Most of those guys look Jewish" says Howard. "That's a shonda striking another Jew."

"I never liked beating up Jewish guys. They bleed too much."

"I always said," intones Neckman, "if Rudy Yid wasn't a Jew he'd hate Jews."

"Yea, I'm an anti-Semite, Neckman. A hundred in my family murdered by Nazis. My one uncle fell in Palestine and another shot it out in the Warsaw ghetto, Jew courage if there ever was any. Where were the Neckmans then — picking their lice and sores in a rag yard on Roosevelt Road?"

Neckman snaps down another cracker. "Well we're not real Neckmans. We were the greenhorn cousins they sent to Stoney Island to move the shit they couldn't sell themselves. But yea, the old Neckmans were ragpickers. How'd Seth Jokko put it — and leave it to a Southside hack with a comp camelhair and lawn dinette to put grubbery to song and cover himself with a few barbs between. What'd he write: 'The both of them four and a half foot tall, shivering over pennies in a clapped-out kiosk . . . four sons brought in labor and to labor set to, growing stooped from work and *shtupped* with gelt . . . taking

14

Americanized Jewish brides, and becoming Chicago's clothiers and outleteers, and Sundays in Skokie at neighbor Sol's . . . SELs parked to the corner for this gathering of seasoned heads, shining collegiates and precocious children, while in the kitchen swathed in charcoal gray, nibbling powdered cookies from old worn fingers, sit the two progenitors nearly turned away from our shore. And gather from a glance that this gnarled little *Zayda* and *Bubbeh* brought forth a shining American dynasty of business heads, respected professionals and leaders in Chicago's future.' "

"He forgot whores and thieves" says Rudy Yid. "Your uncle Bernie is a thief and a prostitute."

Neckman nods, "He stole your mother's chest, right?"

Rudy Yid turns to Howard, "My mother puts a chest with silver and gold thread in their store, the only thing she ever had and when she calls a few months later, they tell her there was a flood and it got waterlogged and thrown out and don't owe her a penny."

"The consignment contract bears no responsibility" says Neckman. "Not to reimburse, not even a phone call to report damage."

"There was no damage. Your uncle Bernie, a furniture truck should back over him tonight, saw a woman who couldn't defend herself and took it himself. It's those little filches a born whore can't resist."

"My uncle Bernie wiped his ass with your mother's complaint. He's president of Uptown Merchants and the Chicago Association voted him Chicago's Leading Jew."

"Leading Jew. He's eaten more pork than he weighs."

"So. A pig's a clean animal."

"Yea, it eats shit from the ground."

"You're mad because we didn't buy Kosher meat at the dirty little store your father had on Kedzie." He nods to Howard. "You ever see his old man cut meat? He used to stop every five minutes to put a finger to one side of his nose and

15

blow on the floor with the other. The only reason you had any customers at all is that the block was full of dirty little refugees who didn't take a bath all winter and drank fish oil to keep the lice from eating them alive."

Rudy Yid says nothing.

"No reply?" asks Neckman.

"What can I tell you?"

Neckman runs the last cracker in circles cleaning up smudges and snatches it in his teeth. "Yea," he smacks, "Rudy Yid, Rudy Valentino Yid, *Southside* Rudy Yid. Why'd they call you that? Not the Jewish guys, the goys."

"It wasn't 'cause of my dick. I must have done something to impress 'em."

"You're not even six feet, are you?"

Rudy Yid shakes his head.

"And what do you weigh?"

"Two hundred."

"You're not two hundred."

Rudy Yid puts two twenties on the table. "You got a big mouth, bet."

Howard warns Neckman off. "He's over two hundred. We went back to the scale at Hi-Lo."

Neckman weighs him up. "Where do you put two hundred pounds? You don't look a buck eighty." He flicks his napkin aside. "It don't matter. Those gym guys in California would make you look like nothing."

"It's not all in the looks."

Neckman nods, "Aha, aha. More than one shagatz had to stay home from school a few days after you got through with him."

"I don't know. I was never the attendance monitor."

Neckman runs his tongue to one side and smirks out some liver between his teeth. "A head full of shit and a smart mouth. I could never figure it. I remember at the Tri-State tourney

16

somebody pointed you out to the Gold brothers of South Bend Scrap and they said '*That's* Rudy Yid?' "

"They just looked like two big zhlups to me. I wasn't scared."

Neckman presses his fingertips together over his empty plate. "Oh, they would have kicked your ass real good. They had kneecaps as thick as your skull and you wouldn't have been Big Rudy Yid in school either if blacks were swarming the halls, stepping on everybody's heels."

"Is that so? I seen a lot of niggers do the sidestroke. You ain't seen the sidestroke until you see a nigger do it."

Howard nudges Neckman. "Tell us about Hollywood, what you were doing."

"Nothing. I failed."

"You what?"

"I failed. I optioned one script in ten years. My writing's not what they want."

"What do they want?"

Neckman leans back. "Phoney baloney and hooey booey, Howie. I don't write that shit. I read the Russians: Pushkin, Peshkov, Nabokov. I read *Lolita* thirteen times. Give me one line, I give you the next. I wrote scripts with dialogue like from *Lawrence of Arabia*. Matters were unfurled, truths told and choices made. They knew me. They knew who I was. They said we respect you, man, but who's gonna get this. I said throw me a scrap then: a rewrite, an adaptation, something to keep my head up. You throw thousands into scripts for national embarrassments like Schwarzenegger and Stallone. Throw me a goddamn crumb."

"They wouldn't do it?" asks Howard.

"Those are the real Nazis" nods Neckman. "The Nazis could have learned from those whores. Those prostitutes could watch a man die of thirst with their hands on the spigot."

"Why not swallow your pride and write some phoney baloney yourself?"

Neckman's voice softens. "Not everyone can, Howie. To do it right you have to believe what you're writing: the sweat, the guns, explosions and erections. You see, when the downtrodden look up from the dust, you've got to believe that big shmuck coming over the rise with blazing guns, muscular tits and a long dick is you."

"Stallone believes that?"

"From what I hear he's the type of grown idiot who'd pretend he's on a horse and shag you through the woods . . . but in simple minds lies simple genius."

"Stallone a genius, c'mon" says Howard.

"You heard me. Stallone plucked two thorns up white America's ass: losing Vietnam to little slanteyed people and national manhood to big black ones, and he rose up, cleaned house and gave the all's-clear; and your typical American closet homo runs out of the theater yelling we won. Everybody knows this is the stupidest populace on earth with the largest per capita of morons."

"How about South America and Argentina?" asks Howard.

"Oh yea" nods Neckman. "There's lots of morons down there. But we have obligatory education."

"So what're you gonna do?" asks Howard.

"I'll have to find a way to make money, won't I? Nothing more pitiful than a failed Jewish artist. Remember those cantors who used to come in from New York and go store to store showing yellowed clippings and asking for cab fare to the temple, like that's where they were going? That won't happen to me. I played the part long enough, going around studios with rolled-up trades, loitering in commissaries with the wags — so-called friends who'd rather starve than see you get a gig — then disappearing from the face of the earth on Saturdays and Sundays in a furniture warehouse in Cudahy and driving back at six in the morning with my eyes sticking out of my head and my hemorrhoids on fire from walking those aisles all night. No. It was time to look it all in the eye.

I just wish I'd done it five years sooner."

"But movies were your life" says Howard. "It's all you talked about."

"Finis, kaput, farkockt. I draw the line; that's it. I quit cigarettes five years ago, not one since. My little interest in movies now is in trends they set, the entrepreneurial orb. Everything I think about now is in terms of product and market, this chopped liver even."

"What kind of market you going into?" asks Howard.

"Beauty fads and sexual aids. It's huge in L.A. The town is a dichotomy. The movie business a closed bordello, a slammed gate. Once a year a new whore slips in. But the rest of L.A. is an awakening. Come call. Bring your own: a topic, a shortcut, something lighter brighter. They'll try anything and their first priority is body appeal. Find something unique, pass it around, let them get a whiff, then go hide and they find you — so unlike your typical Chicago miser sleeping under three blankets with his Talman passbook snapped to his balls with a rubberband. People in L.A. want to be sold."

"They're gullible?"

"They're suggestible. On the look. Who to be, what to be. Everything hyped anew in the sun. It makes me sick to be back here. I got off the plane, the humidity hit my face like wet stink. Just what they call a newspaper here brought nausea up in my throat. I wanted to brech. And all the halitosis and acne all over again."

"How long you gonna be?" asks Howard.

"Who knows, four, five months. The house is too big now. The store's for sale. Big Sid had side businesses with partners. We think he buried money. I've got to find out before he goes. The first thing mental workers do is ply old Jews about what they got stashed. And the tsuris now, she won't make any decisions. She's lost. She used to take a dress back to Weinstock after a year, and that's Jew against Jew. Now it's 'What'll I do? Where'll I go?' I said do what you want. Go to

19

Florida. Sit with your sister and make friends. She says friends are jealous and a husband is truer than a sister."

"Maybe she wants to go to California with you" says Howard.

"First I'd cut my vocal cords and eviscerate myself."

"She's driving you crazy?" asks Howard.

"Oh she was waiting" says Neckman. "I step into the house and it has a glow like it never had when Sid was there. I sit down to eat and she's standing back and asks how's the salad. I said fine; and she leans into the light and says, 'You wanna see cuts on my hands from making it?' "

"Not as bad as mine" says Howard. "I asked her once if there was a day in her life — just one single day when she felt good, and she said *never*. And the water she pours out from spaghetti, she says that's soup in other countries."

Neckman tires of him in favor of Rudy Yid. "Your mother passed?"

"Yea."

"Big Shmuel went to Israel."

"Yea."

"He have Alzheimer's, too?"

"No, he was just nuts."

"What's he doing?"

"He stays with a sister; on her poor bones. Every month he sends me the same letter. Before I go to sleep I want to see you and a girl under the chupa."

Neckman winces. "Rudy Yid married. I can't picture that. You wanna get married?"

"I don't want to wind up an old bachelor."

"You don't?"

"No. Last week I'm in Goldblatt's and old Friedman says to some old lady, 'See that boy. He's thirty years old and ain't got nothin' in his pants.' "

"What kind of girl you looking for?"

"A Jewish girl. She don't have to be a beauty."

"What could you get now — a divorcee maybe."

"I ain't marrying a divorcee. I'll marry a Mexican before a divorcee."

"Where do you work?"

"Calumet Rail."

"You were in a mill when I left. Can't you work your way to manager of a grocery?"

"It's not that bad. Eighty a day and for every half hour you work you get an hour off but you gotta work with shlongs. The place is all shlong now."

"So?"

"*So?* They're lazy. They're always late. They don't wanna work. It gets over a hundred and forty. You pull butts for thirty minutes and look for the niggers and they're not there. Then they show up like they're doing you a favor."

"They're all like that?"

"Enough."

"Why don't you go to the office?"

"They already gave Ozohan one heart attack. He's done me favors. I'm not gonna go crying to him now."

"He's gonna get jumped," Howard says to Neckman. "Like they jumped Joey Week's uncle. You hear about that?"

"No."

"They were waiting for him in the washhouse. Thirteen of 'em hitting him with bolts inside gunnysacks. He had a thick head to begin with. You should have seen. His nose was cracked in half and his jaw off the hinges, one eye looking out the side. His whole head was ripped loose like divots."

"You see it?" Neckman asks Rudy Yid.

"I saw pictures in the office."

"Why'd they jump him?"

"He's a foreman and the shlongs knew he hated 'em."

"You heard they killed Maishe Bik?" Howard asks

Neckman.

"Who doesn't know that?"

"Makes it through the camps, his whole family gone. Comes here and takes fix-it jobs, half the time he don't even know what he's doing. Finally he's fifty he opens a store and shlongs kill him."

"What were they, kids?" asks Neckman.

"Grown shlongs" says Howard. "They came into the store fucking around and he tells 'em to leave and gets out a .22 he must have paid five or ten bucks for."

"Was it real?"

"It was real. It didn't look real. I don't know," says Howard. "As soon as he walks up a shlong steps behind him and *pow!* They didn't even run. They knew they were gonna get away with it. The police came and Maishe's wife runs up, 'Shoot, shoot them. They killed my husband. What are you waiting for?' They looked at her like she was crazy."

Howard takes a breath. "She's still there. People tell her, 'You're crazy. They'll kill you too,' but she says, 'I have no choice. I have to make something of my children.' "

Neckman shakes his head. "Jew grit. And everybody thinks it's the men. Well, he should have never brought out that gun. What did he expect those black guys to do?"

Rudy Yid speaks up. "They knew he was harmless. They saw a chance to kill a little Jew and took it. They laughed at him on the ground."

"How were they to know Maishe Bik was some innocuous little Jew trying to bluff them out?" says Neckman. "Grow up like they do and see if you stand there picking your teeth when a guy comes at you with a gun, and if Maishe Bik didn't mean it, why was the gun real? Why wasn't it fake? Why would they just shoot him?"

"'Cause they're shlongs" says Howard. "If it wasn't for whites they'd still be shitting in trees and wiping their ass with leaves."

"And Jews never shot anybody?" asks Neckman.

"Not like that" says Rudy Yid. "If a Jew shot somebody in the head, who'd ever speak to him again. People would spit on the ground. Like Ricky Skirbo said. They got no papers and they got no neshuma."

"But they do have big shlongs. I bet you see that a lot in the washhouse."

"Yea, I'm jealous. I'd be ashamed in the face of God. It looks like a small animal attached to a bigger one."

"With your attitude," says Neckman, "you're gonna be next, and I hope they're big and black."

"There's gonna be a bloodbath" says Rudy Yid.

"Show him the balabuss" says Howard.

Rudy Yid leans over to block Neckman's way out. Pushing the plates back, he takes a gun from under his jacket, pulls back the slide and lays it on the table.

"Check that individual" says Howard.

The whites of Neckman's eyes dance. "Take that thing away. I don't like that."

"Pick it up" nods Rudy Yid. "It's not cocked."

"Bullshit, it's not cocked. Take it, man. I mean it. I'll go over the fucking table."

Rudy Yid reaches over and twirls the gun on the tabletop. It clatters like a train on old tracks. Howard and Neckman are stiff against the backrest.

"Hey, the cops 'ill be here" yells the Greek from the counter.

He takes the gun and puts it back under his jacket.

"What was that?" asks Neckman.

"A nine-millimeter and I've got a short shotgun in the trunk."

"You'd be surprised at the guys carrying a bix now" says Howard. "Guys you'd never believe in your life would carry a gun."

23

"And you know how to use it?" says Neckman.

"I taught myself."

"You go to a range?"

"That's cop shooting, if you're gonna shoot somebody up against a wall, but I figure it's gonna be like a fistfight, in the legs. Ducking and whirling like the Marines against those bolos in the Philippines."

"You shot anybody?" asks Neckman.

"Tell him" says Howard.

"I get out of the car on a Saturday night and two shlongs come at me in the alley and wanna know the time. Like a shlong is concerned with the time on a Saturday night. I hold the gun behind my leg and tell 'em to take another step."

"And you would have shot?" asks Neckman.

"I'd have opened up their heads like watermelons. I was looking to ring up a couple."

"Where was this?"

"Behind the Arms."

"You live there?"

"I've been there three years."

"Blacks are there now?"

"They're all the way up to Kedzie," says Howard. "You ever believe the Litvaks would let 'em past Western? In the summer you see the mothers walking the little bastards to school, with those Vaselined nobs they call hair, big round wumps and skinny legs and feet like claws with red painted over the dirt. If they caught a white guy fucking one of them they ought to shoot him for depravity."

Howard stops to swallow. "You should see what they did to our little grade school. You walk by you think it's the monkey cage at Brookfield."

"They're expressing themselves" says Neckman. "They don't sit like zombies like we used to. Any whites still there?"

"Half and half" says Howard.

24

"Before I'd let kids of mine go to school with them," says Rudy Yid, "I'd work three jobs and sleep on a bench between."

"Where'd everybody go?" asks Neckman.

"Homewood, Park Forest, Flossmoor" says Howard. "You should see what Shulman built. A mansion. How you go from a shoe salesman to a general contractor I don't know. It's a mystery to me."

"Nobody went north?" asks Neckman.

"Bogoch and Cantor but they'll be back. A Southside guy is a Southside guy. Jerry Mink is in the Marina paying twenty-two hundred a month rent. I don't know who he thinks he's fooling. He married one of those Japanese who was born here."

Neckman leans back grinning. "So it's Howie and Rudy Yid."

"I wanna go myself," says Rudy Yid, "or it's gonna happen with the shlongs."

"What's keeping you?"

"A five thousand dollar payout when the mill closes."

"When's it closing?"

"That's the problem. They've been talking about it five years and Monday it's still there. Everybody's gone and I'm still there with shlongs. Maybe I should kick it all for a gepoorah and go to California."

"Try South Africa or Australia" says Neckman. "There's lots of blacks in California, a lot of them in BMWs with blond shiksas and cute Jewish girls."

"You don't have to go to California" Howard says. "Your mother tell you about Debbie Fines? She married Block. You knew that?"

"Yea."

"She left him for a shvig. She's working downtown for an insurance company, meets a cool young shvig, and she leaves Block and two kids. You believe that?"

25

"If I saw her on the street," says Rudy Yid, "I'd spit in her face."

Neckman flinches. "What gives you the right to spit in her face? They'll arrest you."

"It'd be worth it. Fuckin' whore. Starts fuckin' a nigger and leaves a home and two kids."

"That's up to her," says Neckman, "and none of your goddamn business. Maybe Block wasn't giving her what she needed. Maybe he didn't have what she needed. You don't know what was going on in that house."

"And she was always the prettiest Jewish girl" says Howard. "She used to walk into school Monday morning and even the principal looked. Block is so lost he says he's gonna take the kids and move to California."

"Just what California needs, another Jewish accountant coming out and driving up property prices."

"You know who's out there?" says Howard. "You remember Jerry Sobel? He used to come to AZA on a bike, the only Jewish guy in Evergreen Park."

"Not well" says Neckman.

"Listen to this. He's in some apartment house in San Francisco that's loaded with retired performers and gets the idea to go to every temple and talk to the officers, and starts getting these old mimes and magicians work at parties. Y'know, the Jewish way, slippin' some back under the table. Abrams went out to see him. He told me he makes a thousand a week off these old kockers, just sitting by the phone drinking coffee."

"What's a thousand a week in California?" says Neckman. "What moron can't make a thousand a week in L.A.?"

"It's that good out there?" asks Howard.

"How's a guy get started in L.A.?" asks Rudy Yid. "Where do you go?"

"Go all over" says Neckman. "Wherever you want."

26

"But a guy like me from a steel mill? What kind of job could I get?"

"They got mills in L.A."

"I'm not going to L.A. to work in a mill."

"Oh you want a good job while Hispanics and blacks can't get work. No I don't think I'd pass that on even if I knew. It would just make me part of the net that holds them down. You got something to offer California?"

"What'd you offer?"

"Don't compare what we do. It's bogus. I went out there to make my own way."

"I just asked where I could find a job."

"No. You asked what privileges do I have in California as a white putz over black and brown people."

"Nobody ever gave me any privileges."

"You have no idea the privileges you've had all your life."

"I never got nothin' free."

"Never got nothin' free? Your mother used to go over to Mount Sinai so she could get free meals, taking out bedpans and smiling at everybody so they'd heap it on her plate."

Rudy Yid leans over to him. "*Let* me tell you something, Neckman. You say what you want about my old man; you'd have to look long and hard to find a whore like him but my mother put on her shoes, grabbed a pot and ran wherever she could to help."

Neckman ogles the finger under his nose.

"Say another word" offers Rudy Yid. "I'll slap your teeth out of your pisk right in front of this Greek."

Neckman leans away like he used to, then suddenly stiffens, his back up. "Go ahead. *Slap me*. I'll call the fucking police. They'll throw you in jail where you belong. I'll walk into court like I don't even know you."

Rudy Yid stands up as if he has somewhere to go. "We going to Opening Day?" he asks Howard.

27

"I don't wanna go this year."

"Good seeing you" says Neckman.

"Yea, see me if you ever need a favor" says Rudy Yid and heads to the door.

Howard waits until he's outside. "He keeps asking me to go to games and to the North Side to find girls. It's like we're the only two left and gotta stick together. Hey, I don't feel that way. My life's here on the South Side. Jews who didn't leave Germany after the war all got rich. There was no competition left. I can see why he wants out of the mill. It's dirty and full of shlongs. Hey, I don't like shlongs, but they come into payroll and I joke with 'em. What's it costing me? It's to where if a shvartze can eat like a human being I'll sit at a table and break bread with him. You get along with all kinds now. They're not all mopping floors at Goldblatt's like when we were kids. I like my job. I'm on a clean floor. There's secretaries to joke with. I know if a Jewish guy isn't a moneymaker by the time he's thirty he's considered a shmuck, but there's different ways. I'm making twenty thousand now and getting fifty bonus shares a year. By the time I'm forty I'll be worth a quarter million. No *ifs*. How many guys in business like Levin and Barton can say that? Arnie Barton has coffee provision downtown and drives a Porsche but ask him to write a check for a thousand and he's stuck. Hey, I had a reading problem. I admit it, but I'm neat, I have a memory, so I got into paymastering. Like any yid with some smarts I developed my capabilities. Recently I asked the honcho — a yid by the way — how long it would take a college guy to do my job, and he said a year at least. I said to myself, 'Howie *Shmuck*, you mean something to this company!' And Rudy Yid should go find what he can do. The shlongs relieve him five minutes late; he should shut up and take the rest of the time to study the civil service exam for mail carrying."

"What about the police?" says Neckman. "He could get on with them and take his frustrations out."

"I asked him once, and he says he don't know how you can be a cop and a Jew. He'd feel like he was converting or something. Besides I don't think he could pass the test."

"What was wrong with him?" asks Neckman. "Why couldn't he learn anything?"

"I don't know" says Howard. "The Rabbi took him to get his head x-rayed and there were no tumors or dents. It was always a fist with him. Y'know what he does? He goes to the wheelmill, puts a sack of cement on each shoulder and goes up and down those water tower stairs. He slips once, he's a cripple for life. He's getting ready for the shlongs and for what? He thinks it's gonna be like he used to stretch out the spics and wops in front of school. They'll kill him. He spit in a guy's face out there."

"For what?"

"He said some young hillbilly hired on and an old operator wanted to bone him, so who walks up, spits in his face but Rudy Yid."

"What's this hero act defending young guys? Maybe he wants to bone them himself."

"C'mon" grins Howard. "That's Rudy Yid."

"He's Rudy Yid he's not queer. He ever had a girlfriend? Is he going with a girl?"

"Yea, he was going with a girl from South Bend."

"*Rudy Yid* going with a girl from South Bend? What'd she look like?"

"Not bad. Buttocks like beach balls but a pretty girl. She came here and was going to services and eating dinner at different houses and got fixed up with Rudy Yid."

"So what happened?"

"After a few months she saw it was going nowhere and she picked up and left like she came — smiling, happy. She couldn't find a guy here so she went to Cincinnati. I hear she got married."

"Why doesn't he go to the North Side or Skokie?"

"You think he didn't try? He worked at Diamond Four Star Liquors."

"No."

"Yea he did. He went up and interviewed with Diamond himself. You should have seen. He thought he was out of the mill for good, but Diamond is an exploiter up there. He gets these Jewish shmucks with strong backs and gives them the lantsman spiel. Y'know, pictures of his nieces turned to 'em, crying about not having a Yiddish yingl to help him run the business, his eyes on 'em like prove yourself, boychik, and it can be yours. He puts these shmucks to work for two-fifty a week and runs their kishkas out. Ten, twelve hours a day with responsibilities at the register. He puts a shmuck like this in every store and they do the work of three, stocking and working the registers until they start falling off their feet. Then he cans 'em with a snap of the fingers like he never knew 'em, and these guys stand there scratching their heads, wondering what happened."

Neckman grins as if he still doesn't believe it. "Rudy Yid worked for Four Star."

"Five weeks" says Howard. "And nothing to show. He spent a hundred and fifty a week for a motel and ate in coffee shops. That's his ten-year hiatus from the mill. Other guys go to Florida, Maui; he finds somebody to bone him. It was a month before he looked himself."

"He told you?"

"He told me everything. Sunday nights he went to the Singles Dance at the Skokie Ramada and stood there like a putz with his hands in his pockets. Everybody else is skimmin' around in the latest, rich girls looking for sharp guys and vice versa and he's standin' there in a Sears blazer and doesn't even know what they're talking about. They were laughing at him. He told me himself. Y'know what he said? He came back so discouraged he was thinking about going to Australia or

Greenland, some place where there's Jews."

"What about Solly Stein?" suggests Neckman. "You'd think he could get a start with him."

"He told me Solly Stein took him aside on Kol Nidre a few times, but he says he doesn't wanna wind up in jail and smell other men's shit and dirty feet. He's a fastidious guy in a way like me. He says he can watch blood like water from a faucet but other things turn his stomach."

Howard takes a breath. "I'm a bookkeeper really. I see debits and credits and he's got credits but can't put them to use."

"Like what?"

"He's a good-looking guy. You got to admit. Even the rebbitsin said he was the handsomest boy ever to walk into temple."

"Yea what else?"

"Punctuality. You tell Rudy Yid nine-thirty and he's there nine-fifteen, you know that."

"Yea?"

"And he's honest. If he found a buck on the street he'd ask if it's yours."

Neckman tries not to laugh. "An honest punctual Yiddish shmuck. Where in the world could you find another?"

CHAPTER 4

It's too early to go back to the Arms but he can think of nowhere else to go. He pulls around back making up his mind to leave Chicago before it's too late. It was going to come to blood at the mill any day. He goes to Purl's room. Ten years ago Purl had been a vicious hundred and seventy pound football player in the Catholic Schools League. Growing ten pounds a year, he is now a bloated two hundred and seventy pound bouncer-buffoon at a night spot on 95th. He was raised by the old shul on Prairie and could speak and understand a little Yiddish. The old Jewish women on the corner called him Young Richard Burton for his handsome pocked face and big personality. He moved into the Arms four months back and Rudy Yid went shooting with him a few Sundays in Indiana Dunes. The last time on the way, Purl kept bringing up an old aunt who lived alone in Hammond and kept valuables in her apartment. Rudy Yid played dumb but he knew what he was getting at. Another time he found his door open and came in on him doing oral sex on a mangy-looking black prostitute. Lately a younger girl in exercise tights has been running in and out.

Purl comes to the door with his pants open and belly out. "Hey, what's going on?" He goes back in and starts turning things over.

"You lose your wallet?"

"My keys. This bitch comes up here frying porkchops and poking around in my mail, and you'd think she'd get the idea to clean the place."

He pats his pockets and sends some magazines flying. "It's enough to make you wanna start screaming *motherfuckers*. Yesterday she's picking her toes on the couch, jumps up and says 'Let's have nachos and cheese!' I said 'Aren't you going to rinse your fingers first?' And this is going to nurture our next generation."

"I want to tell you I'm going to California."

"When?"

"Tomorrow."

"For good?"

"I'll see. I've been stagnating ten years."

"It won't be the same."

"I was thinking you wanna buy the short shotgun."

"You're not taking it?"

"I don't think I'll need it."

"How much?"

"One-fifty? I'll take a loss for a hundred."

"I'm strapped. You wanna leave it, I'll send the money."

He knows Purl intends to pay, but Purl is so loose in his ways he doubts he will ever get together a stamp, money order and address at the same time.

"You trust me?" says Purl.

"I trust you. Maybe I should hold onto it in case I come back."

"I was gonna get you" says Purl. "You wanna make a quick thousand?"

"For what?"

"Y'know Sklar TV?"

"The Persians on 61st?"

"Yea, the youngest brother got his skull fractured at Skipper's."

"I didn't know."

"He goes to get his BMW and they hand him a bill for seventeen hundred. He says 'No way!' and they block him in so he panics and they go to town on him. I go to the store and Hamid tells me the doctors drilled holes in his brother's head to relieve the pressure. He says he's gonna close the store but first he wants Skipper fucked up, so Shlagelmilik and I are going over to put a head on him."

"Where?"

"Right there. Shlagelmilik's wife's gonna drop the car off and we're goin' in at closing time. When he hits us with the bill, Shlagelmilik's gonna throw it in his face. That's when you get out with the shotgun while we put a head on Skipper."

"He's got a lot of shitheads."

"You pull the shotgun they'll dive like Jacques Cousteau."

He feels a pinch in his throat. "It sounds okay but I'm

gonna leave. I don't wanna get held up."

"Skipper's time's come. Even the cops know it. At the most we'll go to a hearing."

"I spent a whole summer going to hearings once."

"It's a fast thousand. In and out. You wanna put a heel to some shitheads, I'm sure Hamid will be generous."

"When you gonna do it?"

"Friday."

He pretends to mull it over. "Maybe I better go while I can. A thousand isn't gonna make much difference now."

"Sleep on it. Let me know."

He goes to his room on the third floor and packs two suitcases. Cleaning up, he takes down four rubber pads in the corners of the ceiling, he'd been shooting pellets into. He's sure he won't return and carries a television and a set of plates down to an old guy who knew his father on Kedzie. Coming back he calls Howard to say goodbye.

"I'm goin'."

"Where?"

"L.A."

"You're not gonna wait for the mill to close?"

"How long can I keep waiting?"

"What're you gonna do? You don't know anybody."

"I'll work. I got four thousand in the bank. Maybe I can get into a business."

"You wanna start a business out there?"

"Why not, I'm a goy? I gotta work for other people? It takes a genius? Zulman went to Elgin to start a security lock business. He learned how to drill a hole in a door and put in a deadbolt. I bet he didn't have a thousand dollars."

"What thousand? He did it on nerve. He talked a company into giving him locks on consignment, then got a registry of senior citizens and started calling and scaring the hell out of them."

"Yea, a moron. He couldn't carry on a conversation. He was too cheap to buy Clearasil. He used to boil up some shit out of cornstarch."

"He plays the role now" says Howard. "Drives back in a Lincoln Town Car, in a jumpsuit. He acted too rich to talk."

"He is rich" says Rudy Yid. "I saw his mother at Goldblatt's and she says Stanley and six Israelis went in on a two-hundred-unit complex in Galveston, Texas. Where do they come up with these places? These camel jockeys are over here two years and already know to go buy in Galveston, Texas. She looks at me and asks did I ever believe her Stanley would own income property and drive a presidential car. I felt like saying I never thought they'd ever let him wash a presidential car. Everybody's gone out and done okay. Isky and Riser got into tire disposal. They look like two bums but it's a business. Now they're gonna buy a specialized truck for sixty-five thousand. And I'm still here with shlongs. And it was always me who had money. Eight years old, I was cleaning porches and carrying bags from A&P. Women used to say 'You're gonna be a pistol, and what do I wind up?"

"It's not that bad."

"Nah, it's true. A man's not proud of his job he's not proud of himself."

"Whose fault is it? Who told you to go to a mill?"

"I'm not blamin' nobody. I had him on my hands five years. I'd come from work and see him sitting there in the dark his head in his hands. Finally I talk him into going to Israel and another five years go by and I'm still nothin'. I'm thinking now it didn't have to be a business. I could have learned a trade. I could have gone to Jewel and been a butcher now instead of wasting ten years. I passed up opportunities. Ricky Txik came to me when I started in the mill and says give me a hundred a month; I'll put it into medical technology. In ten years you're gonna have a pile. What was a hundred a month to me? I was working doubles. I didn't think things like that happen — money falling on your head. I thought you had to work for money. And Ricky Txik's done better than anybody. He just doesn't let you see it."

"Didn't Zulman come to you for money once?"

"Yea, he wanted a thousand to go into security locks, before Elgin."

"And you said no?"

"How was I supposed to know? I never had anything to do with him. All of a sudden he's at my door on a Sunday afternoon, sweatin' in a tee-shirt and wants me to go into the lock business."

"Too bad. You could own property in Texas now. Maybe you'll get a building in L.A. Would you rent to me?"

"You, not Neckman. You ask a guy about a new place and he acts like I'm not welcome out there."

"He wonders about you."

"Wonders what?"

"About carrying guns and sticking up for young guys."

"Sticking up for young guys?"

"Yea, why you do it."

"I got some Yiddishkayt. I ain't a fuckin' goy."

"He wonders if you want 'em yourself."

"Want *who* myself?" He loses his breath a second. "What's he sayin'?"

"I don't know what he's sayin'."

"He's sayin' I'm a fag?"

"He asked if you were dating anybody and I said no."

"Who was he dating for ten years — Sally Field and Sally Struthers? Let me tell you, and tell Neckman. I'd rather be a penniless Vietnam vet with one leg and one testicle than a fag. I'd rather have leprosy and live in a basement than be the most comfortable fag on Lake Shore Drive. Shows you, you know a guy since you remember and deep down he always hated you. But I just learned. Now on I wouldn't piss in his face if his nose was on fire."

"I'm sure he'd do it for you."

Rudy Yid sits numb. He hears Howard yawn.

"Be successful" continues Howard. "I mean it, be successful. And call the mill and tell them you have an emergency. You get sixty days grace. Send me a postcard."

It is almost eleven and he could get a foreman on the phone but doesn't want to tell any more lies than he has to. He sets the alarm at five so he can leave a message on tape. Turning off the lights he has second thoughts. He just paid rent and won't get a refund. The blacks will think they scared him off. He had nothing to avenge himself over but wanted to trounce at least one before he left. And how can he walk out on five thousand? He has forty-three hundred in the bank. The payout would make ten thousand, something to show for ten years.

CHAPTER 5

He wakes before the alarm. His bed is by the window and he watches the night fade. Ozohan comes in before six. Getting himself up, he goes to the phone and dials.

"This is Calumet Rail. At the sound of the tone state your name, spell your name, your employee number and the reason for your absence...."

He takes his car to the service station, goes to the post office and fills out a form to hold his mail. He walks to the bank, closes his account and takes four thousand in traveler's checks and two hundred and fifty in cash.

Driving back to the Arms, he carries two suitcases down to his trunk and turns in his key. He stops at Purl's room but his knock is unanswered.

He is on his way before noon. The morning was bright but

the afternoon is bleary over I-55 as he drives across flat farmland. The ground is turned over, nothing growing. It begins to drizzle and he turns off for gas as a rainbow comes over the black dirt.

The way turns toward St. Louis along groves of trees and hills. Five miles from Missouri he turns off the interstate and goes up an embankment to the lot of a country store. He gets a hard roll and pat of butter at the counter. Out on the porch he sees a constable standing by a patrol car blocking the drive. Chinking sounds come from around back and a long-limbed youth in white jeans tears around the side, kicking up gravel. Pimples red with pus, he hands the officer a camera. The lawman pushes a button producing an undeveloped picture that he pinches on the corner and puts on a fender to dry. He's stout with pants coming up low under the small of his back.

Rudy Yid starts toward his car when a thin old man comes out from behind the store with a boy on his arm.

"Over here!" The constable whistles him over.

The old man turns the harelipped boy around and leads him up. He takes off his straw fedora and holds it by his leg.

"What were you doing back there?"

The old man sees the picture developing on the fender. "Relieving myself."

"You see a sign?"

"I did."

The constable picks up the picture and looks at it.

"I had a call, sir."

"You want strangers making calls behind your house?"

"No sir."

"Then why the hell did you do it?"

The old man lowers his head.

"Okay, I'm gonna take you in and they'll set bail." He turns him by the shoulders and the old man looks back.

"Sir, I'm hard up. My great grandson, we're coming from St. Jacob and I don't know what's gonna happen."

"What the hell's that supposed to mean? Stand straight. Don't turn your head."

The old man feels the lock on a wrist and looks to the boy who is gurgling like an infant. "Sir, if you'll let me talk with the proprietor maybe he'll let me clean up."

He bends around and is grabbed under the throat so that one eye bulges twice the size of the other. Rudy Yid starts toward them.

"*Hey*, he don't need that."

The old man is pushed into the car, the boy in with him. Shutting the door the constable turns toward Rudy Yid.

"What's that?"

Rudy Yid says nothing, and the constable gets behind the wheel. He starts the car, sees Rudy Yid still looking and slams on the brakes.

"What was that?" he asks again cocking an ear.

"I said he didn't need that." The quaver in his throat is all he's going to let slip. The state line is five miles away. If he gets out of the car and comes up he'll catch a hook that will take his head half off.

"You wanna complain, follow me" invites the constable, looking him up and down like one would a prostitute on the street. He pulls away with gravel flying back and turns out. The youth in the white jeans catches Rudy Yid's stare and runs for the store. He gets into his car and drives across the lot looking right. The police car is a quarter mile down. Turning after it he stops, thinking they'll be waiting for him in front — whoever is at the station there, and it might make it worse for the old man. He turns back the other way.

He drives thinking he should have gone to the station and paid the old man's fine. What could it be, a lousy fifty or hundred? What is that to him? He has over four thousand. He'd take the old man and boy back to their car and get them on their way. He'd shine in the eyes of God. He thinks it's not too late but can't make himself turn back. He rationalizes that the police won't want an old man around there any more than anybody else would, and they'll get what they can out of him and send him on his way.

The foothills are green from rain and he would enjoy the scenery but is bethought of the old man. By nine that night he's on the other side of Missouri. Steam rises out of trenches aside the road.

CHAPTER 6

The motel is in a clearing of woods and the morning fog and trees are the same silver shade. He warms up the car and drives out onto striped blacktop, swinging by a figure coming out from the thick with a thumb up. He looks back at a stooped form. Braking, he backs up in the fog to a slender hitchhiker in a long wool coat and scarecrow hat.

"Where you going?" he asks, rolling down the passenger window.

"Arizona."

He pushes open the door and puts down the backrest. The hitchhiker unslings his packboard and slides it in back. He gets in smelling like wet soil.

"You taking a piss back there?" asks Rudy Yid getting going.

"I was sleeping."

"In the woods on that pack?"

"Yea."

"You get a night's sleep on that?"

"I'm used to it. I've been traveling two years."

"You just get off somewhere and pitch a tent?"

"No, I zip up a bag."

"Nobody bothers you?"

"Not so far."

"How about animals? They come up?"

"I don't even know what they are. I see eyes. A coyote came sniffing once and snapped at my face. I could smell his breath."

Rudy Yid shakes his head. "I got nerve but I wouldn't sleep in the open. I had an uncle who was murdered in his sleep."

"In the open?"

"No. He was with a few hundred Jews who put up a fight against Nazis in the Warsaw ghetto. When he saw it was over he got out through the sewers and crossed the border. He asked a Ukrainian to put him up and while he was sleeping in the barn, the farmer went in and hit him in the head with an ax."

He sees the hitchhiker wince. "Maybe I shouldn't have told you — you being out on the road?"

"Oh, I had close calls. Once in Oklahoma four guys went by yelling and turned back. It was broad daylight. I didn't think they'd do anything. A feed store was across the way but they went by about eighty and threw a bottle. It came so close I felt it brush my cheek. If it'd hit me — "

"It woulda killed you" finishes Rudy Yid. "On the spot. You'd have been better off getting hit by a bullet. What'd they look like?"

"Three white guys and a black guy. All wearing tee-shirts like they went to the local school. I ran back and bought a bus ticket to go over the state line. I saw your Illinois plate."

"Yea, Chicago."

"I'm from Kankakee, on I-57."

"You must know Chicago?"

"Never went."

"Never went to Chicago?"

"My friends used to go. Even hitchhiking I missed it."

"You didn't miss anything."

"No?"

"Nah, everybody's got a nose as long as a dick and they all

41

wanna stick it in your business."

"It's not like they say, 'city with broad shoulders'?"

"Who said that? All I ever seen was a bunch of filchers. Every one of 'em with some scheme or other to beat you out of something. You remember in the bible about God sending an old guy to a town to find two honest men and he couldn't do it?"

"Yea."

"He'd have the same problem in Chicago."

"It's not a rough tough place?"

"They talk tough but there hasn't been a fighter to come out of that town in fifty years. The last two were Barney Ross, maybe Davey Day, a couple of Jewish guys before the war. You got family in Arizona?"

"No, a friend. We're going down to Mexico to learn weave crafting."

"You speak Spanish?"

"It isn't necessary. It's an open air school. You live with Indians and help them plant and gather food, and in the afternoon when the sun is high the women teach you how to work a backstrap loom."

"And you stay with Indians in huts?"

"You have to build your own but they bring materials. They're patient and like to teach."

"How long's it take?"

"In two years you can get pretty good. One guy who's kind of famous now spent six years in Oaxaca and came back and opened a barn shop in New Mexico designing saddle-blankets and bags and had Robert Redford and the Goldwaters ordering things from him. He took a few years off and built a small ranchero to scale, everything like it used to be — saddles, mesquite beds, rugs, quilts."

"You saw it?"

"No. I heard. It's my hope to live like that. Take materials and wood and make things like they used to."

"You wanna open a shop?"

"Yea or get a van and travel through Arizona and sell."

"Sure. Move around. Find your customers. I'm going to California to get into a business."

"What kind of business?"

"I don't know yet. I've got to find something. Everybody I know got on to something but me."

"Why don't you come learn weaving with us?"

"Go to Mexico?"

"Yea."

"I'm thirty already. I fell behind. I don't think I can lose two years."

"Well they say up in the mountains you step out of time. They say your concentration becomes so pure you can learn in two years what takes six back in the world. And you learn Oaxaca culture and natural medicine."

"It sounds okay but I'm somewhat limited. What I can do I do and what I can't I can't no matter how many times you show me. In school they showed me how to run a projector fifty times and I still couldn't get it. I used to get discouraged but I decided it's not that my head doesn't work, it's that other guys take interest in things. I'm not interested in everything."

Having the rider to talk to makes him forget the old man and boy at the Missouri line and he stops twice to buy him meals. He's sallow-faced and doesn't look like much of an eater but cleans up his plate both times. They go across Oklahoma and down through the Texas panhandle.

Late that night he is filling up at a station close to Deming, New Mexico. A prairie wind as sharp as anything back in Chicago whips between the pumps and he puts his collar up and knocks on the window. The hitchhiker rolls it down.

"You wanna sleep in a bed? It's gonna be cold."

He looks out toward the interstate. "Would you let me take it? You can get there that much faster."

"You're not tired?"

"No."

"I don't think I can stay awake."

"I'll be okay."

The horizon comes up in a silver belt. His first glimpse is of the hitchhiker straightbacked at the wheel. He looks out at a cactus desert coming into light.

"This Arizona?"

"Yea."

He looks over at the fuel gauge. "Pull off when you can. We'll take a piss somewhere."

Just as the sun shines he turns off by a Gulf station at a desert junction and holds out his hand.

Rudy Yid sits up. "You sure this place in Mexico is real?"

"As far as I know. You don't want to come?"

"I'd be out of place" he says letting go of his hand. "You need five or ten bucks?"

"Okay."

He didn't think he would say yes. Taking out his money he hands him a five then another. The hitchhiker gets his packboard and crosses the road to the junction.

He crosses into California stopping at a small sign giving the miles to San Bernardino and Los Angeles. Across the interstate is a line of brush fronting two ramshackle houses with a late-model pick-up in the shadow between them. The sun is bright but he feels a strange chill from the ground as he turns to get back in the car.

The desert ends after San Bernardino and he turns into a wide interstate over farmland, comes into traffic five lanes across and goes on to a rise of freeway where he can see downtown buildings in the distance.

At dusk he comes under a wide sign for Los Angeles. The lane splits and he swings north instead of south toward the city. Seeing he's going wrong, he turns off on a road of low flat stores made of a rough plaster used for building cheap garages in the outskirts around Chicago. He goes a few blocks and U-turns to a motel on the other side. Stepping around a motorcycle, he goes into the office. A clerk shaped like a gymnast is in a swivel chair watching a small television on the desk.

"This L.A. here?"

"North Hollywood."

"Where's L.A.?"

"Down the freeway. It's all the same. What're you looking for?"

"I just came from Chicago. I'd like to get started here."

"What kind of work you do?"

"I was in a steel mill ten years."

"You a tradesman?"

"No. Hot end heavy labor."

"There's plenty of hot heavy labor here. The warehouses and tire outlets down the road are hiring."

"I'd like to get something better."

He nods to a newspaper on the counter. "That's Sunday's. It's full of ads."

Rudy Yid weighs the paper in his hands. "How come there's so much work out here?"

"Lots of money here. You can't find work in L.A., you better pack it in."

Rudy Yid grins. "They say that in Chicago but I never believed it."

"No?"

"Nah, the only work I got was work nobody wanted. This all you do?"

"I'm an actor. I got into a beef with my agent so I'm laying low."

"You look familiar, you're not one of Mickey —?"

45

"No. People ask that. His sons are tall as trees. You ever watch *Rehab, Divorce Court* and *Parole Board*?"

"Yea, Channel 9."

"I did *Rehab* twice. I got 'em all in the first six months I was here."

"I know a guy who was out here ten years and couldn't get work."

"You go gung ho. I was out eighteen hours a day. If there was a party, I went. I didn't care if I had to walk. Every beer I drank, every sandwich I ate, all the straightball I shot was where I could meet somebody. I took care of my grandmother until I was twenty-six; I didn't have time to waste. I wanted to be like Alan Ladd. He was five-three and a tough little monkey like me. But you only get so far without an agent."

"You couldn't find an agent?"

"Yea, I found an agent. Little Marty Small."

"Marty Small who played on the *Tony Rich Show*? He was your agent?"

"Yea, an *agent*. He couldna sold a sandwich in Auschwitz. He said he was going to take me around and introduce me to Merv, Hef and Allan and has me biking him to parties and people are looking at me like they think I'm his buttboy. One joker takes me aside and says you should have seen the losers he used to bring. Guys with pot bellies who spit when they talked. So one Sunday we're going for brunch and I pick him up in the hills and he yells down to fix him a sandwich. It didn't feel right. I'm a Uke Canuck. Up there it doesn't matter what you do so long as you're ready to spit in anybody's eye. So I'm making the sandwich but I wanna slit his throat. We get to the Mansion and I'm still not feeling right and go to the head. I'm sitting there and look up and there's Marty giggling with his nose over the stall. I come up off a squat and Jap-slap him like Toshiro Mifune. I run out and catch him between two Jews, and he starts screaming '*Stawp! Stawp!* Why are you doing this?' You think Hef's is all mellow chat and cool breeze jazz? Like this a Mandingo manservant corkscrews my arms behind me, knees me over and hauls me out like a wheelbarrow with my nose bobbing off the ground. All I could see were the toes and heels of those Playmates digging out of the way, and Marty back up on the grass screaming 'I wanna kick him in the nuts! *Please* let me kick him in the nuts!'

"Next morning I run over to *Parole Board,* see if I can score a few lines and Lonnie Sharm the producer tells me I'm bad news. Word was out. All these Hollywood hebes tellin' everybody they fought their way off the streets. Show 'em some real violence and they squirt dick cheese."

"So what'll you do?"

"Waitin' for an inheritance and I'm gone."

"Whereto?"

"San Francisco, New York." He gets a glimpse out the window of a blonde getting out of a car filled with clothes and heading across the street. "I rode that pony."

"Her?" asks Rudy Yid watching her go across.

"Her or one just like her. They get on the outs and come in here and ask what they can do for a room." He swivels back around. "You and I both know what they can do for a room."

"She would have guys yelling out on the street in Chicago" says Rudy Yid.

"She's nothin' here."

"*Nothin'?*"

"Nah, they come and go. Them and the others."

"Just running around?"

"Yea, the only genuine item out here. The glass buildings, agents, billboards. And what's it all come to — one, two movies a year worth seeing, but that was the goods. The only genuine article out here and the first to fall for the bull. But it has to be that way. The *lore* — not just who gets to the top but all the ones buried underneath."

He feels lucky he stopped here. Everything Neckman wouldn't tell him, this guy would.

"How much a room for a night?"

"Why not a week? You get free calls. You're close to studios and companies. What's the use of running all over 'cause you're new? You wear yourself out."

"How much a week?"

"Usually two-ten. No discounts but one ninety-five for you."

"I paid that a month in Chicago."

"Better forget Chicago. Rent's no joke here. The trick's keeping the landlord off your back."

"I'll take three days. I might get an apartment by then."

He stands up no taller than a boy. "You won't get an apartment in three days. You'll get something you don't want. Give me one seventy-five; it's yours."

"You gonna give me a receipt."

"You don't trust me. I'll put down you paid the rate. I'm trying to help but I see you're strongheaded."

He sleeps for an hour then heaves himself up and goes out to see if the blonde is still walking around. He has a place for her if she's in a pinch. Walking down the street he stops at a nightclub with an Old West front. A country quartet plays to customers. He goes to the bar and looks out on the floor where a few couples dance. The style is shifting both elbows to the left then back to the right, stomping one-two with the heels. Younger than the other patrons, a blondish redhead gets away from two at the other end. Leaning against the bar in a thin skirt and flats she asks for a glass of water. She sees him looking and squints an eye as if she knows him from somewhere.

"You wanna dance?"

"What?" he says, thinking she's hustling drinks.

"I said you wanna dance?"

"I don't know how."

"C'mon." She reaches for his arm but he won't move. "It's

48

easy. You could stand out there scratching your ass."

"I can't."

"Can't scratch your ass? What's your name?"

"Rudy Yid" he coughs.

She holds out her hand. "Madelyn Jenso."

"Marilyn?" he asks leaning forward to shake hands.

"Madelyn with a *d*. You're not from around here?"

"I'm from Chicago."

The bartender brings her glass of water and she winks. "I shouldn't say this but these guys from Chicago sound a little slow."

The bartender goes and Rudy Yid doesn't know what to say.

"You shy too?"

"I don't wanna walk in like I own the place."

She looks back at the dance floor. "That's okay. Nothing bothers me more than a guy selling himself."

A patron in a western shirt and boots comes up with his hands in his back pockets and asks her to dance. She goes out on the floor and he starts dancing too fast, kicking up his heels. She tries to get him to slow down. The number ends and she steps over to talk to one of the guitar players. The western character waits awhile and leaves.

She comes back alone and heads out. Seeing she's on her own he gets off the stool and goes after her, stepping around someone with the same idea. She is across the drive, on the sidewalk as he catches up.

"You need a ride?"

She turns, eyeing him. "I live around the corner."

He looks down the street. "Would you like to stop somewhere and get something?"

She sees he's excited. "I have to get home but we can stop at Jack in the Box if we make it fast."

He steps up alongside. "You go back there a lot? You seem

to know everybody."

"I sing in the contests so I stop in. I don't want them thinking I just come to win money."

"How much you win?"

"Sixty-five dollars." She wags a finger. "I've won six in a row."

"You're just about on the payroll, huh?"

"No, they told me one more and that's it, but they said that after the third time, too."

"They probably figure you bring in business."

"How's that?"

"With your looks."

"I don't win on looks. I'm talented. No luck but talent. What about you? What'd you come for — to get in movies?"

"Why do you ask that?"

"Every rugged guy from everywhere comes to get in movies and winds up driving a beverage truck in Van Nuys."

"Not me. I was in a steel mill ten years. I came to get into a business."

She takes his arm to cross the street. "Well there's every business you can think of here on top of another. People make a living here combing dogs."

"You wanna get six tacos for two-fifty?" she says getting to the patio.

She orders six and two drinks and he gives her a five dollar bill. They sit down at a stone table to wait.

"You had a taco before?"

"Usually I get red-hots. Chicago is a hot dog town. On every corner."

"You'll change" she says. "You get here and become part Mexican. You start eating tacos and green burritos. You learn about fifty words and put salsa all over your eggs."

She leans back crossing a leg over and dangling a shoe. The ridge on her shin runs to her ankle. Some rough characters in jeans and construction shoes eye her across the patio, talking out of the sides of their mouths as though they'd like to get in a few nips on that leg. She stares back but it does no good. When the order is ready she takes Rudy Yid by the arm.

"Let's go to my place."

A blond babysitter with smudged glasses answers the door. Behind her a fisheyed boy sits watching a soundless television.

"Were they good?" asks Madelyn.

"I got 'em in bed. That's all I can say."

Madelyn goes into a bedroom, coming out with money.

"Can I depend on you tomorrow?"

"I'll be here. Let's go, Jeff."

In going Jeff's dull eyes come alive for a glance down Madelyn's cleavage. She closes the door behind them, taking the bag from Rudy Yid.

"Have a seat." She goes into the kitchen and he sits down facing a coffee table.

"You want rum in your coke?" she asks.

"Okay."

"You're not a drinker?"

"I drink. I can swig a half pint of Smirnoff if it's cold out but I never needed one. Same with cigarettes."

Madelyn brings a tray with two red glasses and a plate of tacos. "I'd kill for these." She holds one up with a hand underneath. "I let myself at 'em once a week. Any more and my sides would blow out."

"Your what?"

"My sides." She lifts her top and pinches her hip. He looks at her thin stomach, feeling a twinge in his pants.

"Everybody's fat there" he says.

"Not out here. I see girls at the beach and get so jealous I could flatten their little button noses. When I was in school, if a girl had a chest she was usually on the heavy side. Now they have these skinny stomachs, long legs and still carry a load on top."

"If you went to the beach everybody there would be looking at you."

"Sure, I'm older. Older women look like they know."

"What are you, twenty-six?"

"Twenty-eight. My girl is eleven already. She sees a man and her eyes light up. She'll make me a grandmother by the time I'm thirty-three. Once you're a grandmother no matter how good you look it has to do something to your head."

"How old were you when you got married?"

"Seventeen. Ran away to Las Vegas to become a singer and married a guitar player in Duane Springer's Band twenty years older than me."

"He was thirty-seven?"

"Yea, I'm still trying to figure out how it lasted ten years. He'd be out drinking all night with prostitutes, then wake up at two in the afternoon and come out to the kitchen with his thing hanging out of his shorts. Every time he touched me I thought I was going to get a disease."

Madelyn's daughter comes out of a room holding a pillow and blanket.

"Mom, Tommy's snoring in there. He sounds like a wolf."

Madelyn's jaws clench. "Go in my room. No, wait. Use the couch."

"Can I have a taco?"

"No."

She picks up the tray as her daughter stares at Rudy Yid.

"I'm Cindy."

"C'mon" says Madelyn.

He follows into a bedroom with business boxes stacked up in the corners. She sets the tray down on the dresser and closes the door.

"You see her look at you? I'm counting the days."

He sits down by the bed and Madelyn turns on the television to the movie *Captain Blood* with Errol Flynn. She

52

stands there looking.

"I always liked old movies" she says. "The men were open, friendly. These guys today act like they'd be afraid to talk if they met you on the street."

"You remind me of my mother. She named me after Zachary Scott."

"Zachary Scott, I loved him." She steps back. "I thought your name is Rudy."

"My real name is Zick. My old first grade teacher called me to the front of class and said I had eyelashes like Rudolph Valentino and started calling me that. My last name's not Yid either. It's Yitz. I used to run around with Polacks; they called me Rudy Yid. A yid's a Jew."

"You're Jewish?"

"Yea."

"The Valley's full of Jews. I dated a couple of Jewish guys. They were in telephone sales."

"What'd they sell?"

"One was power tools and the other pens. Right here on Lankershim. They said they came here with holes in their pockets and in six months had apartments, cars and jewelry. I don't know if you can believe them. What is it about Jewish guys? Are they smarter or do they help each other get rich? I heard that."

"They didn't seem any smarter when I was in school. I think it's the people. Anybody else you can be an honest guy they don't care what you do, but you're a Jew and you're carrying mail or working for Sears, you're a nobody."

"They turn their backs on you?"

"More like they grin up their sleeves."

"I worked for Jews in Palm Springs at Bingo Palms. The old men were sweet, but those women wanted to eat my heart out. 'Honey, it's cold; Honey, it tastes funny; Honey, bring me a cleaner glass, please; Honey, the chicken's dry.' All of them had recipes for chicken from their mothers like they were still nubile or something. And the onions were never sweet enough like all they bought at home were Sweet Bermudas for seventy-nine cents a pound. Breakfast wasn't bad because they were stuffing themselves with lox before it was gone, but they came to dinner painted up for war. Those smiles with fifty teeth, and if there was brisket, were you in for it. There was no way to get it right. They wouldn't even tell you what's wrong, just hand you the plate and say 'I can't be bothered,' like they're royalty. And the chef gives me holy hell saying what the hell can he do. And you better not say anything back to those women. They will stand up with a mouthful of food and tear into you in front of everybody. And they take nothing personal. They look at you like you're an enemy to every Jewish person and child ever born."

"You ever talk back?"

"Not me, but a guy named Joey got fed up and said, 'Lady, I'm not prejudiced but if you people hadn't crucified Christ, you'd have nagged him to death.' "

"Or sued him."

She turns from the television, grinning. "You don't seem Jewish. You all or part?"

"I'm all. I'm what they call a real Jew. If there was ever a Jew and couldn't be nothin' but a Jew, it's me. When I was small we were out in front of Holy Angels in the summer and a truck pulls up and the priest tells us to help carry in boxes. I get inside and see that high ceiling and body up on the wall and chills go up my spine. I was never so glad to get back out in the sun in my life. I thought I was gonna faint and I've never been knocked down. And when it comes to pork, if I ever ate a piece of pork, I'd heave from here to O'Hare. I wouldn't be able to eat for a month. If there was ever a Jew and couldn't be nothing but a Jew, you're looking at one."

She stands there. "Yea, I guess you are." She straightens her dresser top and moves some boxes behind the television. "I bet you couldn't marry anybody but Jewish."

"No, I don't think I could." He coughs, clearing his throat.
"That doesn't mean I couldn't know you. I like talking to
you."
She doesn't reply.
"You need help?"
"No just sit."
"You still a waitress?"
"No, I do business support at home. I can't leave her long.
She rides around on her bike with boys. They're already
buying her candy and ice cream. I've got to keep an eye on
her."
"How old's your boy?"
"He's not mine. He's a neighbor's. She leaves him with me
and the smaller one down the street. Y'know some people
shouldn't be mothers. They don't get pangs mothers get. She
stays out all night and her dates drop her off in the morning,
then take her to the door for a last feel — and they're not all
white. But that's okay. It pays a sitter and the light. Her
parents died last year six weeks apart and left her eleven
thousand. The first day she goes over to Beverly Hills and gets
her hair fingers toes done for two hundred and fifty dollars. In
three months she made shit out of that money, not that it
bothers her. By noon she's buying rags at K-mart and the kids
are home swallowing spit."
She picks up nylons from under the bed and puts them
away. "Y'know a lot of people have problems they can't solve
no matter what, but money could solve every problem I have.
I keep thinking something is going to happen with my
singing."
"How do you get to be known?"
"You have to be discovered. I've sung in every contest
around. I used to drive to Santa Ana and sing at the
Longbranch. I won that contest six times in a row, too, before
the manager called me over and said that's it. At the Palomino
here on Lankershim — everybody goes; even the governor

used to stop in. I was singing one night and Burt Reynolds was at a table with his pals giving me the eye. And I was singing, too. People were standing all the way back. I thought for sure something was going to happen."

She folds a tissue box and stuffs it in a basket. "And one night down the street the Red Range Brothers are sitting in front cracking stupid jokes and snapping hankies. There weren't even any women sitting there with them. They were acting that stupid just for themselves. And I had a voice that night. I'd never sung like that. They didn't even give me a look. And the waitress — a heavyset girl — they called her every name in the book, and the bouncer who was no Slim Jim himself stood there grinning. There's no amount of money that could make me take that. Then they get on the radio with that *yes-sir no-sir* crap and *thank Jesus* this *God bless America* that. Those hypocrites. And they jump on that poor girl. It made me sick."

"I don't like that" says Rudy Yid. "My mother used to go iron clothes. Her father sent her to take care of old people. They think 'cause you need money they can say anything they want. Every Academy Awards they show Jack Nicholson telling off that old waitress doing her job. If I'd been there I'd have taken him around back and fixed his sides for him. He'd have been afraid to step into another coffee shop for the rest of his life."

She stops what she's doing. "He looks like a pretty strong personality to me."

"It wouldn't help much. He'd be screaming from the first shot."

She picks up shoes and puts them under the bed. "You sure you didn't come to get in movies? You have a way."

"Nah, I don't like movies much. It used to be one against five, now it's five thousand. And they all want you to see their butt crack. The men."

"There's nobody you like?"

"I used to like Audie Murphy. I saw *To Hell and Back* three times and read the book. He killed a hundred Germans. Some Jewish guy should have gone and done it, but a skinny little hillbilly did so my hat's off to him. I never wanted to be like anybody else."

She looks at him.

"I'm surprised you can't get into the movies," he says, "with your face."

"What's being pretty out here?"

"You're more than pretty. You got a look. And your little girl out there. That's the prettiest little girl I've ever seen."

"Oh, God. Don't ever say that to her."

"You got smart faces, like Jewish faces."

"Smart" she blushes. "My aunt used to tell me if anybody was born to work on an assembly line it's you." She looks around at the boxes. "And that's basically what I do, put pamphlets together." She motions to Rudy Yid. "You play sports?" she asks. "You look so even."

"I never liked sports that much. Just sixteen-inch softball. We called it limeball. You didn't need a glove. I used to like those games in the alley, chasing each other and jumping over fences and garages."

"You weren't afraid of dogs?"

"Dogs." He stands to show her. "Dogs are smarter than you think. You think they come high but they fake high and go low to grab your ankle and snap it. I threw a left hook at a German shepherd once and missed by three feet."

"Sit down" she says. "Relax."

He sits back down and she opens the door a crack and looks out. "You've never been married?"

"No, I wanna make money first. I know what it's like in a house with no money. Besides I've always been bashful."

"Bashful" she says her hands on her hips. "You can't have kids if you're bashful. My own mother used to say that."

She looks over at a clock, slips off her shoes and notices him glance at her feet. "I was a little bashful too when I first got out here but you see so many things and hear so many things you start to feel you don't belong if you don't loosen up. I went to a nude beach last year."

"Nude, naked? Everything or just on top?"

"Everything. I enjoyed it. If you have a good body that's the place. You'd be surprised what a little bikini can cover up."

"Like what?"

"Like sag and bad nipples and no nipples and lumps on the rump. It's not modesty that keeps most women from a nude beach. It's usually pointy little tits."

"And men are looking at you?"

"So what."

"I'd never go."

"You got something to hide?"

"Yea, I got something to hide. What kind of man walks around with his business hanging out? A man ought to have some shame."

She pulls up her top revealing a low-cut bra holding round freckled breasts. "Well I'll show you if you're not ashamed to look."

CHAPTER 7

Twenty minutes later he gets his pants back on.

"I hate to rush," she says, "but it looks bad when a man walks out in the morning, especially when he needs a shave. I don't want to put any more ideas into her head than I have to. Are you coming tomorrow to hear me sing?"

"I'll come get you."

"No. Let's meet. I never know for sure if my sitter's coming and I start getting nervous."

"Well, maybe something will happen tomorrow."

"Not in that place. I'm starting to think it's not gonna happen. I'm gonna leave here."

"Leave California?"

"Yea. I thought my luck would change here but it got worse. My mother died back in Grand Rapids and a few months later my younger brother went with a friend to do landscaping work in Massachusetts, and he was in back of a house and thought nobody was home and starts urinating off the patio and a woman comes out front of the sliding door and starts screaming to high heaven like she never saw anything like that before. She went back in and picked up the phone and my brother went in and hit her with a tool. They gave him twenty-five years."

"He killed her?"

"He panicked. He was just relieving himself. There were no open toilets around there. She didn't have to start screaming like that. He was a nineteen-year-old boy with a junior college background, never in trouble before and he gets the maximum for second degree murder. You can imagine the defense he had. He doesn't even remember hitting her. There was no intent. I talked to lawyers here. They say her insane impulse set him off."

"How much of that twenty-five is he gonna have to do?"

"I don't know. His lawyer is trying something, but my brother says if he stays much longer he doesn't want to live. He's already been raped. And I have a sister who could have saved him. I went to her and said we've got to get him a good attorney. He was the baby. He came when my mother was forty. We used to hold him in our arms like he was ours, but my sister said she'd worked too hard in her life to jeopardize her money. I used to be so proud. I had a sister who'd become successful. We were so poor my father's hands shook when he peeled an orange for us. And my sister's living out in this rural area married to a German handyman and sees it's no good and decides to make a store out of her front room. She just moved everything upstairs, brought in secondhand stoves and refrigerators and learned so much she made those guys at Sears and Wards look like loafers. She gave it a personal touch, and the field workers around there were driving out to see her."

"Your sister look like you?"

"My sister weighs three hundred pounds. She doesn't wear makeup and works sixteen hours a day. The only thing on her mind is the next sale. She doesn't sit on the stool without a manual. Her German husband does all the delivery and hookups. When she's in front, he puts his head down and goes through like the Mexican help. Nothing else matters to her."

"What about food?"

"That either. She doesn't eat that much; but she's got an estrogen problem and no matter how busy she'll go upstairs every day to vibrate herself. I don't wish her bad. She worked for all she has but she'll never be my sister again. During the trial she buys sixty acres in Black Oak. Our brother is in prison and she buys sixty acres in that shithole. If I could get a break, I'd get some lawyers moving. Eight years ago Kenny Rogers was right down the street here on Lankershim in a roach infested apartment. Look where he is now — on a plantation in Hawaii. I went to a three-day seminar and they said go make it happen, but I can't. My voice is as good as anybody's. I don't even think they're all that good. They just have those natural trills from the South. I'm a Michigan girl; I don't have that, but tone for tone nobody's going to run me out of the room. You listen to the radio?"

"I listen in the car. I don't know much about music. I don't get much in one ear."

"What happened there?"

"I was running across a garage and fell through rotten wood, and tore off half my ear. It healed up ruffled and I told the doctor to cut it straight. He said you'll lose tone but I said

I don't care. Cut it straight."

He looks at his watch, not wanting to overstay. "You sure you don't want me to come get you?"

"You could do me a favor. If you get there early get in the corner by the door, I'll get behind you. Otherwise guys come up to talk and it throws me off."

"You get scared up in front of everybody?"

"That's the only place I don't get scared. I've made so many bad judgments in my life I started to wonder what kind of person I am. But up there I forget everything."

Wanting to talk to the clerk again he comes up on the motel and sees a mud-caked Pontiac with an Alaska plate, blocking the drive. The engine is running and a rangy character is at the office door twisting the knob so that the pane shivers.

"You work here?" he calls to Rudy Yid.

"No. He's not there?"

Not answering he gets back in the Pontiac and peels out in reverse. Seeing the motorcycle is gone, Rudy Yid leans over the rail, looking in behind the counter. The television is still on the cash drawer is out and empty.

CHAPTER 8

It doesn't feel real this happened on his first night here. He could have never met her in Chicago. A divorcee like her on the South Side would have every stoop-sitting weasel at the call of an alderman or precinct captain, hieing up the block to report new *talent*, and she'd soon have herself a boyfriend whether she wanted one or not. But out here in this slow-looking place she was alone, like the blonde who'd gotten out of the car and crossed the street. He's made up time but doesn't feel livened up any. It didn't seem right with her daughter in the next room knowing what her mother was doing. It doesn't feel much different than after walking out of one of the Korean places on the South Side. It was only one night but he said he'd meet her again tomorrow and senses he could get entangled before he has a chance to look around. This didn't fall in his lap. She didn't come on in the bar because she was looking for a boyfriend. She was looking for somebody who could help her, and he doesn't think he'll be able to say no. He isn't seasoned enough. She was too much for him — just the way she talked or bent over to pick something up. Still, she said she'd be leaving soon and if he doesn't talk big to impress her and just tags along she can't expect too much.

He gets up two hours later than he wanted to, going out in the sunshine to the soda machine in the bower. In the office window he sees a swarthy foreign man going through guest cards. The empty cash drawer is up on the counter.

Taking a soda to his room he looks through classifieds. Most of the businesses are priced like buildings in Chicago. He finds a popcorn caboose for two thousand and a coin laundry for fifteen. He dials the caboose number and a rough old voice answers.

"I'm calling about your ad. What is it you have?"

"A cornpopper with a caboose front."

"I saw one in Chicago but that was a fire truck. Is yours red?"

"Red. Fifty inches high, thirty wide and a hundred and forty pounds on wheels."

"And you take it to a mall somewhere?"

"Hitch it up and take it where you want."

"I just came from Chicago. I'm in a motel in North Hollywood. You far away?"

"Y'know Lankershim?"

62

He drives east a few miles to an area called Burbank, seeing nobody outside. The houses and lawns are small and neat but everything is still.

He goes to a door and a stocky retiree with a printer's apron comes out from behind the fence.

"You call about the caboose?"

A stubby white dog leads the way into a garage workshop. The cornpopper is on a canvas cover on the floor. The caboose is a lacquered maroon case with a railroad insignia.

"Brand new?"

"Just finished."

He looks behind the glass case at a pullout stool, an umbrella shaft and an aluminum counter with a cabinet underneath. The retiree rests a hand on the case, the thumb missing at the joint.

"The one I saw in Chicago had a bell."

"Put one on. You won't need it. The kids see this and say 'I want Red Caboose popcorn, Mommy.' "

"I see why." He opens the cabinet. "You get corn oil, kernels, bags and salt and go to a mall?"

"Why malls? Malls cost money. The ones doing best get activity calendars from City Hall. There's a couple, three events in town every day. Get there early and set up. You're there just one day, the cops don't bother you."

Rudy Yid steps back. "If you know what you're doing what kind of money can you make?"

"Depends on how you set up. That's the nub of the business, getting there first. I've sold to the ones who put the machine in the garage after a week and I've sold to ones selling two, three hundred bags a day."

"How much a bag?"

"I recommend a dollar bag." He takes a red striped bag from the counter. "Keep it simple. A nice bag, but not enough to share. You sell two hundred of these and you're doing okay for yourself."

63

"How much of two hundred is profit?"

"That's up to you. Take off for kernels, fat, fuel, taxes if you're gonna pay any. You should bring home one-fifty."

"For five days that's about eight hundred, right?"

"If you're a hungry bastard and want to work more, you can make more."

"Can I go somewhere to talk to somebody with one of these?"

"Like I said, the ones doing good move around. They're independent cusses. Most of 'em drove lunch wagons and snack trucks. They can't work for nobody."

Rudy Yid walks round the machine. "I saw a coin laundry in the paper for fifteen thousand; that's a long shot."

"Fifteen thousand for a coin laundry. That's a junker by the Mexicans."

"You make your money. They don't have their own machines. I know a guy who fixed up a laundromat in a Mexican neighborhood. He had a Polish sausage counter up front and in back he sawed out a corner and set up a bower and shipped UPS. The Mexicans were coming in for a wash, a kielbasa and a ship home in one shot. He's king now. A Polack. His father was a janitor."

"You gonna leave a deposit?"

"How much?"

"Five hundred. I'll hold it two weeks."

"If I don't get this one I'll get the next."

"I only make one every two months."

"Just one" he mumbles. "I'm new here. I don't know my way around."

"How long's it take a young fella to learn his way around?"

He could be in business tomorrow, sooner than he ever thought, but how many times has he come across clever new things then found out he could get them for half the price somewhere else?

"I don't wanna do anything until I see the laundromat. If I'm late for this one I'll be early for the next."

He calls the laundromat number from a gas station and gets directions on tape to a boulevard in Eagle Rock. He looks at his watch and decides to skip going out there that day and get a haircut instead. His head wasn't on business. He didn't have any trouble leaving Madelyn the night before but all morning he feels himself twitching in his pants to see her again.

CHAPTER 9

The lights are on and half of the crowd is up. From what he overhears they are mostly cement truck operators for a local rock company and longhaulers staying over. He's been sitting at the end of the bar saving a seat but had to give it up. The contestants, mostly soloists with guitars, started at eight. As it gets close to nine he wants to go down to her apartment but knows he'll lose the corner.

He stands to ease the swelling in his pants when the door swings open. The eyes of everyone outside turn as she comes through in a thin white dress and yellow pumps. She sees Rudy Yid in the corner and gets over to him.

"Where you been?"

"I'll tell ya." She squeezes by him and leans across the bar, asking if she can still go up and sing. Along the line everyone stretches his neck. One of the bartenders finally comes over and takes her card.

Rudy Yid offers her the stool. "Take this."

"This is fine" she says catching her breath.

"What happened?" he asks, feeling her leg against his.

"I wasn't even coming. I was on the phone all day with a cousin in Rockford, Illinois. I could rent a house there for half what I pay here. The babysitters make a dollar-fifty an hour and they're glad to get it. I pay mine three and she won't put a hand in the sink."

She glances around at men staring but seems to have no interest in them. "Then I put on a dress and it has a spot, and I'm thinking 'Tonight's not worth it.' Then I think again. 'It's sixty-five dollars.' I mean go find it on the street so I throw on this summer thing and come running down the block and two cars almost go into each other. Now they're mad at me for coming late."

"They gonna let you sing?"

"I don't even care anymore. I feel like a moocher. I have to wait till closing time and chase 'em around until one goes to the register to pay me."

"Why don't you say something?"

"They're three ex-Pennsylvania state troopers. Try saying something to one of them."

The band is in place. An emcee in a western outfit with kerchief reads from a card and introduces a young female singer and male guitarist. She starts up a lively song, but her voice is thin and she's flat-chested and not ripe enough. Whistles come too soon and she makes haste to finish, going off with tears in her eyes. The host takes the microphone.

"Sonny and Carl Brothers from San Berdu." He takes his time turning to the next card, smiling with buck teeth like he has something good. "From right along the way, singing us back, six-time winner, North Hollywood's Madelyn Jenso."

She slips around Rudy Yid, pushing her way to the aisle along the wall while downfront men turn out of their seats.

Instead of using the side steps, she reaches to the emcee, kicking up a leg which brings yells like from a barracks. Pulling her up he retreats in a crouch, eyes wide. As she straightens her dress to whoops and yells, he springs back.

"You menfolk be kind."

She turns to the quartet, straight in the shoulders and legs. Stepping up so the microphone is between her legs she gazes out over the crowd, humming with the strum of the guitars, and coming in on a piano crescendo.

Sweet dreams of you
Every night I go through
Why can't I forget you
And start my life anew.

They crowd in from outside blocking his view and he gets out into the aisle along the wall, moving down to where he can see her. She is humming now over the guitars, tapping a heel.

You don't love me it's plain.
I should know,
I'll never wear your ring.
I should hate you, the whole night through
Instead of having sweet dreams about you.

She leans back now seeing she has them and lets go like there are two of her.

Sweet dreams of you.
Things I know can't come true.
Why can't I forget the past,
Start loving someone new,
Instead of having sweet dreams about you.

She sidehops off the stage wading into them, coming up the center with every eye hard on her heels. Going left along the bar, she beats Rudy Yid to the corner. His eyes are wide. "I didn't think you could sing like that. I thought you were a church singer or something." He is about to show her the chill on his arm when a bartender puts a drink in front of her and she gulps half, leaning back in the nook with a hand over her lips. In front the emcee thumps on the microphone to get everybody turned around, while a tall figure in a light blue western suit makes his way out, calling over.

"I enjoyed your song. You with anybody?"

"Yea him" she says nudging Rudy Yid.

"I mean representation" he nods as if she knows what he means.

"No."

He reaches over and hands her a card. "I'm Jesse Sparks. Give me a call."

"Who's he?" asks Rudy Yid.

"A recording agent" she says biting her lip.

CHAPTER 10

Next morning she hardly lets him through the foyer. "I called him. He wants to send a picture and tape to every record company and country station. He says nowadays it's a waste of time to go play honky-tonks. He wants a contract up front. I told him how it's been and he said I've paid my dues twice over."

She barely lets him by. "But you know what it costs? Three thousand five hundred. He wants to send out a thousand copies."

"You have to pay?"

"He says I'm new; it's up to me. I called friends in Grand Rapids. I even thought about calling my sister. Where am I going to get thirty-five hundred?"

He knows he's letting himself in for it. "What happens after the stations get the tape?"

"If it plays and people start to call, or if record companies get interested, a hundred thousand dollar advance is nothing to them. It can happen overnight."

"They'll call" he says. "They see your picture and hear you sing, they'll call."

"Yea, but where do I get money?"

He stands there convincing himself.

"I got it."

"*You've* got thirty-five hundred dollars?"

"I told you I came here to get into a business."

"It's no guarantee. I don't know how long it'll take before I sign a contract."

"It won't take long. Who's gonna turn you down? Who won't fall in love with you?"

Tears turn in her eyes. "You're the only one who ever helped me and I could see it the second I saw you. I'll pay you back. For risking your money, for doing this, whatever I get is yours."

They drive over the Hollywood Pass to a building on Franklin and take an elevator to the third floor. They pass an import business, coming to Sparks Talent Agency and Notary Public. Jesse is in front of his desk pressing an imprint on a business form. A man in short sleeves, holding an attache case, hands him a twenty dollar bill and looks surprised when he gets no change back. Madelyn beams at Jesse but he regards her in a plain way.

"Have a seat."

He goes to a back room and Madelyn and Rudy Yid sit down. She leans against him squinting at a row of celebrity pictures on the wall. Jesse returns, lifting a leg across a corner of the desk. His western pants draw up over black buckled shoes.

"Y'know Tanya Tucker?" Madelyn grins, nodding to a picture of her in a leather jumpsuit.

"Yea, Tanya'll stop in when she's in town, but she's not what you might think. The girl will pause to pray and bless her food."

Getting out a pack of smokes he eyes Rudy Yid. "What's your part?"

"I'm with her."

"You sit like LAPD. Anybody tell you that?"

"I'm from Chicago. I didn't go to college."

"We're together" repeats Madelyn.

"Together, okay. Let's talk. You have something. I'm not sure what exactly, but you have something. But you know, don't you, or you wouldn't be here. It wouldn't be worth your while, would it?"

He gets a grin out of her but she expected more.

"You sing good — not well, just good. And that's a compliment comin' from me. Your call needs tonin' down and that's not as easy as it sounds. You're new but I think we can bring this together. Like I said. The plan's direct. We don't waste a lot of time here. Other agents'll tell you go sing in honky-tonks and come back. To me those days are gone. We're gonna send dubs and photos — a thousand each. Most of it I admit is splat to see what sticks but I've been around longer'n I wanna admit and I know the pros still around and not these conceited jerks on toot. Now here's what I charge — and it costs because I've had 'em run out on me after I've busted a blue gut, then call back a few months later with the here's why. Hey, I don't wanna hear it. So hereon I make sure of commitment first, and it's gonna be fifteen hundred up front and another two thousand before recording tomorrow."

"So soon?" asks Madelyn.

"You have time to waste?" he asks. "You're getting a late start. What are you, thirty, thirty-two?"

"Twenty-five" she says back. "Could I sing *Sweet Dreams*?"

"No, we'd have trouble with that. I got a ballad."

He gets a cassette player from the back, puts it on the desk and pushes the play button. Without instrumentation a female voice starts out hoarse like in a rough hymn then smooths out a story about a woman picking up and setting out to find somebody new. It's spirited but does not reach a crescendo.

"Was that Brenda Lee singing that?" asks Madelyn.

"Ain't you gonna ask who it was wrote it?" suggests Jesse

flipping off the player.

"You wrote it?" Madelyn smiles.

"Thank you, but what's that matter nowadays? Well, what'd you think?"

"I think I could do it."

"*Can* you do it proud? That's the point. Some top gals asked me to sing it, but I've been saving it for one of my own."

"Could I make some changes? I think I can open it up."

"Make the changes you want but you get just two hours in studio tomorrow. I don't want your voice flying into the instrumentation. I want it comin' forth hand 'n hand. I don't want 'em thinking you're green."

"Do I sing with a band?"

"God, no!" he yaps. "Your voice couldn't time a band in an hour. You'll work with Jimmy Blevins, one of the best tone and echo men in the business."

"You mean sing into canned music?"

"Can you master a song in one night?"

"I think I can."

He takes a cigarette from a pack and taps it on a thumbnail, eyeing Rudy Yid. "It'll cost me plenty on shipping and follow-up but I think this young lady here is the best prospect I've come across in years, and I'll bet a good cup of coffee she gets where she's going."

On the way back Madelyn sings off a music sheet.

Packing memories in mornin's glow,
Ask me what I did I still don't know.
But I don't stay where I ain't wanted,
It's not my M.O.
Dryin' farewell tears I'll set out on my own,
Find another movin' on.
It's been my way to hold my own,

I ain't no stranger to ways gone lone.

She nuzzles up to Rudy Yid and warbles in his ear.

It's been my way to hold my own,
I ain't no stranger to ways gone lone.

"What's wrong?"

"I don't like the way he was talking to you."

"How was he talking to me?"

"He sits there like a cold fish and asks if you're thirty or thirty-two, then says you don't sing well — just good. Either he was using cheap psychology or he was trying to hurt your feelings."

"So you don't want to give him money?"

"You tell me; you wanna do business with him? The way you sing maybe we could find somebody else."

"I've tried. I've gone everywhere. I've knocked on every door. You see how I sing; whoever lifted a finger to help? Whoever picked up the phone to do the littlest thing for me? Even a guy like Jesse plays hard to get. We don't have to be friends so long as he helps."

He drops her off and takes his traveler's checks to Bank of America and buys two checks. He drives back to Hollywood and hands a fifteen hundred dollar check to Jesse who folds it once and slips it into his pocket like a note.

Next morning he picks her up in front of the apartment house. She's in flats, shorts and a sleeveless blouse, dressed like women do to clean house. As she swings her legs in, he sees old mosquito bite nicks along her shins. The freckles on her nose have spread and she has bags under her eyes.

"I didn't sleep" she says. "I worked so hard on the song I got in bed and thought about it all night. And Cindy knew I had a big day, so she picks this morning to start up about buying her clothes at Zody's. She used to love to run through the aisles there. Now it's not good enough. She ate my heart out first thing this morning."

They drive to a small stucco studio aside a metalworks barn. Dino the photographer and his assistant take her to a mirror and make her up. She strips to her bra and panties and pulls on a white spangled top and tight black skirt. Her breasts are half out and Dino, a silverhaired old-Hollywood pretty boy in tight maroon pants all but moans through his nose then out of the blue brings up he used to date Virginia Mayo.

They try a red wig but Madelyn takes it off, so they roll up a bang in front and spray it stiff. Dino sits her on a low stool with her knees cramped under her chest, and has her twisting so that her nipples almost pop out, which appears to be what he's after as veins protrude in his neck. He snaps pictures prefacing each with "So pretty" and "Once upon a smile."

Dino tells them how to get to a recording studio on Lankershim and sends them over. It is a converted garage behind a liquor-grocery. Jesse leads them into a bare room except for a recording table and disco ball. Rudy Yid's eyes are getting used to the dark when a pale hand comes up under his nose for a check.

A technician sits Madelyn down and explains the process. She puts on earphones and starts humming and tapping her fingers, fitting words phrase to phrase and catching a breath between. She leans forward trying the phrases until she figures it out. Uncrossing her legs, she sits up and starts singing, missing and catching herself until she's in a timbre that pitches between the walls. Jesse winks over at Rudy Yid.

"She's guaranteeing it now."

She finishes and heads around the table out of breath. "Truthfully, Jesse, how long do you think it'll take?"

"Slow down. Whoa." He holds his hand up. "It takes awhile but this mail-out tactic gets us on the road." He checks his watch. "Okay, you'll have the dub and picture by Wednesday."

Back in the car Madelyn slumps in relief. "I didn't think it would happen," she says. "To get out a song and picture to radio stations and record companies."

"We're not there yet" says Rudy Yid. "When it's all sent out and the record companies have the tape and see your picture, then we're there. Right now he's got the money and we got nothin'."

"You gave him the two thousand?"

"He had his fingers under my nose the second I got in there."

"You're broke?"

"I still got some money."

"What're you gonna do?"

"I saw an ad for laborers. Forty a day and they cash your check."

"You're gonna do that?"

"It's okay. It'll pay the motel and gas until something happens."

"You think it will?" she asks, her eyes glazing over.

"Do I think it will? You should have seen Jesse in there. He was twitching."

CHAPTER 11

He drives out at six in the morning to Day Hire in Van Nuys. The door is on the backside of a vacated state employment building. A score of derelicts are in line with their backs to the wall, talking sidewise to each other as though afraid of losing their places. Groups of Hispanics stand around drinking coffee, unconcerned about a place in line. A few loners like Rudy Yid get out of cars with out-of-state plates and look around. He feels in disguise here with these characters in need of a few dollars. He's almost forgotten now the old man and small boy he'd abandoned. They faded from him as soon as he parted with the thirty-five hundred, but he promises himself that he will make up for it down the line. The door opens at seven and one at a time they go in, give a name and social security number and take a number.

The first employer vehicle is a bus from a movie service company. A jobber gets off, saying he needs bodies for a flophouse scene. The derelicts come to him holding up numbers. He lets on one to sixteen. Those over ask if they can go but are turned down and taunted from bus windows by the others. Turning their backs they tear up their numbers and walk off the lot.

Next comes a small pick-up driven by an Aussie wearing a bush hat, shorts and construction boots. He wants two for landscaping work. Those with numbers before Rudy Yid don't want it and he gets on the truck with a sturdy Mexican who speaks no English. They are driven to a northern corner of the Valley up into foothills. The Aussie wants an area leveled aside a hill. He gives the Mexican and Rudy Yid a wheelbarrow and shovel each. They roll them up zigzagged boards and start to dig, loading the wheelbarrows with loose red dirt, then roll them back down to dump out in the shade of a tree. The Aussie pushes a third wheelbarrow up the boards to work with them. He looks as tanned as a white man can be without chancres. He starts to dig and the stringy muscles in his arms snap like a hammock in the wind.

Rudy Yid figures him good for a wheelbarrow or two but he works right along with them until a break at noon. Driving off, he leaves Rudy Yid and the Mexican to rest under the tree. He is back at one and works with them until four when he collects the equipment, writes two vouchers and drives them back to Day Hire. Rudy Yid waits inside with the Mexican for their pay and overhears the Aussie at the counter saying that tomorrow he needs two faster men.

He drives to the motel, his arms and face powdered from the silt he dug and redder underneath from sun. Feeling good he's done some work and been paid he lies down on the floor to rest before he takes a shower and calls Madelyn.

Next morning he is driven from Day Hire to Glendale, to a used Chevy lot across the street from a dealership. On the boulevard there one car lot comes after another. The lot manager gives him rubber boots and a hose, and has him go from car to car hosing them down and wiping them off. He finishes one side of the lot, takes a break and starts on the other. He's done by three and goes into the office. The manager is a strapping man with crisp blond hair creeping out in front. In a short-sleeve white shirt and black tie he looks like a Mormon but the name on the deskplate looks Italian with three z's. Behind him is a shelf of signed baseballs with two Pittsburgh Pirate caps. He puts down the phone and the hair on his forearms shines like spun wool.

"You want this job?"

"No, I don't do this."

"You don't do this? What the hell you doin' here if you don't do this?"

"I'm working day to day. I might as well move around."

"If you're drifting, watch yourself. Glendale isn't L.A. They got an eye around every corner. The cops don't even like out-of-state plates. I was here five years before they accepted me on the row. I didn't like it at first but I appreciate it now. You got settler stock here. Iowans. John Wayne stock. They might be running businesses but you still see the pioneer and animal herder in their eyes."

"That so" says Rudy Yid. "They got pastures here where they go fuck sheep?"

The manager leans back. "What's that?"

Rudy Yid shakes his head between his hands. "Sorry, things come out of me sometimes."

"What're you, a two-bit actor waiting for a break?"

"No. I invested in a singer."

"*You* . . . invested in a singer?"

"Yea, she sings country songs. Her name is Madelyn Jenso."

"How much you invest?"

"Thirty-five hundred."

"Thirty-five hundred. What's that gonna do?"

"It makes a thousand pictures and tapes."

"That's not gonna get it. You need a syndicate to get a singer off the ground. I know the business. I used to play rhythm guitar. When my brother and I got out here we played with Gary Busey. This business is staked out by agents, front men, publicists and shills. They have their territory and don't just let you by. You get in with them, and they turn you out. It's a big pie with a lot of thumbs."

"I ain't worried about nobody's thumbs. People hear her sing one time, that's it, she's famous."

"They'll never hear her. It's fixed. I had a buddy in Pittsburgh who brought black girls to Motown. He told me there's ten thousand girls who could sing as good as The Supremes. You could find them on street corners, but he couldn't sign up. He didn't have the connections to promote. He knew 'em all up there — Smokey Robinson, The Temptations, Jimmy Ruffin — and still couldn't do anything."

"Maybe it's different with them."

The manager reaches into the drawer for a voucher.

Wednesday he and Madelyn are outside her apartment house. The mailman comes up and hands her a padded envelope. Tearing it open she holds up a black and white glossy and the color leaves her face. He looks and doesn't recognize her. Her face is round as a pie with a silly smile and half-closed eyes.

"Where'd they get this? This isn't you."

They go in, put the tape in a player and stand listening. The singing doesn't blend with the music, but when he turns it up her voice rings out.

Madelyn sits down numb. "Do I sound like that?"

"It's okay" he says. "It's like you sing. But why'd he pick

this picture?"

"Call him up" she says. "Get it changed."

He picks up the phone and dials. The answer comes in a number: *9678.*

"Jesse, that you?"

"Who's this?"

"I'm the guy with Madelyn."

"What can I do you for?"

"I'll tell you. We just got the picture and it's no good. It doesn't look like her. Who'd know this is her?"

"Nobody knows her anyway. What's the difference?"

He angers that Jesse isn't wise to this. "We were counting on the picture. She has a special look. It would catch a good eye. She looks like nothin' here. You send this picture and they'll throw it out."

"I already sent it."

"You *sent* it!" He looks over at Madelyn whose face sinks in her hands. "All thousand?"

"Yea."

"What was the hurry? You didn't have time to give us a look?"

"I told you we're working fast."

"Fast! How long's it take to look? You couldn't give us a call? We'd have come up there. And you couldn't pick a better picture?"

"Hey, I'm in this business twenty-eight years; I know what Country likes; it's not the smart-ass look you think. They want a done-up sweetie looking up at 'em with invite. Now, you wanna do it again we can follow up with a press release but it costs."

"How much?"

"A thousand and I'm lowering it five hundred."

Rudy Yid shakes his head. "Hey Jesse, this wasn't right. You sprang this on us. We put good money in your hands and you played it fast and loose."

"How'd I play it?" he asks.

"Fast and loose."

There is a click in the line. "I have another call, let me know."

He puts up the phone and sits down by her.

"Three thousand five hundred for a bad picture and off-key song." She stands up, turning back and forth.

He stops her and runs his hand up under her shorts between her legs.

"Is this a time?" she asks. "I feel sick to my stomach."

"It'll be okay" he says. "Out of a thousand somebody's gonna notice."

"Who?"

"Somebody. Who can hear you sing and not think you belong on radio?"

He goes back to the motel. He tried to show he was a sport and wasn't worried but he knew the tape was no good either. And who was to blame, letting himself get led around by the nose by an old hick? Sitting down he counts what's left of his traveler's checks, sorry now that he didn't at least get himself a little place and phone to get a start from. Now he'll have to look for a room in a house somewhere.

Next morning he gets a work slip with the address of a production company in the east Valley near the studios and drives to a small building on a curved lane. The first hour he sits in the air-conditioned lobby looking up at pictures of film crews on location doing commercials for trucks and tires. A pick-up arrives at the side door with another laborer and tools in back. A construction honcho gets out and takes him and the laborer behind the building, gives them two spades and starts them digging. The dry dirt sends up dust with each shovel. After an hour under a hazy sun he thinks he's never worked harder. He and the laborer don't have gloves and he can feel blisters swelling. During the break he sits in some shade with the laborer, a young drifter from Texas who tells him if the company had brought in a backhoe to do the work it would have cost five hundred dollars.

They dig a ditch along two sides then turn toward each other and meet in the middle, shovels clinking together. Rudy Yid climbs out with a stiff back and numb hands.

The drifter leaves with the honcho in the truck, and he goes inside and washes up in the restroom. All the while he splashes his face, his eye sockets look as if he's come out of a mine.

The secretary writes out a voucher, asking if he wants to be paid for an extra hour and deliver an envelope on the way back.

He follows her directions up into a shaded area of expensive homes. A breeze in his face, it looks here the way he thought all California would. He pulls into a drive sloping up to a home with a front like a greenhouse. As he gets out he recognizes who's coming: Lowell Stoker, who plays the suave neighbor on *The Abby Allen Show*, whom she and her friends make goo-goo eyes at when they see him over the fence. A black dog of the type that pulls milk carts in Europe romps out on the lawn behind him.

"You're Lowell Stoker, right?" he says handing him the envelope.

"Yep" he says tearing it open and pulling out a folded check and note.

Rudy Yid looks at him thinking he's exactly like on television, tanned and not a silver hair out of place. He waits for him to look up, but Lowell gazes back and forth from the check to the note until Rudy Yid wonders what could be on a check and note of no more than twenty words that would have him turning his head from one to the other.

He waits a little longer. "Well, I'll be going."

"Hold on" says Lowell still staring at the two pieces.

The dog sniffs up alongside Rudy Yid and he pats his head.

"Keep your hand off the dog."

"I was petting him" says Rudy Yid.

He snaps around. "Keep your *goddam* hands off the dog!" He stands quiet until Lowell motions to him to go.

He gets into his car ten feet away then is about to fling open the door and go back when Lowell pivots on the grass, heading to the house.

He coughs up everything he can from the dust he'd dug up and spits it out in the drive.

Next day, he meets Madelyn at a corner coffee shop.

"I'm nervous" she says. "I called three record companies this morning and none of them got the picture or tape."

"Maybe the mail's not there."

"The mail takes a day here. And these are the most important ones. I don't even think he sent them out."

"Why wouldn't he? It's his chance to get big. He knows that."

"Maybe he never had them made. Maybe he put the money in his pocket."

They go out to a pay phone in front. She sits down on a ledge and he makes the call. The answer comes again in the number: *9678*.

"Jesse, that you?"

"Who's this?"

"It's me. Any news on Madelyn?"

"Yea as a matter of fact, a few calls from out of state. A station in Nebraska and one in New York."

"New York. They gonna play her song?"

"They wanted info for now."

He puts his hand on the speaker, nodding to Madelyn. "He says a few stations called from New York and Nebraska and wanted info. You wanna talk?"

She shakes her head no and he lifts his hand from the speaker. "Jesse, Madelyn called record companies here and

81

none of them got the tape or picture."

"It takes 'em a awhile to sift through mail. They're disorganized."

"Yea, anyway Madelyn and I want a list of some executives you're sending copies to."

"Am I her agent or you?"

"You're the agent but we wanna know what's going on."

"I'll tell you both what's going on when it happens."

There's a click in the line.

"Jesse . . . Jesse."

He hangs up. "He's lying. He never had 'em made."

"What are we gonna do?"

"I oughta go over there and kick his lyin' ass" he says turning away.

"*Hey!*" she says.

"Hey what?"

"Hey, you don't talk that way around here. That's okay in Chicago maybe but you go blowing your stack around here and you'll be lucky to get work on a garbage truck."

"And just let him take my money?"

She doesn't answer and he leans over her. "C'mon, we'll go for a ride."

"I have to go home" she says.

"You gonna stay in on a day like this?"

"That's where my pay comes from. Staying in."

He sits down next to her on the ledge.

"Thirty-five hundred" she says shaking her head. "Like we never had it."

"Don't give up" he says. "I see how it works. You get burned you learn. We didn't need him. We'll get another picture, a place to sing — something to shoot for. I'll go talk to these companies myself. Let me at it once I see the way. Just don't lose hope. It's money. You lose money you lose nothin'. Lose your spirit you lose everything."

CHAPTER 12

She calls early next morning.

"I wake you?"

"No, I'm up. Any news?"

"Yea, I think they repossessed my car."

"Who?"

"A lot on Lankershim. My ex-husband sends payments from Vegas. He must be late, but I've got money."

"Let's go straighten it out."

"You're coming?"

"I'll be right there."

They drive to a corner lot with lines of streamers strung around. Two young salesmen sit on a trailer stoop.

"Anybody pick up a white '63 Cadillac last night?"

"I don't know" says the one sitting higher. "You check the cage in back?"

"I saw it" says the other stripping a cigarette. "It's back there."

"I have the payment" says Madelyn.

"Speak to Max. He'll be in after nine."

An Eldorado pulls into the lot, the driver a thick-necked character in a check sportcoat and white tie. The two salesmen get off the stoop.

"Mornin', Max."

"Mornin'."

"That little beaner called last night and says he can get together eleven hundred for the Mustang."

"The '69?"

"Yea."

"Tell him to roll it up tight like they do in the slammer and work it up his ass with his thumb. Better yet, get him down here and tell him."

Max turns to the other salesman. "You get that shit straight with your girlfriend?"

"I'm okay, Max."

"You better be, mister. Nobody buys a car from a sore-ass punk."

The other salesman nods toward Madelyn and Rudy Yid coming up. Max turns his thick neck, looking them up and down.

"What can I do for you?"

"My car was picked up last night" says Madelyn. "I think my ex-husband is late."

"What's his name?"

"Bart Jenso."

"Yea I remember. Tall thin dude. A musician or something."

They follow him into the trailer and sit down on a vinyl couch with a razor slash. He takes a ledger from a cabinet.

"Your number's disconnected?"

"Changed" says Madelyn.

"You working?"

"I'm a singer. I cut a demo. My agent's lining things up now."

"What do you sing?"

"Country. Just about everything really."

"What's he doing?"

"He's sending a demo and picture to everybody in the business."

"That's *not* how you do it. He's using buckshot. What you need is long deadly rifle fire. You've got to meet the *one* person in town with the power to make you a star. So what if some graveyard disc jockey in Omaha digs your sound.

84

Where's it getting you?"

Madelyn shrugs. "Nowhere I guess."

"Nowhere's correct. I'll give you an example. I had a kid selling cars for me. Good-looking kid in a sissy-boy way. He was out here three years, couldn't get a walk-on. Tried everything — schools, agents, portfolios. One day he meets this squeaky little producer buying a sportscar for his nephew. You remember *The Pullmans* on TV?"

"The family in the railcar."

"Remember the oldest son?"

"Yea, *Buzz*."

"That's him. He saw the bottom line and walked it or should I say bent over and caught the mustard." He flips his wrist flashing a gold bracelet and ring. "Back to business. You got this month?"

"Right here." She reaches into her bag. "I appreciate this."

Max pushes a pad and pen to her. "Put your horn there in case I run into a powerhouse." He regards Rudy Yid.

"You a neighbor?"

"Yea."

A salesman leads them back to the cage.

"Too bad he's not an agent" says Madelyn so the salesman can hear. "He could probably get a contract overnight."

"He's a bag of wind" says Rudy Yid.

The salesman unlocks the gate and heads back. Rudy Yid corners Madelyn as she opens the door.

"I'll meet you."

"I have a lot to do. Call me tonight?"

"What if I stop by for an hour?"

"No. You can wait until tonight." She gets behind the wheel with her legs spread. "Call, okay."

He drives to Day Hire and waits with other latecomers,

seeing it's useless. On a hunch he drives out to Glendale and parks at the curb of the Chevy lot. The manager is dealing outside with a wholesaler, and he waits until he's finished and follows him to the office.

"You need a guy?"

"You wanna wash cars in those clothes?"

"I'll wash cars."

"What's the matter — your singer's not famous? You're letting out air."

He closes the door. "I think I got taken. The picture was no good and the tape didn't turn out. I don't even think he sent them out."

"You know him? Anybody vouch for him?"

"He looked okay. He had an office."

"Hell yes, he looked okay. How else is he gonna get your money?" He puts a lozenge in his mouth. "Who let you out?"

Rudy Yid shakes his head. "It's not the money. It's the chance. She'd be famous."

"Who's she sing like?"

"I don't know much about singing."

"Then how do you know she can sing?"

"Anybody would. She makes the hair stand on your arm."

"Who's she like? Juice Newton . . . *Cher*?"

"Cher, nah. Cher could go hide under a bed compared to her."

"She that good?"

"How she's not famous I don't know. Everywhere she goes she wins contests."

"Bring her over with the tape" he says. "Ray Miramonte the general manager at KLIW comes by to shoot the shit on paydays. She's that good I'll call him."

"What can he do, play her song?"

"He might. What's the use of talking?" He checks his Rolodex, picks up the phone and dials. "Ray there? Ray

Azzuzi at Corner Chevy . . . Yea, have him give me a call."

Rudy Yid leans forward. "We'd give you something. We'll let you in."

"Go wash the cars, big shot."

CHAPTER 13

He gets back to the Valley before five and goes to Madelyn's door. The sitter answers the knock, and he sees Cindy on the couch.

"Where's Madelyn?"

"She went to pick up a job in Santa Monica. She said she'll be late."

"What time?"

"She said she'd call."

"She leave a number?"

"No."

"She calls, tell her I have news."

Going to the coffee shop, he sits at the counter, stepping outside to call at six and seven but she's not home. He walks up and down the way there until dark then crosses the street. Her car is still not in the lot, and her sitter answers the door.

"She's not here."

"She didn't call?"

"Not yet."

Cindy glances up from the couch then looks back to the television. The times she'd seen him before she stood up tall looking at him.

"She gave you no idea what time she'd be back?"

"She just said late."

He sits outside on the back stairs beside the bushes, watching cars go in and out of the lot. He imagines how the two Rays at the car lot and radio station will look when they see her and he'll be standing there the one who brought her.

He'd gotten into something he knew nothing about but he sees now you don't have to know everything. The biggest car dealer on the South Side was Chaiken an old Jew who didn't know a carburetor from an alternator. You just need to know the goods when you see them and hold on. Even if it doesn't work out tomorrow he'll go around until he gets it done. Who won't have a minute to look at her picture and listen to a tape? The night chill in his shirtsleeves, the whole of it turns in his mind.

The stone stairs get cold and he stands up. A white Eldorado turns in, pulling up near the walk. It's not so much the car he recognizes as the way the driver pulls in, his face red even in the dark. The engine stays on, and he steps down. His eyes on the light from the dashboard he comes up on the Cadillac from behind.

Max is behind the wheel in his check jacket from the morning but without the tie. Madelyn is lolled up next to him with a leg up and a shoe off. He budges over to kiss her, working a hand up under her leg. She leans up on a knee to let it through and lets him wiggle his tongue into her mouth. As her lips bulge against his she opens an eye at someone looking in from the side. Rudy Yid raps on the glass and she bucks back with a chirr in her throat. Max takes one look and rises up on his haunches. Plucking the handle up he heels the gas. The Cadillac rears into the drive. Swerving back it smashes through a cinder block abutment, squeals out on the street and heads straightaway.

Tenants come to windows and he goes down the street, getting behind a tree. He'd wanted to get his hands on him, not so much for now but for the way he'd come on to her in the trailer while he sat watching. But she was no better. She met him more than halfway with her eyes and voice, drinking in everything he said. If she had the decency to wait just one more day he'd have her out to the Chevy lot tomorrow and the two Rays would do something to get her on her way. Her luck would have changed but she ruined it for herself.

He waits for them to come back then goes to the coffee shop. He stands out at the side then goes to a pay phone and calls getting a busy signal. He tries a few more times while the waitresses inside fill up sugar dispensers, then goes to the motel and is about to call again when he gets a feeling to keep a Jewish head about this. Why should it all be finished and he go away with nothing? He'll be at her door in the morning, tell her what Ray Azzuzi said and get her out to Glendale before she can call Max. If they can start her on something and promise they won't cut him out in the end, he'll go his own way.

CHAPTER 14

Up a little after five, he goes out in the dark. At the coffee shop, he sits at the counter with earlybirds. As dawn breaks and traffic thickens, he heads across the street, down the block to Madelyn's building. Her car still isn't in the lot and he wonders if she came back, doubting she's the type to leave her daughter all night with a babysitter.

Standing out front an hour he watches people leave for work, then goes down the hall to her apartment. He hears the television on and knocks. There is no answer.

"Madelyn, you in there? I got news. I met a guy who knows a radio station manager in Glendale. He wants to see you and hear the tape."

The television is turned down.

"Madelyn, that you?" He hears nothing. "Madelyn, let's go see what he says. He wants to help. He wants to see you."

He knocks harder. "Madelyn, let me know if you're in there." He looks down the hall at somebody going out and lowers his voice. "Madelyn, let me know. I'm not going to do anything."

Thinking it might be the babysitter inside afraid to answer, he taps the door one last time about to leave, when she calls.

"*Rudy*, go away. I don't want any trouble."

"Madelyn, open up. I know a Chevy guy in Glendale who can help us. We can go now."

"Rudy, I can't."

"Madelyn, let him get a look at you. His eyes will pop out. What's there to lose?"

He hears the lock turn and stop, and tries the door.

"Madelyn, what's there to be afraid of? What am I going to do to you?"

She won't answer.

"Madelyn, how could you do it? You let that slob feel you all over. You got no pride? Sucking his tongue and letting him dig his fingers between your legs. He's got some two-bit car lot and he's gonna make you a star?"

He looks down the hall at a male neighbor standing there watching and knocks again. "Madelyn, don't do this. It's not that bad in your life that you have to do this. Open the door."

"Rudy, please, I don't want any trouble."

"What trouble? What about my money? You expect me to forget it?"

"I'll pay you back. I swear to God I'll pay you back, just *please* go away."

He would say more but the shriek in her voice reminds him of his mother's when she wanted his father to leave her alone.

He stops down the street at a car lot with a sign: *Buy Sell Trade*.

"You need cars?" he asks the salesman.

"What do you have?"

"A '79 with forty-seven thousand miles."

He swings a leg off the desk and goes out for a look, walking around the car. "It's big, out-of-state and creased along two doors."

"You can't sell a car like that?"

"Not many looking for a big job like this. You from Chicago?"

"Yea."

"You have to sell? This is L.A."

"I can get by."

"You guys come out thinking you can sell a car for a stake. People keep cars here twenty years. Cars don't rust here."

Rudy Yid looks down the road. "You know anybody who might be interested?"

"Yea for a hundred and fifty. I'll give you that."

"It's not enough."

"You have to sell right away?"

"I can wait."

"If it's not urgent get the crease taken out, get plates and put it in the paper with forty-seven thousand miles. Some Mexican with eight, nine kids will bring you seven or eight hundred for it."

"It'll cost me two hundred just to get the crease out."

"There's an old-timer named Harvey up on Lankershim behind a sandblasting place. He's half blind but does good work. He's done cars for me. He'll charge you fifty for that."

"Fifty?"

"Go see what he says. He likes to talk."

He drives north on Lankershim into a dusty area of old lots and bungalows. Turning into a path between a sandblasting company and liquor store, he drives into a grass lot with a shack not much bigger than a toolshed. Cars from the Forties and Fifties are parked along a fence, spattered with twigs and buds. A modern car with body filler on the side stands under a eucalyptus tree. Hunched between the car and a workbench is an old-timer in a grayed undershirt, sagging fedora and old suit trousers. He straightens up, his jaw hanging as Rudy Yid comes closer.

"You wouldn't be kin to Tyrone Power?"

"No."

"I coulda sworn you was Jesse. I called him that."

"You knew Tyrone Power?"

"Never met his acquaintance. Saw his movies."

"You kind of look like one of those movie characters yourself."

"No, they never asked me. I done cattle-milking and dishwashing in winters, but I never done movie work. That and barkeeping. I did some road work in Texas. Not that they paid me. Isn't safe to go through there down on your luck. Hardest people I ever saw. Won't even smile unless they want somethin'."

"Where you from originally?"

"Oklahoma. The Osage Hills. It's been forty years."

"You never went back?"

"No sir, packed a bag and lit out. I was like my daddy. I liked peace and quiet. The rest of my relatives was armed robbers and roughnecks. All my uncles served time. One uncle and brother-in-law was machine-gunned. The school was all cousins trying to kill each other. The hallways was impassable. It wasn't safe to go through. It was in the blood. We was kin to the James and Youngers of Missouri."

"You were kin to Jesse James?"

"My mother was Sister Opal James. Jesse's mother was her great aunt. My mother helped her in the house. She only had one arm."

"You knew Jesse James?"

"He was gone even before my mother was born."

"Was he like they say?"

"Worse. Five, six times. Jesse, Frank and two Youngers rode with Quantrill when they was boys. Straps in their teeth, navy Colts in each hand, drivin' strong horses. The Union boys weren't no match for 'em. No tellin' how many they left for dead. They never counted that high. But Jesse wasn't the toughest. Jesse had a fancy about him but Cole and Frank were tougher. Cole rode back for his brother in Northfield and got hit eleven times. His horse got hit in the jaw, slid and rit up. And those farmers could shoot. Nothing more practical than a farmer. I remember a male teacher sayin' it might be the bravest act done on American soil. Educated people formin' interest in it, but I never cared for it. I liked working for honest people and getting paid. Excuse me."

He takes a minute to pry the lid off a container. "About ten years back, I was getting too old to keep shuttlin' for myself so I had to find work that finds you. I only been doing car work since I was sixty-nine. Can you believe that on a lotus worm unicorn?"

He looks over at the visitor's car. "You bring work?"

"On the other side."

He goes around the car and runs his hand down along the crease. "This one's sharper than it looks. You want it painted over?"

"How much would it cost?"

"Forty-five, fifty, but I need it a week or two to fit it in. I get jobs from lots to finish in a day. Can you leave it?"

He takes the ignition key off the ring and hands it to him.

"Come by on a Saturday with two Miller and we'll sit. I got a picture of Cole and me when I was an infant on his porch in Sedalia, Missouri. I got it inside in a box and need somebody to help me search for it. People would pay good money to see that picture."

He walks south on Lankershim, going twelve blocks in the sun. He turns a corner not far from the motel, stepping into a market for a carton of juice. Going down the meat aisle he watches a slender butcher placing a tray of packaged meat in the case.

"You hiring apprentices?"

93

The butcher puts the empty tray aside and adjusts his glasses. Except his swollen red fingers he looks more like a shipping clerk.

"You got experience?"

"I can do some boning. I used to clean cutting rooms after school. My father was a butcher. I know the machines."

"You working?"

"I just came from Chicago. I worked in a steel mill ten years."

He doesn't look impressed. "I don't know how it is in a mill, but this is steady going eight hours. No stopping for a cigarette every five minutes. What makes you want to be a butcher after ten years?"

"I'd like to learn a trade."

"I'll tell you now, you got to be a certain type. It's not for everybody. You're learnin' as you go or I have to let you go."

"I understand."

"You look like a butcher. You live around here?"

"Down the street."

"I'll call the office and tell 'em we're taking you on. It pays five-fifty an hour but you get raised every three months. Can you get by?"

"Yea."

"Be sure. I don't want you comin' next week saying it's not enough."

"I'll get by."

"I'm Tom the manager. Be here Monday at seven and we'll make a butcher out of you."

Monday morning he steps out of his room at six-thirty and walks to the market. In the cutting room Tom hands him a pencil and application sheet, then fits him with a white coat, hat and apron, and chain mail finger glove. He puts him to work carrying in boxes of ducks and chickens from the cooler.

When he finishes he goes to stuffing frozen beef strips into the grinder and cutting slabs into stew meat. Seeing he can handle a knife Tom brings him a box of ox tails to cut into pieces. As Tom rolls in a rack of beef shanks, Rudy Yid grabs one off a hook and bones it clean in two sweeps of his knife. "Look at that!" calls Tom to the butchers as Rudy Yid laughs.

At ten-fifteen he goes to the back with a carton of cottage cheese and sits down across from Ted the other apprentice who's past his break.

"How long you been here?"

"Two months."

"You like it?"

"I don't know. I thought I was okay, but Tom told me this morning I'm not fast enough."

"Not everybody's made for this."

"And you are?"

"I didn't mean it like that. My father was a butcher and his father. You gotta feel the knife in your hand even when it's not there."

The explanation doesn't impress Ted. "I wanted to be a journeyman," he says. "I want to keep moving. I can't stay in one place anymore. A lot of vets doin' that now, but you need a trade so if you tap out somewhere with your ol' lady you can go knock down ten, twelve bucks an hour at the local market and won't have to go cleaning yards and collecting cans."

"You a Vietnam vet?"

"Everybody's a Vietnam vet. I was Light Infantry on the Cambodia border. They did a story on us. We ambushed an NVA company coming across a river and cut 'em to pieces."

"How'd you know they were comin'?"

"Kids told us. We thought they were lying but we set the ambush."

"You paratroopers?"

"No sir. Straight leg. The best. One blood all, and you knew the ones going to make it. I picked every one. I just didn't know about myself. I thought if I got out in one piece nothing would stop me, but it's been one trap after another. I couldn't get anything down. Five years ago four of us got together in the same situation. Divorced, busted, nothing to lose. We thought nothing's gonna stop us now. We started a janitorial service and in two weeks we were bitchin' about who wasn't doing their share. We would have taken a bullet for each other and now we were arguing about who wasn't getting in corners. It threw me. I didn't want to live but I came to realize you got to do whatever you can for yourself. It's you first and what you can spare for others but no more."

He is wiping down steel trays when Tom comes up. "That's a day. See you tomorrow."

The next two days he works as if he's been there a month, rolling and tying roasts, boning shanks and wrapping packages. All the butchers seem happy with him except the saw butcher, a bullneck called Red for his face or temper.

Wednesday afternoon the butchers are at one table, cutting slabs into cubes for stew. It is a slow time and they gab as they work. Saw Butcher Red is at one end.

"You get it last night?" he asks Tom.

"Fuckin' A" says Tom.

"You probe the old bat cave?"

"She don't let me fuck her till I do that."

Rudy Yid brings in a tub of suet.

"Hey Rudy," says Tom, "how old are you?"

"Thirty."

"You been married?"

"No."

"Why not?"

"I got time."

"These guys today don't want responsibility" says Red. "Look at your boy Ted. You say something and he goes

AWOL."

"He'll be back" says Tom.

"Yea, for his check or send his wife."

Tom breaks out laughing so that he has to hold a finger under his nose.

"Yea laugh. That's why this country is going to shit. Send 'em to fight a war against some slanteyed niggers weighing a hundred pounds apiece and they come back crying with shit all over their face. They embarrassed this country. They embarrassed me."

"That was ten years ago" says Tom.

"Look around" says Red. "The world's laughing and they're still crying, with head bandanas yet. One of these days they'll let Russia and China over here and they'll bring Mau Maus from the Congo to come get theirs — rape our daughters and fuck our wives in the ass."

Tom puts the knife down before he cuts himself.

"Think it don't happen?" says Red. "Look at the Greeks and Italians. They used to be blond. Their women all looked like Sandra Dee. And you think the Jews are gonna be any help? Show me a Jew yet who can't figure the odds on the spot and know whose boots to start licking. Mark my words. This country is gonna turn into Brazil where everybody's half nigger and half queer and all they want to do all day is dance on the street with their butts out. We'd be lucky to kick their ass."

"C'mon" urges Tom. "Ted did a job over there."

"Yea a job. Open up on some mountain assholes with their balls in the water and it rates *Time* magazine. In my day it wouldna made the *Army Gazette*. Audie Murphy was a soldier. Fought his ass off day in and day out."

"That he did," says Tom, "but it was different times then."

"Times don't change. Just the weather and quality of your men."

"Yea," sniffs Tom, "and the spring in your hard-on."

Next morning he is grinding hamburger meat when Tom comes in from the front and goes to Red.

"They're grabbin' up that pork chop special."

"I got a hindquarter for Elks."

"It's gotta wait." He calls to Rudy Yid. "Get the pork ribs in back and pack for Red."

He brings out two boxes of ribs and Red piles them up to his right, running them through the saw. As chops stack up, Rudy Yid packs them into Styrofoam trays.

"Use two hands."

He tries two hands but they stack up higher. Red stops the saw, grabs a tray and arranges eight chops, flipping the tray aside.

"Like that. Let's go!"

He saws again and Rudy Yid can't keep up. He stops the machine and shoves him.

"You can't do the job, get the fuck outta here. I'm not losing a finger for you."

Feeling the thud on his shoulder, Rudy Yid flips his cap aside and steps to the right. "Don't ever lay a hand on me, red face. I'll turn your day black."

Tom steps between them. "What happened?"

"Teach him how to pack trays or get him out. I won't work with him."

Tom takes Rudy Yid aside. "Grind these flanks. I'll pack."

At quitting time he has finished washing steel trays when Tom comes to the sink.

"You cooled down?"

"Who's he shoving me?"

"Hey, Red's the best butcher in the company. Bite your tongue or you're gone. Take off tomorrow and be back Saturday."

He eats at the coffee shop and is back in his room with a newspaper before five, wondering if this is for him — just to have a trade to fall back on. Everybody he knew was making money and he was taking two years out to learn how to cut meat. It would give him an excuse to wind up a butcher. He rests awhile, deciding he'll take a walk and go somewhere and think it over.

At eight that night he is in a movie line at a theater a mile from the motel. In the lobby he picks up a free movie magazine and goes inside to a middle row. As he looks through the magazine four teenagers pile into the row behind him spilling a drink.

"This movie better not be boring" says one.

"Suck my drawers. Who asked you to go?"

One leans over to another. "Let me have some popcorn."

"Get your own popcorn."

"I just want a handful."

"I'll give you a handful with a root and a head."

"Keep your lousy popcorn."

The lights dim and a preview comes on.

"Candy Bradley's in this. My brother says she's got some good pussy."

"Your brother is a lying gorp."

"Your mother's a gorp."

Rudy Yid turns. "I'm trying to watch this."

He turns back and a teenager snatches some popcorn.

"I said get your own popcorn."

"Give me a dollar you owe me."

Rudy Yid gets up and moves down six rows.

"See, people avoid you."

"Nobody avoids me." The teenager throws a gumball that flies past Rudy Yid's head and bounces between seats. He looks back.

"You better quit fuckin' around."

"*Oooh!*"

An usher comes turning a flashlight on the boys. "You're

making too much noise."

As the feature starts the teenagers move down behind Rudy Yid. Their chuckles turn to wheezing, and he rolls the movie magazine tight. A bare foot comes up on the backrest next to him and he looks back at the teenager.

"Get your foot down."

The teenager pulls his knee up to his chin, holding it there until Rudy Yid turns, then stomps the backrest. Rudy Yid turns back smacking him with the magazine. The one on his left jumps up as if to fight and is yanked over the backrest, and slammed down between the seats. As the crowd yawps he holds him down ready to let go but the teenager begins to kick and curse.

"That's it!" He bangs him side to side and drags him out bleeding from the nose. Getting him up by the hair, he pulls him through a side row, knocks open a door and shoves him out in the alley. He pulls the door shut before he can get back and returns to some cheers and boos. The other teenagers have left and he sits down with no one around him.

Fifteen minutes later the usher leads two patrolmen down the aisle, pointing at him. A light shines in his face.

"Over here!"

He moves to them. "What's wrong?"

"There's a complaint of battery against you" says the patrolman turning the flashlight down. From the reflection Rudy Yid can see stripes and hashmarks on his sleeve. His young partner stands watching.

"You have an altercation with two boys?"

"Yea, they wouldn't leave me alone. They put a foot up next to my head and kicked the back of my chair."

"They hit you?"

"No."

"You hit them?"

"I slapped one with a magazine. His buddy jumped up like he wanted to fight; I pulled him over the seat and dragged him out."

"Come with us."

He goes through the lobby to a patrol car in front.

"You have identification?" asks the patrolman.

He gets out a wallet and hands him a driver license.

"You know how old those boys are?"

"No."

"Fifteen. You get the feeling they were going to jump you?"

"No" says Rudy Yid glancing over at a line of people looking on. He eyes the younger patrolman, who stands to the side with half-clenched fists watching every move he makes.

The patrolman hands him back the license. "Face around and lock your fingers behind your head."

He's patted down; his arms are pulled behind him and his wrists locked. ·

"You're under arrest. You have the right to remain silent. Anything you say can and will be used against you. . . ."

He's put in the back and on the way to the station he looks out at the streets he just walked, wondering why he didn't get out of the theater when he had the chance.

In the station lot, he's taken through a back door into a holding room and locked to a ring on a bench. He sits there while the patrolmen fill out a report making calls to the emergency room and theater.

The veteran patrolman approaches him at the bench. "You're charged with two counts of battery on minors. You'll go in front of a judge within twenty-four hours to plead guilty or not guilty."

He's unlocked from the bench and taken through a security door to a caged counter and turned over to a pug-faced jailer wearing khakis.

"You got two hundred for bail?"

"I got traveler's checks."

"Cash only." He points to a phone on the wall with

business cards around it. "A bondsman there makes the exchange for a fee."

He looks over at the wall. "I might as well stay the night."

"Put everything you have on the counter."

The jailer takes him into the next room where he's fingerprinted and photographed. Next he's taken down a corridor to a steel door and let into the bullpen, a high-ceilinged stone room with vulgar carvings in the walls. A few blacks in sportswear stand near the middle and ragged whites sit on the floor against the wall. An old bum with a dry red mouth approaches.

"Hoss, you gotta match?"

Rudy Yid steps around him, holding his breath.

"All I want is a match. Is that too much to ask a man?"

He sits down on the floor next to a longhaired white with military tattoos.

"That old guy needs to be fumigated."

"Wait till he shits his pants. You'll wanna stuff your shorts up your nose."

"What're you here for?"

"Possession."

"I throw some teenagers out of a movie and they charge me with assault and battery."

"You can commit assault just by looking like you wanna kick somebody's ass."

"I don't think I hurt 'em."

"Don't matter. If they're minors you're not supposed to lay a hand on 'em."

"How serious they take this?"

"Depends. You know anybody?"

"No."

"Better hope they don't either."

The old bum who'd asked for a match comes over. "You gotta match?"

The longhair hands him his cigarette. "Smoke it over there."

He sits with him until the lights dim then goes into a narrow cell and lies down on a bare rack putting his shoes under his head.

CHAPTER 15

A breakfast cart is rolled in and he gets in line for a tray of toast and syrup and a cup of coffee. He and others are called out of the bullpen by name. Marshals lock them four to a chain and take them out across the lot into a holding room next to Arraignment Court. The chains are removed; the prisoners sit on a bench and a marshal plays a tape that informs them of their constitutional rights. Each prisoner is asked if he will hire a lawyer, defend himself or wants a public defender. An hour later Rudy Yid is called into a room divided by bars. A pudgy lawyer with a short red beard sits at a table on the other side. The room is warm but he wears a jacket of a heavy knit.

"I'm Sol Nathan, a public defender."

He unzips a frayed briefcase, taking out a report. "Y'know the charges?"

"Assault and battery."

"Two counts battery on two minors fifteen years of age. What's your side?"

"They came into a movie and started bothering me. They threw a gumball and kicked the back of my chair. I moved away but they followed me and put a foot up next to my head, so I slapped one with a magazine and threw another out. I had a reason."

"You had reason but you may almost never lay an angry hand on a minor. Not only that — you picked the wrong ones. *Boy* did you pick wrong ones. These boys have names. I recognize the addresses. This Donco boy's grandfather is a Superior Court judge. I've argued in front of him and he's no nice guy. The Spoegels kid, if I'm right, is lawyered up on both sides — in the Valley and over the hill both."

"I don't have a right to protect myself?"

"Your right to defend yourself is limited to physical attack and there was none. You admitted as much to the officer here. If you had the savvy to say they kicked you in back of the head, that's different. A good little lie takes some starch out of any charge."

He turns his head to some sun through the window. A thick double chin shows through his red whiskers. "Why the honesty?" he asks. "You think they deserved honesty?"

"I didn't hurt those guys."

"Well, they've been to emergency. There's a medical report of a fractured nose and a concussion. They'll probably sue the theater."

"So what's going to happen?"

"I suggest you go in front of the judge, hat in hand, and say you're awful sorry."

"Then what?"

"You could get anywhere from a suspended sentence to a year."

"It wouldn't be good to ask for a jury and tell them what they did?"

"You get formal with them they can get formal with you. You could get a year on each count, plus thousand dollar fines and be required to pay the county back for legal services."

"And if I tell the judge I'm sorry?"

"Since it's your first arrest here you might get a month. I don't think you'll get road crew on this."

"When would I know?"

"You'll know today. You plead guilty the judge sentences you."

"And I go to jail?"

"Probably."

"And if I say not guilty?"

"He sets a trial date four weeks away."

Rudy Yid sits not knowing what to do.

"What's it going to be?"

"I don't know."

"You don't want to plead guilty?"

"No."

"Can you get together enough money for a private attorney, about a thousand dollars?"

"No."

"Okay, when you're called plead not guilty and ask for a public defender." He passes a card through the bars. "Call me if you change your mind. You got two hundred for bail?"

"I got traveler's checks."

Nathan takes the card back and writes a name and number on back. "Call this guy. How long you been out here?"

"Two weeks."

"You have anything to go back for?" he half jokes. "They wouldn't come looking for you."

On the way to the bullpen he calls the number and leaves a message. An hour later he's taken to a counter to meet a bondsman, a type he knows from the South Side, a wiry Slovak tough guy wearing a short-sleeve J.C. Penney shirt and straw hat. He never thought he'd see the same out here. The bondsman cashes ten traveler's checks of twenty dollars each taking two more as his fee.

On the bus back to the motel, he thinks what to do. He has a hundred and sixty left in traveler's checks along with a little pay coming from the market. That will be enough for the week's rent. He saw a cheaper room down the street with torn red carpeting and wallpaper but he knew it would depress him.

He has another check for about two hundred coming from the mill. He planned to get his car from Harvey, sell it for eight hundred and use the money to rent a small apartment. He'll have to hold off now until he sees how the charges against him turn out.

Next morning Tom has him out in front, away from Saw Butcher Red. He takes out cartons of picnic hams, removes the pieces from the cans and slices them on the machine for the lunch meat special. During the ten-fifteen break, Tom comes to the back.

"Red complained to the office; it's your last day. They're transferring you to the store in Hollywood."

"How do I get there? I don't have a car."

"You take three buses."

"I'm not taking three buses. I'd sooner go down here to Day Hire and get paid every afternoon."

"You won't go to Hollywood?"

"No."

"I'll call the office and ask to keep you until we get another apprentice. After that I have to let you go."

"That's okay."

"Stay away from Red."

The rest of the day he keeps the case filled with the packaged meat brought out on trays. When the delicatessen case runs low, he goes to the cooler in back, bringing out packaged coldcuts and pricing them. Alone in back he sneaks an apple out of a box, rinses it at the sink and polishes it off.

The few times he crosses paths with Red he stands aside. When he finishes the day he buys a bag of rolls and carton of cottage cheese to take back to the motel.

He kept his mind off his predicament at work, but at night in the room he gets a bad feeling about sticking around when he knows he's going to jail. Nathan joked they won't come looking for him if he goes back to Chicago but he knows nothing will change for him there. He'll go on day to day on the South Side like he used to.

He stays out front. It's hardly work compared to what he was doing before and the other butchers give him the eye, but Tom says nothing. Having him in front saves him the responsibility of running out to check the case every ten minutes

With just a few dollars to eat on he sneaks an apple in the cooler when he can, then brings home hard rolls and cottage cheese. At night he goes to a library and reads classifieds getting to know the jobs available. He remembers an Armenian in the neighborhood who never had much to do with anybody. He finished high school and was on the corner at five the next morning waiting for the Kedzie bus. His mother packed him a lunch in the morning and at night he came home to supper and got ready for the next day. It never looked any different but in ten years he bought into an air-conditioning company and was supporting a wife, mother and mother-in-law. When the Armenian saw him on the street or at Walgreens he'd tell him the way: go job to job, one to another so long as it pays more, no matter how hard the work and somewhere along the line a boss who's old, tired or doesn't want to put in the hours anymore will offer a part of the business. It's the hard way, not like Jews do it, but it might be the only way for him.

His court date is the next to last day in April and he gets a form from Nathan in the mail to fill out and return. He takes walks at night getting the notion again not to let them lock him up but to pick up his check on Friday morning, get his car from Harvey and head out. He'd only be out the forty-three hundred. Other than that he was the same, but when he gets back to the room he wonders if going back to Chicago broke and starting in the rail mill again is any better than going to jail for a month or two. He was born in Chicago; he knew Chicago and always had the feeling it was for a scrounge.

CHAPTER 16

On the morning he puts on a pair of pressed pants and long-sleeve shirt from his suitcase. Directions in hand, he goes out into a hazy morning, walking to Lankershim and waiting on a corner with a group of day laborers.

The Municipal Court is a modern building next to a police station, a lower structure with security screens along front. He gets off the bus and comes up a courtyard laid out in cinder slabs with open squares for twin trees. Going across the patio to locked glass doors he looks into an empty marble lobby.

Courtgoers come from every sidewalk crowding the doorfront. Deputies check the clock and open up. He takes an elevator to the third level, going down a polished hall to Division 100.

Inside a bailiff sits chatting with a young deputy city attorney. They are alone and turn a cold eye to him. He goes back out to sit on a bench.

Nathan gets off the elevator wearing a tweed jacket on this humid day. He approaches a pair of young blondes in tight faded jeans sitting near pay phones, bringing up a court matter. As one listens, the other lifts a spike heel up on the bench and clips a red toenail. What Rudy Yid makes of the talk is that their boyfriends, not they, are in trouble. Nathan turns to go without thanks from either one.

He stands and Nathan recognizes him. "Let's go in here."

He takes him into a conference room just inside the door. "The city attorney recommends thirty days if you plead guilty."

"The judge goes by that?" asks Rudy Yid.

"That's a chance you take. He's an old western hardnose. He's been sick. I was hoping he wouldn't show."

108

"And if I stand trial?"

"First, I don't think you can win. And it would be nothing for this guy to give you a year. You have two counts."

He sits thinking.

"It's up to you" says Nathan.

"Okay, I'll take thirty" says Rudy Yid.

"You mean plead guilty." Nathan takes a form from his briefcase. "This is a Waiver of Rights. Are you literate?"

"I don't exaggerate" says Rudy Yid. "It leaves a bad taste in my mouth."

"Can you read?"

"Yea."

"Read through this, put your initials next to the marks and sign it."

Rudy Yid goes through the form, signing at the bottom. Nathan looks at his watch. "You wanna get yourself a cup of coffee or go in?"

"I'll go in."

Nathan has him sit in front to the right. He greets the court secretary with a tease and goes over to join the bailiff and deputy city attorney who barely keep from turning their backs on him.

Courtgoers spread through the rows. A group of tall lawyers with New York accents stand around quipping, their hands in their pockets. He looks back at the clock. It is nine-fifteen and the teenagers aren't there. A buzz sounds. The secretary picks up the phone, calling to the bailiff who calls the court to order.

"Everyone remain seated. The Honorable Jay Ruch."

An old judge with a high right hip staggers in. He pulls himself up a handrail to the bench and says good morning into a microphone. Reading the docket he sticks out a deformed tongue to lick the corners of his mouth.

The door opens and Rudy Yid looks back. Four teenagers in jackets and ties come in with two attractive mothers and a successful-looking man in a black suit and silver tie. As they file into a row the judge holds a gaze on them, savoring their appearance in his court.

The deputy city attorney and Nathan are called to the bench. Nathan steps away and beckons Rudy Yid through the gate to the defense table.

The judge looks toward Rudy Yid. "You're charged with two counts of battery, last April four, against two minors fifteen years of age. How do you plead?"

"Guilty."

The judge holds up a form. "This is your Waiver of Rights. Do you understand and did you initial each of the rights given up?"

Rudy Yid clears his throat. "Yes."

"Is there a justifiable reason for your action?"

Nathan sits down beside Rudy Yid, with a yellow writing pad in his lap. "Your honor, at the time defendant had been in California a few weeks and was already working at a meatcutting job. He'd put in a hard day and that evening spent hard-earned money for a movie seat when four young men moved into the row behind him, starting loud talk. Defendant's request that they be quiet was mocked. An usher warning them was ignored. Defendant moved to a lower row and they followed to taunt him."

Nathan puts the pad on the table. "Court might suggest here that he could have gotten up and moved again, but defendant is a person with pride like anybody else, and when a foot was put up near his head and the back of his seat kicked, he turned and slapped one young man with a rolled-up magazine and bounced out another who jumped up at him. He did not use his fists. He did only what it took to remove him. He felt a right of defense. It didn't occur to him they were minors, but he accepts the strict liability and is anxious to have it over and get back to work at the market."

The judge looks amused. "Court notes your working-class

spiel, counselor, but not so fast. The conduct here was extremely dangerous. I'll ask defendant a few questions."

He curls a finger at Rudy Yid. "When you turned to strike with the magazine, did you have a boy picked out or didn't you care who you hit?"

"I hit the one behind me. The one who kicked my chair."

"And the boy you bounced, why him?"

"He jumped up like he wanted to fight."

"He throw a punch?"

"He didn't get the chance. I pulled him over and pinned him down. I'd have let go but he started to kick so I dragged him to the door and threw him out."

The judge puts his fists under his chin. "You talk tough, defendant. You one of those fellas who comes to California to show you're handy with your fists?" He holds up his hands in the pose of an old-time prizefighter.

"I came to find work" answers Rudy Yid.

"Where from?"

"Chicago."

"That a tough town, Chicago?"

"They wouldn't take this serious" says Rudy Yid knowing it's not true.

"Oh" remarks the judge. "Did you go around Chicago beating up people with impunity?"

"I never beat up nobody puny in Chicago" sneers Rudy Yid, having enough of him.

The judge looks over at the prosecutor, nearly laughing, then clasps one hand over the other. "Now, when one strikes another in anger one risk of many is that who is struck is of legal age and if no, there's no defense other than that to bodily harm. Heckling and taunting by law offer little mitigation. A kick to the back of one's chair is battery but hardly here a physical threat."

His head shakes as though he's tasted something bitter. "I

myself can't stand noise in a theater. I *just* don't like it, but those of us responsible must not use our hands even at a loss of pride. This is the grace of seniority. How light our dignity among polite juniors, but the polite junior California we knew is now a volatile willful tribe testing us at every turn, one with which our restraint is damn near everything or we'd have some state of affairs, let me say. You see that just driving through the Valley here."

He straightens the waddle in his throat like a necktie, following his nose back to Rudy Yid. "No, we won't have our teenagers manhandled and so you remember, young Chicago fella, you'll jail thirty days and think it over."

The short thick-necked bailiff comes up to Rudy Yid. "Let's go."

Rudy Yid taps Nathan on the arm. "Can you call my motel and —"

The bailiff lunges. "I said let's *go!* You *hear* when I talk?" He is flushed under an eye as if ready to use his fists. Rudy Yid looks at him as if he's crazy.

"Put your hands out."

He holds them out and the deputy locks his wrists and takes him to a side door.

CHAPTER 17

A bus with barred windows rolls into a stone yard where he stands chained to three others. There are eight in all, four to a chain. The transportation deputy, tall and mustached, resembles television detective Magnum. He takes charge, checking booking slips against wristbands and moving the prisoners on board. Rudy Yid leads the way past the driver to the back, sitting down with a husky blond wearing a Blue Hawaii shirt as if on his way to the beach.

He looks through the window at the open gate.

"Don't look so happy" says the husky character. "They'll send you back home."

"You been here?" Rudy Yid asks.

"I've been in the tank, never here."

"You heard anything what it's like?"

"Bad, real bad. All I know is I can fight my ass off for ninety seconds and if the job's not done my ass is theirs."

"What're you here for?"

"Nonsupport. My ex-wife's giving nob jobs to all the beans at Cesar's lounge and I'm supposed to pay for that, huh. My name's Yarbrough, what's yours?"

"Rudy Yid."

"We'll stick together."

The bus goes down a side street snapping back tree branches. Turning left and left again onto a boulevard of car dealers and coffee shops to a freeway, it goes up a ramp heading east.

Passing over grids of bungalows and low apartment complexes, the bus veers around the bluffs of a high park where the freeway widens. Building up speed they come up on downtown buildings, changing into an exit lane looping through a tunnel and coming out a few blocks from the jail. The driver steers around a wall topped with razor wire, nosing up to a gate and pulling into a waiting area. He opens the door and sits back. The two buses ahead are filled with newcomers bobbing their heads for a look around. A deputy with a clipboard passes the first two buses, coming up to the transportation deputy. "Go to old Federal. They're receiving."

Rudy Yid hears that much before Yarbrough bumps him. "They're moving us."

Backing up the driver heads to an old road alongside railroad tracks. On broken pavement they cross a stone bridge over a railhead, wind around loading docks shaped like baseball diamonds and go on to a redbrick structure that looks to Rudy Yid like old packing houses on Pershing Road.

Through the gate they pull into a gravel lot on the backside.

The door opens and they're called off. He moves down the aisle behind Yarbrough, stepping out on the gravel. The transportation deputy walks them past the food service and laundry docks. Workers humped over hamper buggies and bins give them the eye. They go down a concrete decline and shouts come from behind screened tiers above. Through a tunnel they go into a stone corridor to a counter where the transportation deputy pulls out the chains and removes the cuffs. A jailer puts a brown bag in front of each man.

"Everything out of your pockets, off your wrists, fingers, over your neck. Whatever you're carrying: chains, medals, rings, smokes, medication, money. Keep one unopened pack of smokes if you got 'em and up to twenty dollars at your own risk. The rest in the bag."

He takes out his keys, wallet and thirty cents, watching Yarbrough pick four fives out of a wallet for himself. Guards called prowlers come into the corridor and after some shoptalk with the transportation deputy move the newcomers into a hall with rows of benches, where each is given a cup of hot chocolate and sandwich. He smells the glazed lunchmeat and offers his sandwich to Yarbrough who takes it. The others eat with sallow faces. From what he overheard in the holding pen they're there for theft. The two tallest wearing saggy mustaches and worn-out jeans were caught removing materials from a construction site.

Two prowlers stand watching. They are beginners in jail for their first training with offenders. They don't look the new arrivals in the eye but over their heads as if ashamed to be in contact with them.

They move to the end of the corridor to a technician at a table aside the wall. The first in line sits down and after having blood taken, takes a step and drops. The prowlers pull him to the wall and sit him up. Yarbrough peeks back at Rudy Yid, turning out a plump forearm with no trace of a vein.

The next five get blood drawn and get in line. Yarbrough

sits down on a low stool, tightening his lips and exhaling through his nose as a needle breaks his skin. His eyes look ready to roll, but he gulps, clenches his teeth and stands up. Rudy Yid sits down and puts up the wrong arm.

"The *right* one!" glares the technician. He looks to Rudy Yid like any white guy you'd see on the street but he's never seen such hate in two eyes. He puts his right arm up flat. A vein stands out in the crease but the technician slants the needle in underneath, staring into his eyes. It's sharp but he stares back at him. He started boning meat when he was twelve and has nicks all over his fingers. The technician taps the needle across the vein and slants it underneath from the other side, simpering in his face. His left arm is free and he's ready to hook it around, the prowlers there or not, when the technician realizes he's open to a shot, onlookers or no, and takes care. He breaks into the vein and Rudy Yid is still okay until he sees his blood draw up. Rising with a chill in his throat, he gets behind the line, clenching his teeth.

Moving to a stone court with yellow marks, they take off their clothes and fold them up. Putting booking slips and underwear in shoes, they get in line for a skin search.

One of the lanky thieves who'd been caught stealing from the construction site steps forward and sticks out his tongue. The civilian examiner is short and has the prisoner bend at the knees. As he balances on his heels, his member curls down under his testicles as if trying to look out the other end.

The examiner, wearing cuff links and tasseled loafers, tussles his hair and moves his tongue side to side. Bending him over with a stiff arm, he snaps on a glove, works a finger between his gaunt cheeks, and pulls it out smeared to the knuckle. He looks around at him. "Toilet paper's free here, pal. Use some."

The prisoner snaps back up as if joining the army.

After the skin search a guard sprays them for lice then they get under a nozzle for a shower and wipe themselves off as much as they can with blue paper shams.

Moving to a counter they get blue pants and tops, a bedroll and toothbrush each, then go to the yellow marks to dress. Still wet they move across the gravel yard to an auxiliary building. A prowler opens the door with a rod key and the newcomers go into a landing at the base of a steel stairshaft. There is a rumble of voices from above and a smell like from urine and bad meat. About to see what they'll be faced with, they go up alongside new standpipes and sprinklers, looking into the blocks. The third tier is full of blacks and Hispanics who go still for a look at the newcomers. Still lightheaded Rudy Yid dizzies more at the thought of going in there. A devilish-looking Hispanic sergeant with bushy eyebrows curled up like thumbs comes over to the landing, getting ahead of the prowler and leading the way up to the fourth level. The block here is almost empty. A few whites look out from cells at one end and two blacks and a short Hispanic stand at the wall at the other. The bad air is not as thick up here.

The sergeant does some paperwork at a station. There is a door to an elevator to his left and a narrow skylight in the ceiling behind him. Finished he addresses the newcomers.

"I'm Velez, supervisor tiers one through four. No horseplay here. Follow the guy in front. A deputy calls 'Catch hole!' it means get in your cell. No excuses no exceptions." He points back at the staircase. "A pickup by the pipes lets a horn go. Yell for help, make it count. We run up here for a joke, you lock hole twenty hours."

He pulls a lever drawing back the gate. The newcomers go into a high stone block with a row of narrow cells. Two metal tables are bolted to the floor. The ceiling is slanted, one end wall higher than the other. The newcomers move off to the left toward the white faces near the short wall. Yarbrough nudges Rudy Yid.

"This don't look so bad."

They go into a cell near the middle. The commode is full of turds and Yarbrough puts his foot on the handle, getting a rush of water. They put their bedrolls on the racks and step back out, going over to a bench near the door. Yarbrough opens his cigarette pack, glad this much is over with. Rudy Yid leans forward rubbing his right arm. The Hispanic leaves the two blacks at the long wall and comes over, his hands in his pockets.

"What you guys down for?"

"Nonsupport" says Yarbrough.

"And you?" the Hispanic asks Rudy Yid.

"Battery."

"Who?"

"Two guys at a movie."

"Some fags come on to you, man?"

He doesn't answer and the Hispanic crouches in front of Yarbrough. "You say your wife put you here?"

"Her and her lawyer. She's fucking him. Let him pay support."

"Your wife good-looking?"

Yarbrough cocks an eye from a wisp of smoke. "Your tongue would drop like a trap door. I wish I had a picture."

"I believe you, man. What kind of work you do?"

"Lay tile."

"And you?" he asks Rudy Yid.

"A butcher."

Yarbrough takes out his pack and taps out a cigarette to Lupe.

"Camels, eh. A lot of flavor."

"If I wanna suck steam I'll stand over a tea kettle."

The Hispanic grins. "I enjoy your sarcasm. My name is Lupe." Yarbrough thinks he means to shake hands with him as a friend, but he grips the pack in Yarbrough's fingers. "Two for my partners, eh?" He nods back at the two blacks watching from the long wall.

Yarbrough looks dumbstruck and Lupe tightens his grip.

"*Okay*, that's it. No more."

117

Yarbrough taps out two. "What the hell you in for?" he asks putting the pack away.

Lupe shifts his weight from knee to knee, rolling a speck of saliva on his tongue and spitting to the side. "I cut some little dude's liver in Long Beach."

"What's it like in here? People get along or what?"

Lupe twists around on his heals. "I can't tell you, man. It's a mental thing. You hold your own."

"I got a feeling," says Yarbrough watching him go, "the first thing you gotta learn is who can and who can't jump up your asshole."

At five o'clock the block is opened and two trusties roll in a meal cart and coffee jug. Lupe and the two blacks get in line first. The taller is reddish-brown and with splayed freckles like dots. The other is short and angry-looking with shimmering black cheekbones.

Rudy Yid gets a tray of frankfurters and beans, sitting down with Yarbrough at the first table. He smells the wieners, tastes the beans and drops his spoon.

"What's wrong?"

"It smells like pig fat."

Yarbrough's cheeks are full. "That's the lard in those beans."

"You can eat it?"

"My ex-wife's from Alabama. She cooked everything in lard."

Not all have come out for a tray. Two whites in the corner cell at the short wall move around barechested eating out of snack cans. They are quick-looking characters not too tall. One is a tawny redhead almost maroon and the other stockier and lighter complected with sandy features that blur at a distance. The redhead puts a cigarette in his mouth, brushes his fingers aside his pants and asks for a match, lighting up as if he has it made in there.

Two cells down a white inmate lies limp on the upper rack,

his chin to his chest.

Across from Yarbrough a dusty-faced drifter circles his spoon through the beans. Looking up through discolored bifocals he eyes the reddish black.

"Hey, Reggie, I'll trade you these eats for a smoke."

"Those rotten hot dogs for a Viceroy? You crazy?"

The bifocal man checks the other side. "Anybody take my tray for a smoke?"

The newcomers say nothing. "C'mon, fair trade."

Reggie holds up a cigarette butt from his shirt.

"C'mon, Reggie. How long's that gonna last?"

"Forget you then" says Reggie putting it back.

"Okay, okay." The bifocal man leans over to pass his tray when Reggie's eyes double.

"Get your *thumbs* out of those beans! I don't *want* it if your thumbs are in those beans."

The bifocal man flicks his thumbs up and takes the butt. Reggie dumps the tray onto his and resumes eating with rippling cheeks.

"Wolf them beans, Reggie," says an admirer.

After supper Rudy Yid and Yarbrough are back at the bench by the door. Straight across the bifocal man sits on his haunch. He watches Yarbrough light up and comes over.

"You got a smoke?"

"I'm giving out too many."

"One, please. I'll pay you back when the store comes around."

Yarbrough lets his breath go and taps one out. The bifocal man crouches, lighting up. "Man that's good. The butt Reggie gave me was torched. You just book or get moved?"

"Just got here."

"What'd you get?"

"Thirty days."

Rudy Yid nods he got the same.

"You'll remember every minute if you don't get a permanent concussion. It ain't safe to take a deep breath in here. I'm a vagrant. I don't belong in here with these coldbloods."

"You talking about Reggie?" asks Yarbrough.

"He's one. There's seven others in isolation. That's why it's quiet."

"What'd they do?" asks Yarbrough.

"Kicked in a guy's eyesocket."

"For what?"

"He was a feisty kid. He took a swing at Reggie and didn't have the ass to back it up. He got knocked down with the first punch and it set the others off."

"What about the guards?" asks Yarbrough. "What do they do?"

"Don't expect Johnny-on-the-spot. Velez down there, Duncan Renaldo's stand-in, is divorcing his wife to marry his niece. He's ready to retire and don't bust his ass getting up here. He gets a crew first."

"How come Reggie's not down there?" asks Yarbrough.

"Reggie's smarter than the others. He hit that kid and backed on out. He's a no-good motherfucker but compared to the others he's civilized. Wait till Junior Bravo and Trashbucket get back."

"Who are they?"

"Junior's the cell boss and Trashbucket is a psycho hillbilly. He wasn't in town a half hour before he ground a beer bottle in a guy's face. Don't look in his eyes."

"What do they do?" asks Yarbrough. "Just come up and start fucking with you?"

"You're lucky if you get that much warning. I wasn't mopping the floor fast enough one morning and Trashbucket come up behind me and swung his big foot up between my legs. It's one thing to get your nuts kicked from the front. Try catching one from behind you when you don't know it's coming. You *taste* it. All *up* in your *gums*. Now every time he gets behind me I feel I'm gonna faint."

"How long they gonna be?" asks Yarbrough.

"They could be back tomorrow if that kid won't stand and point 'em out."

Yarbrough nods toward the corner cell at the long wall. "How about that little Spanish dude Lupe and the other black guy?"

"I don't know he's Spanish" says the bifocal man. "I think he's white and plays the role. I heard he used to work at the stables. The other is Short Reg. There's two of them. He and Lupe are mostly instigators if he don't scare you to death with that black face."

Yarbrough has another question. "How about the two white guys in the corner? They look like they're getting over."

"That's Rhymes and Tapia. A couple of road agents from Arizona. They both got three, four girls sending 'em letters. They think they're quick but the coldbloods are gonna be at their door."

He edges up. "I'll let you in on something. For what it's worth to you."

"What's that?" asks Yarbrough.

"They might be letting out low misdemeanors in a spring sweep."

"When?"

"Next week."

"Even if you just got in?"

"Don't matter. You're low you go, just so you book."

"How you know?" asks Yarbrough.

"It's going around but don't come at me if it don't happen."

Yarbrough nudges Rudy Yid. "Wouldn't that be rich?" Getting out the cigarettes he taps out another. The bifocal man looks at it as if he expected more.

As the skylight turns dark, Rhymes, the stockier of the two in the corner cell, comes out and starts a poker game at the first table. Getting newcomers around with a smart tone of voice, he sets himself up as house and dealer and sells small tokens at eight for a dollar and has single cigarettes and hard candies at his elbow for a token apiece.

His redheaded partner stays in the cell smoking a cigarette and writing a love letter with such concentration and design he seems to be decorating every word. He puts another cigarette in his mouth and comes out.

"Gimme a light."

Rhymes flicks a matchbook over his shoulder and his partner has to snap it up from the floor.

"You just wanted to see me bend over!" he curses.

Rhymes deals out seven card poker, the house taking a chip from each pot. Yarbrough and Rudy Yid go over and watch.

"Let's get in" says Yarbrough.

"I don't have money."

"You didn't bring money?" Yarbrough asks.

"All my money went for bail."

Yarbrough buys five dollars in tokens, sits down and introduces himself. Rudy Yid goes back to the bench, exchanging looks with the bifocal man sitting at the second table. The slumped inmate sleeping during supper is on the commode and after a few squirts comes out on the floor. His ears are shaped like handles on a consommé cup and his hair is piled up on top like a patch of jute. He sits down next to the bifocal man like a younger brother. The bifocal man takes out a half roll of Lifesavers and makes a show of holding it up and peeling the top. The cellmate looks on but the bifocal man ignores him, flicking one into his mouth before getting up. Rudy Yid looks over at the cellmate. He is over six feet with a good chin and wide shoulders and Rudy Yid wonders what could have happened in his life to sit slumped like this and have to ask for a dirty piece of candy.

He sees Rudy Yid looking.

"You been here long?" Rudy Yid asks.

"Ten days."

"How many you get?"

"Ninety."

"Whew" sighs Rudy Yid. "I just got thirty."

The cellmate comes to him heeling to a side, the arm tucked in. "I'm Eusluss."

Rudy Yid feels for him. "Everybody's good for somethin'."

"It's my name."

His smell is similar to the smell coming out the back of small poultry plants on the South Side. He shakes his moist hand, sorry now he started up a conversation.

"Sounds like a country name."

"I'm from Montana."

"You own your own horse?" asks Rudy Yid, taking short breaths.

"No, I worked in a smorgasbord. My brother is in the painters union here and kept calling to come out and he'd get me in. I had nine dollars, so I put everything in a bag and went out on the road."

"You hitchhiked?"

"Partway. I met a guy and we got on a railcar. It was January but we made it to a mission in Salt Lake City and they got us work loading boxes and gave us new shoes."

Rudy Yid looks down at a pair of black work shoes.

He shrugs as if it didn't go good after that. "I got to my brother's house in Las Palmas, and every morning we drive to the paint hall and come back and spend the rest of the day at a tap. After a few days he starts asking why I didn't bring more money. So Friday night he wants to go and I ask if I could skip it, and he leaves by himself and comes back with a guy named Herman and tells me to get my bag and get out."

"Maybe he was drunk."

"No, I saw the way he was standing there. He wanted to

fight. I got near Hollywood and found an old garage with couches inside. An old movie couple lived in the house. They knew I was there but didn't say anything."

"You going back to Montana?"

He shrugs.

"There's work here if you want it. Day Hire in the Valley. It's forty a day and they cash your check. You can catch a hard day, but I had a couple where all I did was hose down cars and wipe 'em off. The thing is to get a room so you don't eat up the forty at a motel. Then you can look around."

He nods along as if enjoying every word. "You done hard work?" he asks Rudy Yid.

"Yea, but I never worked hard. I think that's been my problem."

Eusluss twists away to cough. It doesn't break in his throat coming out a croak. He looks back with a flushed face. "You wouldn't have a sour ball or piece of candy?" he asks, his face glistening.

"Wish I did." Rudy Yid looks toward the card game. "Wait."

Rhymes flicks in a pot with his fingertips. Rudy Yid comes up behind Yarbrough and drops a quarter in the pot. He points to the candies.

"Gimme two."

Rhymes looks up, his face puffed round with pores like pinholes.

"Two chips. Eight for a dollar."

"I don't want chips, just two candies."

"Two chips."

He nudges Yarbrough but Yarbrough doesn't look up. "I'm not payin' a dollar for two penny candies."

Rhymes points the way. "Hit the *fuck* outta here."

Looking into Rhymes' yellow rimmed eyes, he reaches across and takes his quarter.

He sits with Eusluss awhile longer running out of smalltalk.

He notices the tucked-in arm is crooked. Peeking down he sees that the muscle under the forearm is missing, as if it had been scooped out, and the elbow is so sharp it doesn't look as if it can straighten. The work he'd suggested to him he probably couldn't do. Eusluss slumps and gets up, going back to the second table.

Yarbrough is quicker than the other newcomers and plays up to Rhymes, raising hands with the remark "Price of living's gone up, fellas." He rakes in a pot, whistling.

"I hear there might be a Spring kick-out."

"A what?" says Rhymes.

"A Spring kick-out for low misdemeanors."

"Says *who*?"

Yarbrough nods over his shoulder to the bifocal man crouched in front of his cell.

"That *tramp!*"

"It's not true?" asks Yarbrough, glancing back as the bifocal man stands and goes inside.

"Hey cocksucker" he calls after him. "Ask me for another smoke."

Short Reg sticks his head out at the other end and comes to the game. Rhymes stands up to slap hands with him.

"What's up?" says Short Reg looking around.

Rhymes nods at Yarbrough. "The face here says they're gonna let him go on a kick-out."

Short Reg eyes Yarbrough. "Who told you?"

Yarbrough nods over his shoulder. "That tramp."

"You give him anything?"

"A smoke." Yarbrough is twice his size but looks as though he thinks Short Reg could beat him to a pulp.

"Don't be givin' out nothin'. If you interferin' in somebody's play he got the rights to call you on that."

Two eyes look out at him from a cell and Short Reg swings around the table. The bifocal man flops across his rack, bringing his knees up for cover. Reg grabs the bars and feigns swinging in.

"Pitiful motherfucker."

Seeing the newcomers hanging on every word he turns to Eusluss at the second table. "Don't be handin' out nothin' to this hardup mope either. He got the gripe and be walkin' around askin' for sweetmeat."

He puts an arm around him. "The man be hidin' from the world in a garage, eatin' out tuna cans with cats and got his gut infected. He eat a spoon of beans and be in there squirtin'. Ain't that right?"

Eusluss grins as Reg flicks his stiff hair with strong silver nails. "The man climb over animal regulation to get his cats and they shine a jacklight in his face. Am I right?"

Eusluss nods it is so.

"Why you grinnin'?" asks Reg. "You think it's funny, riskin' yourself for cats. Don't feed a cat once it'll hate you the rest its life. Livin' in that stink. Ain't nothin' meaner 'an cat piss. It burn your lungs out. That right?"

He nudges him to look up. "Nothin' for nothin' right." Eusluss nods and Reg rakes his nails down over his ear. Eusluss leaps and twists around. Staggering to his cell he sticks his head under the tap. Reg turns. "Cryin' shame, put somebody in here like that. Anything he touch he infect it."

He eyes the newcomers. "Better none of you be here for child molestin'." He honks up his voice. "I repeat! Don't be in here for child molestin'! And if you new you last. Don't run up in line. It don't mean nothin'. And morning bring mops and buckets, don't be layin' up in the rack 'cause if a hardback get stuck with a mop and you layin' on you dick, he gonna be with you shortly."

He gets a nod from all except Rudy Yid who eyes him from the bench. "You hear me, man?" Rudy Yid says nothing waiting for him to come close. His arm is still stiff but it'll work for now. Reg notices he's edging up and his eyes flare. "You feelin' froggy, jump," he beckons, his nose holes like barrels. "You catch one up yo windpipe you ain't gonna be lookin' so hard." He eyes a prowler coming up the stairshaft. He watches him sit down and pick up a magazine. An eye back on Rudy Yid he heads to the other end and brings out Red Reggie and Lupe for a look. Rudy Yid looks across to the bifocal man's cell, where Eusluss has climbed up on the rack and turned to the wall with a clump of wet toilet paper to his ear.

Rhymes calls for the tokens buying them back at ten for a dollar. The newcomers gripe but they can take it or leave it.

A muscular young sergeant comes up on the tier.

"Catch hole!"

The inmates head inside and the sergeant lets in a trustie who moves down the row slamming doors.

Rudy Yid sits on the rack while Yarbrough takes off his blues, runs a toothbrush through his mouth then climbs up with a suspicious glance.

"You were taking a chance staring like that."

"I'll spit in his face. Tries to tear that guy's ear off then says we better not be child molesters."

"Hey" hushes Yarbrough. "You're not here to prove anything." He shakes his cigarette pack. "You look like you got some badger in you. I can tell on a white guy. I lived over a boxing gym in Minnesota, but these guys trade in beating and kicking. You hear what that hobo said?"

He lights up and lays back. "Well the first one wasn't so bad."

Rudy Yid stands up. "I'm not gonna be able to sit around like this. I'm gonna ask if they have a work detail. Maybe I can get into the kitchen. I can't eat this shit. I need a piece of brisket and cole slaw."

"A meateater, huh? Where were you working?"

"Sunset Market near Lankershim."

"I know that place. What were you making?"

"Five-fifty an hour."

"You can do better than that. That's sub-Mexican."

"I was an apprentice."

"Nobody comes to California to apprentice. You come to smarten up. A guy like you should be making three, four hundred easy."

"Doing what?"

"Doing anything with a head on your shoulders."

"Is that what you were making laying tile?"

"I was making three, four hundred a week making appointments for laying tile. But I got eyes. I'm a Minnesota boy. I don't sleep on my feet. I see I'm taking home three, four hundred and my boss is pulling down two, three thousand a week."

"Two, three *thousand!*"

"Right. Like a medical doctor and always telling me I was the one who had it made 'cause I sat on the phone all day while he hauled ass. But I know he's hiding something. He's working seven days, won't take a day off and can't keep help. Even Mexicans quit on him. And he's a lightweight. A freak with blond hair down to his ass. So I kid him into taking me along one weekend. I watch him lay tile and see a monkey could do it. Right there I figured what it would take: a float for grouting, a couple of buckets, trowels, wonderboard, wire mesh. I'd have to undercut everybody, bootleg the license, no insurance no tax — just like him. I go home, tell my wife and she says I won't make the rent. This time I don't listen. I go out there killin' myself. I didn't think I could work that hard. Sixteen hours a day and running to Tijuana Sunday mornings for Mexican tile then getting back to finish a job or follow up a referral. I'd get so tired I didn't know the day. One day I stood behind my truck for ten minutes and didn't know who or where I was. And while I'm out killing myself, she's layin' home like dead flesh, can't get a message or call right and gets smart with my customers. So one Friday night I come late from a two-day job. No supper, no beer, nothin'. She's in bed watching *Dallas* and I sit down in the dark there with a beaucoup check in my pocket to tell her about my day and she turns her ass to me. So I let her in on how things are, how women I see are split from big honchos and they get me in the house and tell me landscapers, pool guys and handymen are always offering to trade for services until it dawns on me they're fucking these ham 'n' eggers and want it from me too. She doesn't even blink; so I ask her straight-out what she'd do if she was alone and roofers, landscapers and pool guys wanted to take it out in trade. She leans back and says 'Why just *guys?*' Bent doublejointed bitch. After the divorce she called the IRS on me."

He looks down and sees Rudy Yid with a hand over his mouth.

"Laugh, cocksucker. Get those guys after you and see how funny it is." .

"It's the way you said it. You going back in business or are too many getting into it?"

"You kidding? There's sections out here, one after another and you can cop a stake in any one."

"If you need help I'll work."

"Yea," says Yarbrough, "until you get wise, then you're competition. You don't want competition don't train it."

"Why should we be competition? Let's go in together and make more. With your personality, anybody would give you business."

Yarbrough looks down over the side again. "Why do you say that?"

"You're a people person. Anybody could like you just talking to you, and I'd bring some things to the business."

"Like what?"

"I'd make up for what I don't know. You won't lose money on me."

Yarbrough leans back again. "Yea, why not. We can get into marble and store fronts but this time it's not all work.

Weekends we get on new duds, a couple of Rolexes and hit the Palm."

"Go in and write down names and addresses?"

"No, for a good time. I used to go before I got married. You know *Laverne and Shirley*?"

"Yea, I watched 'em."

"They used to be in there looking for sharp guys. We could have taken 'em out."

"You and me?"

"Yea."

"You don't have to be an actor?"

"Nah, a sharp glib guy. You'd be surprised at the guys getting over. If they're still around we'll go in and start joking with 'em and take 'em for a ride. You can have Laverne, I'll take Shirley."

"*Oh*, thanks a lot."

Yarbrough drops over the side, pulls down his shorts and sits on the commode grinning. "Guess what. For the first time today I know what I'm doing."

Rudy Yid looks away giggling.

He lies awake thinking that if he hadn't been sent to jail he wouldn't have met Yarbrough. He pictures himself going to homes, whipping out a tape measure over counters and walls and learning more on each job. How much is it worth in life not to be hidden in a steel mill or meatcutting room, but to go out and make your way? It's true what his mother said to him: to me come for a clean shirt, to people go learn.

CHAPTER 18

A dirty foot swings into the rack, rattling him on his side. He eyes flick open on a blond thug with hair down his shoulders.

"*Ass up!*" He slams the upper rack with Yarbrough on top. "*Out!*"

Rudy Yid gets up as the thug takes the middle of the floor. He doesn't look much older than twenty but goes about two and a quarter with a lumped face. His right foot is bare and he wears a filthy white sock on the left. The block is opened and two trusties roll in buckets. Snatching mops he flings them on the line. Newcomers leap legs spattered, but wherever a mop hits, they know enough to pick it up and start swinging. Catching the thug's glare Yarbrough turns toward the short wall with Rudy Yid behind him. As they go by, the bifocal man whispers "*Trashbucket.*"

A breakfast cart is pushed in on the wet floor. Trashbucket is first in line and the two Reggies and Lupe come up behind. As the newcomers move up there is tromping in the stairshaft. Five inmates come up on the tier and go into the block grinning. The one in front is hailed as Junior. He gets in front of Trashbucket who says nothing. The others cut in front of the newcomers. A last inmate tromps up the stairs with facial cheeks like buttocks. Cutting in behind the rogues he doesn't like where he is and humps his neck, pushing ahead. The others prop up like a gate to block him off. The line moves and as he gets his tray the trusties give him extra hotcakes and syrup, calling him Baby Uey and Baby Universe. He goes to the second table with the rogues but won't sit down until they let him in next to Junior.

Rudy Yid sits with Yarbrough at the end of the first table, noticing good appetites the rogues have in fetid air. They remind him of young blacks who came to the mill on summer programs and after twenty minutes were giving the supervisor looks. They joke as though they forget they are in jail. An old Southside guy once told him that a lout doesn't much care where he is so long as he's with his own kind.

They begin to jabber about stomping the feisty white inmate and how Baby Uey pushed through trying to pull his pants down.

"You were gonna cornhole him?" asks Trashbucket.

Uey smacks his lips. "I meant to have some."

Trashbucket pshaws in disgust but Junior is with Uey. "Ain't nothin' wrong with some hardleg."

"Nothin' wrong!" repeats Trashbucket. "It's not natural that's what's wrong."

"More natural than soapin' it up and whackin' it loose" says Red Reggie.

Short Reg nods. "I see a man bustin' his nuts in the shower where I'm walkin' with bare feet, I'll fuck him up with my fists."

"I suppose you never busted no girl in the ass?" suggests Junior.

"Big difference" says Trashbucket.

"What difference? Boot is boot just 'cause it come hard in the leg."

Red Reggie licks a drop of syrup from his knuckle. "You gonna tell me if they take you out the world and a sissy punk come inside, you not gonna hold that optional?"

"Any man fuck a punk is a punk" insists Trashbucket.

"*Nah, nah!*" the rogues protest. "You makin' a punk. You turnin' a punk."

Junior nods. "It's being the man any given place and time. Like you in a social situation and you take the best girl out from under everybody's nose and they all lookin' at you like they know they not the man you are. On the inside you take the trimmiest punk and when you go back in the world you leave it there."

"Forget all about it, *huh*?" says Trashbucket.

"Put it aside. You one man in here another out there."

A rogue on the end speaks up. "My cousin was inside with Davey Breen of Detroit and he say he run every punk in the stir and used to bust their ringhole so they keep Tampax up they ass. Then he got out and got him a white girl and he and his wife doin' those retarded children commercials."

Lupe points across the table at Trashbucket. "If a punk put an eye on you and you don't put him down, he misconstrue that and think you a punk, too."

Trashbucket slaps his hand away. "No, *you* the punk. They'll punk you the first day you get there and pull their dicks out and not know if it's loose shit or refried beans."

He's off his haunch and Junior tries to calm him. "You talkin' proud but on the inside the only thing save you is doin' the most with what the man put you to, because if you on the rack at night thinking 'bout big fine legs and red toes stickin' out spiked heels and start misusin' yourself, your head do a spin and no woman gonna have you. My own auntie tol' me that."

Trashbucket pinches his nose for all to see. "Sticking your dick up another man's ass. *P.U.*"

After breakfast the rogues go into their cells for a nap. Rudy Yid and Yarbrough sit near other newcomers in the corner at the short wall. The newcomers look through the skylight at a gray morning and start to talk about music clubs and not missing a night when they get out. Rhymes and Tapia are doing exercises in their cell. One does a snappy set then the other gets down and matches it. A deputy comes up on the tier calling for a volunteer for the kitchen. Right behind him a trustie holds back a grin. Rudy Yid nudges Yarbrough.

"Not me" says Yarbrough.

He stands up, raising his hand. "I'll bring you back something." He's let out and taken down the elevator and through a cold breezeway in back of the kitchen. The deputy turns him over to a wiry cook who shows him a cold pantry cluttered with boxes. Some are open and missing a large can or container. The cook smells stale of cigarette smoke and there is a red sore on his cheekbone with a white snip in the middle.

"Get the floor swept and boxes stacked."

He looks the clutter over. There are about thirty. Some are a foot high a yard wide and have to be lifted at arm's width. He decides to bring them out, sweep and put them back.

The cook sits at a counter with coffee and a cigarette, facing toward the front of the kitchen with something on his mind. He doesn't turn his head once. At his elbow a cut peach pie glows like red gold. Rudy Yid eyes it thinking he'll ask for a piece until he notices smoke curling out of the cook's mouth settling on top. Next to the pie is the knife used to cut it and he knows the type, an old butcher knife sharpened down like a dagger and used in the back of markets for cutting nubs from lettuce and cabbage heads. He's seen them used for digging out the black under fingernails.

Getting the boxes out he sweeps the pantry and carries them back. He puts the wide ones down, stacking smaller ones over them. Finishing he calls the cook who comes over to look then goes to a phone to call a deputy. Rudy Yid comes up halfway.

"You wouldn't have a couple of apples or oranges?"

The cook doesn't answer.

He takes a last look at the pie, thinking he'll go to a bakery the day he gets out, get one like it and take it to a table somewhere and have it all with a quart of milk.

The deputy takes him back up on the elevator, letting him into the block. The rogues are still napping and Yarbrough and the other newcomers in the same place.

"What'd you bring?" teases Yarbrough.

In the other corner Rhymes and Tapia have finished exercising and stand barechested at the tap taking a sponge bath. Two cells over, the bifocal man crouches in front the way day laborers stoop in front of old hotels, cupping cigarettes from the wind. Inside Eusluss puts on his shoes and looks out through the bars. Seeing the rogue side is clear, he comes out to the first table with a red ear and a scratch down the side of his neck.

He sits down sideways toward the short wall working

something in his mouth. His ear is swollen red but he sits not raising a hand to it.

The rogues come out from their naps and go to the long wall to stretch their legs. Junior Bravo wearing a nylon tank top prances like a boxer, throwing combinations.

"The man's hands are fast" preens Short Reg. "Fast as any man's alive."

"Junior hit a man five times in the blink of his eye" says Lupe. "And hurt him with every punch."

Trashbucket watches from the end of the bench. "A man's hands don't have to be fast. Landing is the trick."

Junior shuffles by. "Just how you gonna land if you get hit five times going in?"

"Sometimes it's worth getting hit five times to land one big punch."

Junior stops to spread his legs. "You country motherfuckers always talkin' about one big punch. Close your eyes and reach back for that Missouri mule." He does a bowlegged imitation getting a laugh. "This is the city, Jack. You got to stick and move."

Short Reg comes at Junior from the side and catches the wind of another combination. He jumps back wildeyed.

"Junior part Apache, *Kiowa*."

Lupe taunts Trashbucket. "Those fists cut a man up like a Sunday pork roast."

Trashbucket ignores him. "You're fast, Junior, but most times a haymaker is all it takes."

Junior wheels by again. "If I didn't respect you as a man I'd put my fists up against your haymaker and we'd see who gets off first."

"And I got respect for you as a man, Junior, but what black guy can't dance and punch air."

The rogues rear up. "Fuck you, man! You ain't shit!"

Trashbucket holds a finger up to Junior. "Can you drop a

man one shot open hand?" He shows the thick of his hand. "Before I come here I went upside a punk so hard he went into convulsions."

"What's that supposed to mean?" asks Junior.

"It shows the strength in a man's hand, slappin' another man down like a bitch and standin' over him. One hand, straight-up: dude stands or falls."

"Who?"

"Don't matter *who*. It's *you*."

Junior has enough of him, turning his back. He looks toward the short wall at the newcomers in the corner. They huddle closer as his gaze goes to Yarbrough and Rudy Yid on the side. As he looks interested in Yarbrough and his blond hair his eyes turn to the first table. "Bring me that Useless Eustus motherfucker" he decides and flips his hand.

"*Uh-Oh!*" echo the Rogues from the bench.

Lupe strolls over to Eusluss and taps him on the shoulder. "C'mon, Junior want to see you."

Eusluss turns his head back at Junior standing out in front of the rogues; his shoulders looking twice his waist.

"Let's go; he got something."

He staggers turning the wrong way and Lupe pushes him to get going. He sees the newcomers watching and grins over at Rudy Yid shoulder to shoulder with Yarbrough. Rudy Yid says nothing. He sits still.

"You look like an intelligent dude" says Junior as Eusluss limps up to him. "Where'd you work, in a hospital?"

"A smorgasbord" says Eusluss.

Junior pulls his tank top over a wide chest muscle, flicking his thumb over the nipple. He is buckskinned but the nipple is liver-colored and shines like a worm.

"I got a pain in my titty. See if you feel something there."

Playing as if it's a joke Eusluss shies back.

"Go ahead" says Junior.

Peeking around him at the rogues to see if they're smiling,

he pushes a finger to the nipple.

"Rub it" says Junior. "It's not a button."

Eusluss puts the finger back and rubs in a circle.

"Feel something?" Junior shifts his weight, shoulders rocking.

Eusluss shakes his head no.

"You sure?"

Eusluss is about to say when a hand tries to rip off his head. It bounces off his brow sending him back on his heels. Seeing he's not going to fall Junior lunges with another hook and trips like he'd slipped in a pit. Eusluss falls back and Junior jumps up and kicks his rump.

"Get up motherfucker! I'm not through."

The rogues run up showing their faces as Eusluss covers up with both hands. "Get up! Get your ass up!"

It looks like they're about to stop when a rogue sees an opening between Eusluss' hands and kicks him in the face, clicking his teeth. Eusluss' head hits back on the stone and the rogue howls jumping over him with both feet.

Yells come up from the rogues below as though they can smell blood. Rudy Yid goes along the side to the gate and yells through the bars at the pipes as if it were the rail mill at four in the morning and he's yelling into the dark. The horn blares and stops. Through the yells below he hears heels clicking across the stone floor and shouts in relay. A second horn goes off and a steel door flings open on the first landing. Newcomers head from the corner to their cells. Eusluss turns up on all fours with strings of blood hanging from his mouth. Seeing he has time Trashbucket jumps over and kicks him in the ribs, flipping him up. Rudy Yid comes up grabbing Eusluss under an arm and pulling him back as Trashbucket kicks again. Getting in the way he catches it high on the hip and turns toward Trashbucket who bounces on the balls of his feet. "*C'mon!*" he yells.

Hearing the stairshaft rumbling right below he ducks back into his cell.

Eusluss lies gasping. Rudy Yid tries to steady him but he bobs his head, unable to get his breath. Letting go of him he goes into his cell alone. Yarbrough is not there.

Velez and six deputies come up on the tier. Seeing Eusluss doubled up on his side, Velez pulls the lever and deputies go in taking the floor.

"Get out!"

Rudy Yid comes out like the others, turning to the bars. Deputies around Eusluss tell him not to move as his teeth chatter.

"His jaw's busted" one calls.

Eusluss's head strains up, gasps going up his nose like honks, getting a laugh from the rogues. Rudy Yid looks right. Trashbucket is grinning but the others stand with such blank faces that if he'd not seen what they'd done he'd have thought them innocent. He's just one cell over. He could step around and be on him.

Velez turns toward the row. "Who saw this? Sound off."

Rudy Yid itches to step back and point a finger. It is up in his throat.

"If you saw," calls Velez, "step out."

"Step out," warns Velez, "or you lock hole."

The rogues sound off, ready to stomp the floor. Velez motions the deputies up.

"Lock hole! Get in there!"

Yarbrough comes from a cell over, going in with Rudy Yid. A prowler slams the door shut.

Deputies bring in a litter with wheels, lift Eusluss up on it and get him to the elevator. Velez and the others leave slamming the block shut.

After they're gone, the rogues press up to the bars yelling *"Punk! Punk! Punk!"* It's not meant for them but as a chant for what they did to Eusluss. Going strong they stomp the racks until they twang. Water scooped from commodes splashes out on the rogue side, then white newcomers join in as though they'd been in on it. Trashbucket pushes his snout between the bars.

"*Who's the hero, Jack?* I seen your ugly face. You got fuckin' *eyes.*"

The rogues join in. "We'll fuck you up, *Jack!*"

Lupe calls out "I know you, Blanco. You ain't *nawthin!*"

Rudy Yid looks out their way, while behind him Yarbrough has gone from the rack to the commode and back.

"He means you."

Rudy Yid looks back.

"What'd you yell for?" Yarbrough asks.

"They would have killed him."

Yarbrough climbs up. "What business is that of yours?"

"You could watch?"

"I'll watch. If it means my ass I'll watch. I'll watch all day. Sounds cold, sorry, but guess who I'm looking out for? How can you look out for yourself if you're looking out for somebody else? You put me on the spot just being here with you."

He lights a cigarette. "I told you these guys' business is beating and kicking. You see Junior whip up on that guy?"

"He knew he wasn't gonna fight back. He could have hit him anyway he wanted to."

"He's fast just the same. You see Trashbucket boot that goot and flip him like a pancake? He got one in on you."

"You admire that? They call a guy over and bust his jaw and kick in his side."

"Maybe it's not right but they don't have a place in society so they make one here — and don't say it's wrong. *Don't* say it's wrong 'cause they're the ones who go fight a war when you need them."

"Who, Trashbucket and Junior?"

"Yea, Trashbucket and Junior. You see those two coming head-on, if that wouldn't make you wanna turn-tail and

139

bouquee in the weeds."

"They're two pieces of shit. They got those niggers behind 'em. And those whites are no better. They see a guy get kicked in the face and start yelling, too."

"You should have told him not to go over. He looked you right in the eye."

"I didn't think they'd do that."

"Now you know, and they know you but I don't want 'em knowing me. If I was you I'd ask for protection tomorrow. That's all I'm saying."

He steps out of the corner. "They're not gonna get me."

"You're gonna stall 'em off twenty-eight days?"

"I'll think of something. I had an uncle in the Warsaw ghetto. A thousand Nazis couldn't take him. And these shitheads aren't gonna get me. I'll tell you this. If I had a knife like I had in the mill, we'd see who'd get who."

"You'd get 'em all, huh?" says Yarbrough, putting out his smoke. "What if you had a knife and saw Trashbucket alone in an alley?"

"I'd need a knife for him in an alley? I'd go hide my fuckin' head in shame."

He comes closer. "I'll tell you this. I'll get him anyway for kicking Eusluss while he was choking for air."

"What about Junior?" asks Yarbrough.

"Him too but Trashbucket's first. You got my word. One of us is going out of here sideways, or I don't wanna go out at all."

"*Woo boy!*" chirps Yarbrough.

Yarbrough doesn't seem the same. He skips the bag lunch passed through the bars, turning to the wall to sleep. In the evening he sits up over the side for a peanut butter sandwich and a carton of milk.

"What's wrong?"

"I don't know. Twenty-eight more days in here then I gotta go start over."

"You started with nothin' before."

"Not exactly. I had companionship. Somebody to go home to."

"You got me. We'll go out and get that first job and you'll forget you were ever here."

"I'm not gonna be able to start right away. I need money for materials. I'll have to go back to making appointments."

"You said all you need is a couple hundred for tile and tools. I got a car we could get six or seven hundred for."

Yarbrough turns his head. "I don't wanna work that way again. This time I want a license, a girl in the office, truck and a decal. I wanna do it right this time."

As the skylight turns dark, he sits thinking he played himself too far. What chance did he have? He remembers the boning knife he left in the mill never wanting to see it again. What he'd give for it now. His hands on his head, he mumbles, hearing himself calling, "Put something in my hands. Let me go against them."

CHAPTER 19

A jab of lightning like a bough with limbs flashes across the skylight. A short fall sweeps the glass in clouts, running from gutters. Getting up he washes his face and brushes his teeth with cold water. He knows they will come at him on first whim but they're lazy and sleep after breakfast. Thinking it will be afternoon before they get around to it he fancies he can draw Trashbucket over. It won't take much, a look a glance and by the time the others get there he'll be catching it from both hands. They might not even jump in, but he won't count on it.

A little after daybreak, a deputy lets in two trusties who bring around bags and cartons of milk. Taking theirs, Rudy Yid shakes Yarbrough's leg.

"Put it down" he says. "I'll get to it."

Rudy Yid sits and has an egg sandwich with ketchup and a banana with milk.

Velez arrives at nine, puts a wet slicker across the desk and goes in with two prowlers.

"On the grills!"

Yarbrough rolls over as a prowler pulls the door back. He drops down looking for his pants, and Rudy Yid goes out without him. The rogues stagger out grabbing the bars. The one who looks half awake, Trashbucket, works his neck and sees Rudy Yid looking. His eyes narrow.

"*Who* you looking at, punk fucker?"

Getting no answer he kneads the bars as if he's about to let go at him. Rudy Yid eyes him, feeling his ears pin back, when the name *Arterberry* is called. It sounds to him like *Yarbrough* but it's Trashbucket who pushes off. Ogling Rudy Yid like he can't wait to get back, he goes to Velez. Rudy Yid glances back, thinking he's going to be questioned about the beating. A prowler locks his wrists and takes him out.

Velez slams the block shut, leaving down the stairs with the other prowler. Still groggy the rogues go back in. The block in front of him and some sun in the skylight, Rudy Yid goes to sit near the door.

Yarbrough goes back in to use the toilet. He wets his hair and goes out to Rhymes and Tapia's cell. Told not to block the door he talks through the bars.

Rudy Yid eyes him playing up to them when he hears a truck clanging, backing up to the kitchen, and remembers the knife he saw down there by the pie. If he could get down there, get his hands on it and bring it back, he'd turn the tables. He'd cut through all of them to get to Trashbucket and Junior.

Hardly able to sit now he glances over his shoulder for a deputy to come up. A few whites go out to the corner at the short wall looking at him the way recruits in barracks look at a suspected thief in their midst.

Short Reg, Lupe and two other rogues come out to the long wall and sit down with long faces as if not interested in him for now. There is tromping in the staircase and he looks. First up is Trashbucket. He wasn't gone ten minutes. Hope of the knife gone, his next thought is it might as well be now as he's let in, with a deputy there. Edging up he feels in his fists the shots he's going to throw. He has him in eye as Trashbucket gets to the gate but Trashbucket takes no notice of him. He curses to himself, going straight in.

"Cocksuckin' motherfuckers, I'm not pleading guilty to no manslaughter. It was self-defense."

The rogues at the bench get up. "Cop manslaughter" says Reg. "You sent up on second degree murder you be smelling your fingers after a fish dinner."

"He came at me with a beer bottle. What was I supposed to do?"

"You could have kept your hands out from between his wife's legs" says Lupe.

Trashbucket sees Junior coming and raises his voice. "It took me a half minute to kill that motherfucker. You think I'm gonna do seven years for that? I'm gettin' my ass out."

"Gangbusters!" intones Lupe in the way of the radio program. The rogues mock sirens sounding and Lupe leaps at the wall, staggering back. Spread wide he squeals "*Oooh, so well, Jumbo.*" Trashbucket starts after him but Junior and the others block the way.

"Be cool, man."

"I'm gonna glom that horsejockey's teeth against the cement." He pushes until Junior shoves back. Trashbucket turns on the rogues with a clenched fist. Bending, Red Reggie slips something out from under his pant leg, cuffing it in his wrist. Rudy Yid gets up straining to see what it is.

Trashbucket's eyes dart around as if he's ready to fight

143

them all.

"Be cool" Junior warns him.

"I'm gonna start bustin' heads around here, Junior."

He stomps off to sit alone. The rogues close up as though they'd scared him off. Junior goes over and sits next to him, taking out a twist of cellophane with dark pellets inside.

"What's that?"

"Preacher Trank. You smoke some you won't care if you get seven years or you out tomorrow. You think you *Jesus*."

"You took the name of the Lord in vain" sniffs Trashbucket. "That's cold."

The rogues smell hot food and rush to the door leaving Trashbucket and Junior. A deputy arriving with two trusties has them push the lunches through the hatch at the bottom. As the rogues hump up to get a tray, Rudy Yid slips away, getting a glimpse of mash potatoes and applesauce on the side. His stomach rumbles and he would like to get a tray, but he'll be too conspicuous eating at a table.

As the whites go to get theirs, Rhymes and Tapia come out and sit with Yarbrough who quips to them like a salesman. Catching his breath he sees Rudy Yid looking out from the cell and whispers down his sleeve. Rhymes and Tapia look up from their food, their morning eyes opening. Yarbrough has given him away and they won't sit on it long. Feeling any pressure they'll use it to stay in good with Junior and the others.

After lunch the skylight dims and dank air fills the block. He stays put looking again for a deputy to come up on the tier. Yarbrough has struck up a conversation with two newcomers. Asking for a cigarette he goes into their cell to talk. The floor is clear until white newcomers go out to the corner and sit with nothing left to talk about.

Red Reggie, Short Reg, Baby Uey, Lupe and two others come out to the long wall. The two sit apart from the rest as though a split is forming between them. The one on the end looks as the skylight brightens and talks about what he'd be doing on Saturday night.

"I be shiftin' up and down La Brea in a little red Corolla checkin' out bus stops. I picked up a girl on La Brea. She half Korean half sister. She so fine the tips of her toes glowed in the dark."

Short Reg leans back against Baby Uey, calling the one on the end. "Why you don't go to clubs? You too cheap to pay a tab?"

Red Reggie picks up for the rogue. "Why he got to go to clubs, pay tabs and throw his money out? Why he just can't be black?"

Baby Uey's chuckles spur Red Reggie on. "Why he got to spray himself up, wear gold and sport a ride? That sorry as the white man thinkin' he know how to aphrodisiac a woman with his crib and stereo, sayin' he an expert on where a girl want him to put his tongue and fingers. Why he can't just make her happy with his dick? He wanna get all up in your face with his breath and tell you he a champ pussy eater."

"White man can't even keep a woman," says Short Reg, "unless he eat pussy because his dick too small. Only one person eat pussy better than a white man . . ."

"A *Mexican*" offers Baby Uey.

"No. A white girl. Angelique over at C.C. say white girls see a strong sister and get a hop in they walk and start eatin' that big sister pussy and like it. They havin' a baby and man at home and eatin' that strong sister pussy. And if you know them big sisters you know it look like the Creature from the Black Lagoon down there."

One of the rogues points to the white newcomers at the other end. "Them white boys listen to everything we say."

"White peoples jealous black peoples," says Baby Uey, "watchin' everything we do, thinkin' we take they women. Martin Luther King was first to say that. Martin Luther King was a great man."

The rogue on the end calls over "You had you some white girls big and black as you are?"

Lupe leans around Uey from the other end. "My cousin go with black guys. She say bigger blacker better."

Red Reggie winks. "That's right. That blonde lady in *King Kong* wasn't screaming 'cause he was big and black; it was 'cause his breath stunk."

"Big as he was," notes Uey, "they say he had a brain the size of a pea." He leans back, whining at all the talk. "When we gonna get some? My pud need some work and we just sittin' here with all that hardleg over there."

"Them skeeters?" asks Red Reggie nodding at the whites in the corner.

Baby Uey means the other corner. "I want that red Hiawatha motherfucker in there walkin' around barefoot with his butt all uppity like he proud. He probably some two bit half-breed used to wipe windows at a gas pump. Split that red booty and see if he buck back like ol' Warpaint."

He begins to buck at the groin. "Work *good* with me, baby."

"Junior say he cool" says Lupe.

"He cool with Junior, why he got to be cool with me. *Shoot*, just 'cause Junior and he down. My pud need work and we just sittin' here."

"*Get-it-from-yo-momma.*"

It comes like a rivet from a bush, and Baby Uey looks down at the two on the end. He doesn't know who threw his voice but calls to both.

"You don't know my *momma*. Yo mommas smell like piss, but you don't know my *momma*."

Red Reggie and Lupe hold him back. "You two must be jokin' because you don't know my *momma*. Yo mommas prostitutes. Yo mommas put theyselves up for public sale."

It looks to Rudy Yid the two on the end could double up and split him like a banana pie, but they don't seem eager for him to come over.

Two whites in the corner head for a cell.

"You scared them white boys" points the rogue on the end. "*Hey*, where you goin'?" They pretend not to hear and the two rogues run to the cell left of Rudy Yid. He listens as they bail water from the commode. Thinking they're going to wet down the two whites they scared off, he hears pats on the stone floor and sees them one behind the other at the abutment with shirts off and bare feet.

"Your leg's on fire" points the one in front.

He looks down and a bucket swings around, splashing his face with ice-cold water. He jumps up gasping, pulling off his shirt and squeezing water from his pants. The two rogues head back and the Reggies, Lupe and Uey run up to look. He pulls the shirt back on standing there wet to the crotch.

"Look like he peed on hisself" says Uey.

The two rogues swing by with a full bucket. Showing themselves next door, they fling in the water and run from shrieks of "*Cut it out, you bastards!*"

The others move over to look, when a deputy comes up on the tier. His glance turns them back to the wall.

Rudy Yid throws his doused bedroll atop Yarbrough's and sits down on the bare rack looking out at the deputy. He'd been waiting and now can't approach him.

His empty stomach twists and he knows he won't be able to go out for the supper tray either, but even that might not help. Trashbucket will come out hungry from a long nap and this time he'll notice him in the cell alone. Until now the rogues have stayed on their side but he has the feeling that tonight they will rampage.

The deputy sits looking at a magazine and goes back down. The floor is empty when Red Reggie wanders out to the bench at the long wall. Taking off a half boot and sock he brings his foot up and starts picking his big toe. Straining for more light he picks up and goes to the second table. Under the lamp above he pokes a thumbnail under an infected cusp at the corner of the toe. His other leg is out stiff, a jag at the back of the cuff. Rudy Yid edges up. It's not the cut of the boot. It's what he pulled on Trashbucket. At first he took it for something to load up the fist but wonders now if it's the handle of a knife or something to hack with.

Snipping with long fingernails Red Reggie tweezes a jut of nail he's about to pull when he sees Rudy Yid looking.

"Can I help you?"

He says nothing, moving back just enough that he still has him in his eye. Reggie plucks the nail squeezing blood out of the toe and wiping it with his thumb. Pulling the sock back on, he picks up the half boot and swings his leg up under the table. Leaning on an elbow he scratches his scalp mumbling to himself.

Rudy Yid goes to the door. Reggie's eyelids have sunk. He doesn't look asleep, but his legs are trapped under the table and he isn't going to get them out asleep or not.

He remembers when he was small, old Germans who'd fought in the First World War sitting in the park and telling of being in trenches in no man's land when roughnecks among them would roll up their sleeves, take knives and entrenching tools like clubs and go over the top. They called it: *Auf Tod und auf Leben*. He stood near listening, and they thought he didn't understand but he knew: On life on death — one or the other.

Easing out to a draft of air against his wet clothes he's in line with a corner of Reggie's temple wanting an angle at his eye, not to swing down at the back of his head. Reggie twists, turning his face flat to the table, the left eye up.

He comes still. It's a step back and three ahead. The next rogue out will see what he's about to do. Under his breath he calls "*Hey!*"

Reggie stirs, no more.

148

"Hey!"

He lifts as if he heard. Ears up, he senses something behind him. The eye turns, filling the corner, when a fist hooks in with a clap. Turned over, his hip catches under the table. He strains to right himself, the eyelid filling up, when another shot hooks in squirting blood out the corner. He sinks trembling to his heels.

Rudy Yid drops down under the bench grabbing Reggie's pants leg. He lifts the cuff up over a taped handle at the back of his half boot and pulls a short screwdriver sharpened like a pick. Gripping it like a roll of dimes, nob down, he lifts his head by the collar and hammers the heel of his fist into the eye until he sags swallowing his own blood.

He turns and sees the two whites who'd been doused looking out, and nods to them to get back. To the other side of his cell the pranksters who'd thrown water sleep. Crossing to the next cell he sees Trashbucket on the top rack, snoring like a sow. Nobody is below. His mouth is soughing, catching air in back of his throat. It is not getting through straining his gills.

In the next cell Short Reg is on the top rack and Baby Uey on the bottom filling most of the space. He wants to go in on them but Trashbucket is first. First him then he'll get to who he can. Turning the pick in his hand he slips in.

His head up close looks twice a normal size and the lumps on his cobbled face are piled up like slick suet in a butcher pail. Leaning closer he gets a stale waft of his damp neck, noticing a rough outcrop under his chin like string with knots. He means at first to slap a hand down over his mouth but he looks strong enough to twist out. The first shot has to leave him dumbstruck. Reaching to the hair hanging over the side he tugs closer.

Trashbucket's eyes flutter. Gasping to catch his breath, he looks up, mouth apart when the pick swings into his teeth. Opening wide he gasps *"ooh!"* He means to yell. His tongue twists but can't get out a word. The next one breaks through snaring his cheek and tearing it open to the corner of his mouth. He bucks from the heels, hacking up a spurt of blood, nearly splitting the rack from the stone. Eyes wild he doesn't know what's happening. He holds his cheek together with one hand and kicks a leg out as thick as a log but trembling with fear.

Gripped in his hair he tries to catch his eye, showing him the pick for the next one, when Trashbucket swings up his rump for cover, scraping his head down the stone. Rudy Yid lunges across his haunch to let him have it, when a hand shoots up as stiff as a rod breaking loose and jabs his eye.

Flinching, the eye shut tight he can hardly get the other open. Trashbucket's leg comes alive from up high. He feels one jolt on the shoulder; another bounces off the side of his head. Flinging back blind he breaks the next kick at the knee, rolling him up on his head, when the rack jolts in the corner, swinging Trashbucket back at him. Feeling him spit and hiss with his nails at his neck he is no longer gripped in his hair but holding him back with both hands. An eye open he marks him across eyes and teeth. The rack bends and Trashbucket is on him, slapping him on the ear and hammering away with the same hand. Catching fists on top of his head, knowing he has seconds no more, he pulls a fist out underneath and hooks it around bouncing it off the side of his head. Feeling him shake he wrenches free to the right and chops into his hip. Trashbucket jerks, twisting away uncovered. Yanked with him, his right arm loose, he hacks the pick up his side and shoulder driving one under the blade. Trashbucket flips back his head letting out a shriek like an animal being splayed of its skin.

The grip breaking at his neck, he twists him halfway back. His arm going like a bilge pump he hacks into his face, bits flying, until his head bounces over the rack. Driven over, Trashbucket slips through his grip, his tongue sliding out in the corner like a steer's hung upside down. Rudy Yid turns, letting him fall in a thud against his legs as Lupe and others pile up at the door but don't rush in, looking around him at

Trashbucket buckled on the floor. An ear ringing, his neck thick he strains to get his left eye open. He hears yells at the gate and more coming from the tier below. A prowler coming up to look sees the commotion and hits the horn at the pipes. The rogues back away at the blare. A door slams open on the first landing, a rumble starts up the staircase and the rogues scatter as deputies get to the top, pointing to the cell. *"In there!"*

The gate is pulled back and deputies go in. Seeing them come he drops the pick.

"Get out! Out!"

He staggers to the door getting a foot out when he's jolted forward their weight on him. They try to pull his arms back so he'll hit face to the cement. An arm hooks under his chin but he twists under it hitting on his shoulder. His arms are pulled back and his wrists bent together, a knee to his neck. A deputy over him yells to lie flat.

He presses his brow to the stone floor glistening in his open eye, when he's yanked at the collar.

"Get your head straight."

Holding up, he thinks he can't strain any harder when a tremble works through the back of his head until the eye waters over. The burn slips at the point, easing toward the corner as if it'd been no more than a speck from under Trashbucket's nail. Easing his head he numbs from the tone in his bad ear as cells slam shut and rogues yell back through the bars. He feels a rumble from the stone floor, the rogues below stomping away as if somebody has been killed.

The floor tilting in his eye he sees deputies make way as Trashbucket is brought out flat on the floor. His legs are spread like a drunk's. His face is swollen round, seeping blood, but his eyes are wide open and he nods to the deputies' questions. Along the cells the rogues yell they were asleep. Hearing one voice over others he turns his head back and sees Lupe pleading for Red Reggie bent over on the toilet holding a gob of soaked red toilet paper to his eye.

Coming into the block with the watch commander, Velez sees Rudy Yid looking around and calls to the deputy to get him up. He's pulled up in back and led out, getting a glimpse of Yarbrough talking to two deputies with a look in his eyes as though he sees a way out of there.

He's taken down the elevator and out across the yard in a drizzle that cools his face and neck. He hears Velez alongside cursing in his throat the paperwork he'll be faced with. "It's not worth the *Gawdam* trouble." Passing the docks they go to a small square building.

A thickset jailer with hair combed back like an old banker lets them into a stone entryway.

"Watch him" the deputy says. "He shanked a big hump in his sleep."

The jailer shows a split-tooth grin. "Oh, he won't try that here." Showing him the palm of his thick hand, he pats around his waist and down his legs. He notices the poked eye.

"You been crying, lad?"

About to say he's slapped. Seeing stars he goes at him with only his head and the jailer jumps back cocking a fist.

"C'mon. Forfeit your teeth."

The deputies hold him and he can only look. The jailer's smile returns. He opens the block gate and a sour stench comes into the entryway along with shouts from down at the end. Motioning the deputies he opens a solid door with a two-inch slit of window and points to a mark inside.

"Get on that, partner."

He steps in on the mark, turning an eye.

"Stand still" the jailer says, his thick fingers at his wrists. "Don't move" he warns. "*Don't* you move on me."

The cuffs snap open and as Rudy Yid brings his arms around the door slams shut.

He turns to the window, watching them go. Turning back he sees a metal commode with no water and a tap for one hand at a time. Moving up he spits down in the commode and cups

152

a handful of water from the tap to his eye. Hearing shouts from the end of the block, he goes back. One voice is rough and deep. "Introduce yourself, man; tell us who you are, bitch." The other flows like an Indian chant. "In one hand I offer knowledge, in the other power; accept that fact."

He bends aside the tap, letting water glance off his eye. Sitting down at the end of the rack, a wet hand against the eye he adds up what he did. He punched holes through Trashbucket's face that won't fill. He's seen it. It will look as if worms tried to eat him. Women and children will turn their heads. He would have settled for it before but it doesn't feel half enough now. He sees he could have gotten to Junior and the others. He could have washed his hands in their blood. They wouldn't have gotten that pick from him. They would have pulled a tooth from a wolf before they got that pick from him.

The block gate creaks. He hears footsteps to the door. The latch at the bottom flips up and a tray is pushed in. Going to the window he sees a new jailer going down the block, straight in the collar as though just come on. He thinks a second, putting the time at three or four, times shifts changed in the mill. He picks up a tray with two chicken pieces cut small and roasted so dark he can't recognize the parts. He thinks he's being tricked with pigeon or rodent. Watching the jailer turn back he gets a look at his face. He takes the biscuit and milk, pushes the rest back through and eats looking out the window.

He lies down on a thin mattress and stretches the left eye open. The ceiling is high with a caged yellow light like a canary. It smells worse here and he eyes a stone wall with faint circular stains like knots in wood. Leaning closer he sees they are rosettes. Someone had defecated in his palm and rubbed it into the stone. He swings his legs over, sitting up at something at the base of the wall. Swaying forward he watches a slick black mouse disappear into a hole that would hardly fit a pencil.

He sits kneading the eye when the block gate creaks again.

He hears footsteps and a click in the door. It slides open. The new jailer stands a foot back with a deputy and prowler behind him. He motions him to the line.

"Up here and turn away from me."

He goes to the mark and is cuffed from behind. The deputy and prowler take him across the yard to the main building. They go through a back entrance and turn into a dim hall. Two plainclothesmen stand waiting down at the end.

He's taken into a narrow room with a one-way window. They sit him down facing out and go back in the hall closing the door. He leans forward putting his forehead to the table as the sweat cools on his neck and arms.

Thinking he has enough to say he hears voices outside and looks up. The plainclothesmen come in. The one in front holding a computer sheet is stout and mustached. He looks a mix of Spanish and white.

"I'm Sergeant Roa, this is Sergeant Stobb. We're L.A. County investigators." He checks the computer sheet. "You're in for?"

"Battery."

"On two juveniles in a movie theater?"

"Yea."

"What kind of battery?"

"I hit one and threw one out."

"That all?"

"What's it say there?"

Roa doesn't like the question. He looks impatient late this Saturday afternoon. "You're being charged with attempted murder and assault with a deadly weapon. You have a right to remain silent. Anything you say can and may be used against you. You understand so far?"

"Yea."

"You have a right to have an attorney present during any questioning — "

"I don't need a lawyer now."

Roa snaps his fingers and points. "If you can't afford an attorney the court appoints one. You understand that?"

"Yea."

"You want an attorney here?"

"No, what I have to say won't take long."

Roa sees he wants to talk and points up at a camera. "You agree to what we say being taped?"

"Yea."

He goes behind him and unlocks the cuffs. Rudy Yid brings his arms around, wipes his face and cups his eye with his palm. Roa sits down opposite him, his eyes like onyx in a man's ring.

"Before I start," says Rudy Yid, "the one who got laid out up there, Trashbucket, he and some others beat and kicked a guy named Eusluss. They broke his jaw and kicked in his side. I'm sure you càn check on that."

He expects Roa to nod but gets nothing. The shine from his black eyes doesn't lose a point. He sees he should have led up to what he said.

"Okay, I got here Wednesday with some guys from the Valley. They put us on the fourth tier and a guy tells us the reason it's quiet up there is that seven of 'em were in isolation for kicking in a guy's eyesocket and that's another thing you can check."

He takes a second. "So the next morning we get breakfast trays and these same guys from isolation walk in to the head of the line with Trashbucket and another guy Junior in front. And what's the first thing they sit down to talk about when they eat but sodomizing other guys in jail if that gives you an idea of the type they are."

Roa still says nothing, and Rudy Yid glances over at the partner at the wall. "So after breakfast I volunteer to go down and work in the kitchen and when I get back the same ones are arguing back and forth about who can punch hard when this Junior sees Eusluss by himself at a table and calls him over."

He leans forward, appealing to Roa. "This guy was harmless. He never hurt anybody. He shouldn't have been in jail. He was sick and Junior calls him over and starts suckering him and leading him on when *boom*, he lets go with his left hand. Eusluss falls back, and Junior kicks him from behind, then the rest of those dogs run up and one kicks him in the face like you'd kick a box in an alley. That's when I went to the door and yelled."

Stobb speaks up. "Who was Eusluss to you?" He is taller than Roa, with a ranchhand's mustache and boots.

"I talked to him once" says Rudy Yid.

"You talk to him once and try to *save* him?"

"I ran to the door. It's all I could do. The horn goes off and they run to their cells. Eusluss turns up on his hands and knees with blood hanging from his mouth. Then as if they didn't do enough to him, Trashbucket runs back and kicks him under the side. I get in the way and he kicks me too and dances back like he wants me to come on."

"You go?" asks Stobb.

"No."

"You scared one on one?"

"Scared of *him*?" says Rudy Yid. "I wanted him like a tramp wants a ham sandwich. The guards were coming."

"Who was the tier sergeant?" asks Roa.

"Velez."

"He ask who did it?"

"Yea."

"You answer?"

"No."

"You didn't want to snitch?"

"I'd have told. I couldn't right then."

"Why not?"

"I don't know."

"What happened then?" asks Roa.

"We were locked down" says Rudy Yid. "Trashbucket and the rest started yelling they'd get me for helping Eusluss and you can check on that too."

"He ever threaten you before?"

"No."

"You report the threats after lockdown?"

"No."

"They put you in fear?"

"I was looking for a way."

"What kind of way?" asks Roa.

"To help myself."

"You had a weapon?"

"It wasn't mine. It belonged to a guy named Red Reggie. He kept it in his half boot."

"What was it?"

"A screwdriver with a sharp point."

"How'd you get it?" asks Stobb.

"Go take a look at him" he says feeling them closing in on him now. "Hereon I better only say whatever I did I did to defend myself."

"You said you'd tell what happened" calls Stobb.

"I don't need much to get the idea. I don't think you came to help me. I tell you what they do to some guy who never hurt nobody and I see it makes no impression. I tell you to go look for yourself and see you don't like it. But you wanna know who he was to me. They were trying to kill him so I ran to help. That's who he was to me."

Stobb says nothing but Roa gets a look on his face. This time Rudy Yid looks back at him saying nothing. Stobb watches from the wall then goes to the door to call in the deputy.

Brought back across the yard, he walks hardly feeling the ground under him. Taken into the block, he steps in on the line. The jailer unlocks the cuffs and the door closes behind him.

He sits smarting that they didn't care what went on up there before he got his hands on the pick. They wanted to get him. He could see it in their eyes, and he'd left them a clear way to Trashbucket with those deputies around him and the rogues yelling that he got him asleep.

He looks up. The door whisked out the vomit smell but it forms up again. It is a smell he could never get used to. When he was ten he spent a night in a room with a cousin who threw up in his crib and the smell soured all night. The next day he told his mother before he'd sleep like that again he'd go find a patch of grass somewhere.

He lies on his side feeling an itch developing on his back. Thinking a louse from the mattress has burrowed into his skin he tries to squeeze it out. Standing he lifts his shirt and rubs his back against the wall. It feels better then swells hard as a knot and he stops before it gets worse. Putting an eye to the window he listens to the one chanting. "It's my brother's birthday today and I'm trying to get a cake. I washed my hair and it's all wet."

Sitting with his head between his hands, he hears the block gate creak. Stepping to the window, he watches the jailer go down the block and back. He puts his shoes under his head and lies on his side. Dozing from hot air through the vent, he feels his skin start to itch and his hands smell of the stench in the air. He gets up and rinses them off but the smell returns. Feeling the yellow light on his back he thinks it will sicken him more than the smell. He sits mumbling, singing to himself, getting the idea that he'll speak to a Rabbi and ask him to put big heads together to get him out of this, and that he will pay them back out of wages or work it off.

CHAPTER 20

Hearing yells he gets up with a stiff neck. His left eye is half closed and blurred. The tone has eased in his ear but the bump on his back hasn't gone down. He feels his pants and shirt; they haven't dried. He uses the toilet, washes with cold water and sits back down looking at his wet hands.

The block door creaks, footsteps come and the latch opens for a tray of gravied biscuits, diced peaches, and milk. He goes to the door and looks out at a black jailer going down the block. Watching him come back, he wipes off the biscuits and eats facing the window.

He lies on his side holding wet toilet paper to the eye. The block gate creaks again and he looks up at two eyes peering in. The door opens on the black jailer and a prowler behind him. The jailer takes cuffs off his belt.

"Up here!" He motions him to put his hands out.

He goes to the mark holding his hands together and the jailer's eyes flare.

"*Hold 'em out!* I ain't reachin' in for you."

Snapping the cuffs on, the jailer walks him down the block to a room, pointing to a phone on the wall and closing the door.

He gets the phone up between his hands and hears an excited voice. "*Rudy,* that you?"

He thinks it's somebody back in Chicago. "Yea, it's me."

"Sol Nathan, your lawyer."

His breath lets go. "You the one they told to call me?"

"No, listen. I pick up the Sunday paper; I see a jail stabbing; I see your name: '*Whoa!,* it's my guy, they killed him.' I call over and they tell me it's *you* being held. What went on up there? What happened?"

"I had to defend myself."

"*Defend yourself.* A guy was killed in his sleep."

"*Killed?* He's dead?"

"A massive brain hemorrhage against the lobe. Splints of bone were driven into the brain."

"He was looking up at the guards. He was nodding to everything they said."

"He didn't make it. He went out. I called. They don't wait. They make a few calls and disconnect. What was the beef up there?"

He stands numb. "They attacked a guy on my floor and I ran to help, so they said they'd get me."

Nathan's voice rises. "So you let a guy have it in his *sleep*?"

"It was more than that."

"Have they questioned you?"

"Yea."

"Who?"

"Two cops."

"They tell you you could have an attorney there?"

"I didn't want one."

"You didn't want an attorney? What'd you say?"

"I said I had to defend myself."

"You told them you did it?"

"I told them what went on up there, the truth."

"The *truth*. They twist the truth. They'll use every word to make the case and fill in the cracks. Nothing you said will come out like you said it. The truth out of context is better than a lie. It has a ring a lie can't match."

"They threatened to get me. The whole block heard."

"How many were up there?"

"Twenty."

"And they'll come to your defense? You were pals? You know their character? There was kinship after two days?"

"If they get on the stand they have to say what they saw, don't they?"

"No, they can deny they saw or heard a thing."

"All twenty?"

"Yea all twenty. Going oh-for-twenty with witnesses is

nothing. You don't know disillusion until a witness who's seen everything starts to play dumb and pick his spots. Are you lucky? Are you lucky with people?"

"Me?"

"*You*. You lucky with people?"

"Not that lucky."

"Don't count on anybody."

"You go just by that?"

"So far I do."

"That guy Trashbucket and the blacks up there tried to kill a guy. He'll tell you what they did."

"You're gonna depend on a poor shmo they roughed up to take the stand for you?"

"This Trashbucket ground a beer bottle into a guy's face when he got into town. He's there for killing a guy himself."

"Doesn't matter. In court he's name age hometown — stabbed in sleep. That's a murder easy to prove. Intent and act are aligned. Like a man walking to a refrigerator. You basically know he's going to help himself. You wanna know what they did in Florida to a dope mooch named Shophelp? You got the patience?"

"Yea."

"This Shophelp does a couple years for theft and is driving through a snowstorm in Nebraska one night when he stops to pick up another ex-con, a big bohunk wearing those pop-bottle glasses. Shophelp has a little money and they stop at a motel for the night. So the bohunk repays the hospitality. He pulls a gun and sodomizes him. Then he takes him along on a robbery spree down into Florida subjecting him to every degradation he can think of, until one night Shophelp hides the bohunk's glasses and shoots him up close with his own gun. So, what's society's loss? What's a little shmo deserve for eliminating this predator to anyone crossing his path? Maybe you wouldn't want to shake his hand, but those prosecutors down there knew he'd spared innocent people harm. They could have turned an eye and cut him some slack. Nobody would have raised a voice, but they're not hicks down there for nothing. Shophelp has no money, no pull and rolls over like a retarded fourteen-year-old girl. The newspapers play up the sad-sack name and he tightens his noose, admitting he didn't shoot in rage but worked up the courage. What more could they ask? They stamped prime murder on him like on a side of veal and he went through that greased Florida justice like shit through a goose. The day comes and they take this little moocher with bleached hair and racoon rings under his eyes into a room, strap him in, lock his head, and pull down two and a half thousand volts. The blood turns to brown paste in a second."

"They electrocuted him?"

"Yea they electrocuted him and I see this as similar. They're not carrying out executions in California now, but they put you in line quick as anybody."

"I didn't have a right to defend myself?"

"One. It's pre-emptive. It's getting them before they get you."

"That's what I did."

"Listen: it stands when there's no other way. You had no choice. You felt trapped, and so would a reasonable person in your place. I can make this defense. I can go to my boss and put everything down to get to this."

"Could you go to a Rabbi out here and tell him I'm Jewish and had to defend myself against schvartzes and a hillbilly?"

"You're *Jewish*? You look like a Polack. You must be removed from it."

"No, I speak Yiddish."

"What would going to a Rabbi do?"

"He must know people."

"They do that in Chicago? I wouldn't know where to start. What Rabbi would mix himself up in this? They'll be wound-up for the death penalty here. They'll read the *begats* to you. All that can save you is a lawyer willing to put heart and conscience into this. I'll be honest — I want it as much for me."

"I better see who they send first."

"Who do you think they have up there? They'll send a hausfrau who did law school at night or some young guy who's gonna go through the motions and chalk it up to experience. It'll mean your life. You need somebody to go in there and paint the picture they were worse than you. You convince one out of twelve, that's all and everything slips back a notch."

"Let me ask. What happens now?"

"There's arraignment, probably Monday. They set a trial date at six months to a year."

"What then?"

"What do you mean?"

"They got me in a cell that stinks from vomit and keep the light on all night."

"You don't think you're going back in the population, do you?"

"They're not gonna move me?"

"Why would they move you? You're ten minutes from court."

"And I sit until trial?"

"You go back and forth to court on motions. That's the preparation."

The black jailer looks in. "That's it."

"I gotta go" says Rudy Yid.

"Rudy, you want me to go to my boss on this?"

"I don't know yet."

Getting back, he sits numb. Nathan tried to scare him but he doesn't doubt what he said. If he hadn't taken a second to toy with Trashbucket to show him the knife and be poked in the eye for it, if he'd kept hacking away, then pulled him to the floor and gotten out to Junior and the others he could have left a mess up there. Where could they start on him? What could they say or prove? Who'd believe he went against all of them? They could kiss his ass then — no more.

He's lost ideas of a Rabbi or anybody helping him. He has one place to go, to an uncle in Argentina who manufactures shoes. This uncle, Eleazar, came to Chicago when they still lived on Sawyer, a blackhaired hairychested man who didn't look like the Polish Jew he was. His uncle saw the dark apartment they lived in and the little store they lived from and asked to take him to Argentina. After that, whenever he looked at a map in school, his finger would go down to Argentina, as if he had a place there.

Two years ago his father sent him a letter from Israel, saying Eleazar had been there with three grown daughters and asked about him, what he was doing and his address to get in touch. His father once told him that Eleazar was a blowhard and showoff, but he was sure the least he would do was hide him on a ranch on the pampas somewhere, and he would take a name.

He had a car back at Lankershim. If he could move it down over the border, he'd sell it and the guns in the trunk, then find a way to Argentina. He thinks of what Nathan said about going back and forth to court on pre-trial motions. Somewhere along he would break away. He has a hurt eye. If they take him to a clinic he'll look for a way there.

Lunch comes with a tray of stew, cornbread and milk; and supper is cold cuts, a banana and cup of coffee. He eats everything but the cold cuts, deciding he has to stomach the vomit smell now and do enough pushups to sleep good so that when the chance comes he'll be ready.

He drowzes and wakes from the itch in back. He leans back in a corner by the door, getting some relief from the stone.

Lying back down, he dozes again, waking with a nauseating headache. He sits up eyeing the floor.

CHAPTER 21

He's slept for a few hours, when a jailer and two prowlers come.

"Get up. You're going to court."

He stands and they lock his wrists. The prowlers walk him out across the yard in the dark to a building near the gate. They take him to a room and give him a safety razor and paper towels, unsnap a cuff and look on as he wets his face and shaves.

They take the razor, snap the cuff back on and leave him in the room. He goes to a stainless steel bench at the wall and lies down on his side with the towels under his cheek. For the next few hours in this ventilated room he sleeps like a boy.

He is sleeping, when the door opens and he is called out by a rawboned deputy whose nameplate reads Hoje.

"Hold 'em out."

He extends his arms and Hoje runs a chain through a ring between locks and around his waist so he can't move his arms without shifting his shoulders. He checks his wristband.

"You're Rudy Yitz?" he asks, his rough skin glowing from aftershave.

"Yea."

"You're going to arraignment. Any attempt to break free will be met with lethal force. You understand?"

"Yea."

"That's the end of the conversation. Don't say another fuckin' word."

Leading him out he takes a pistol from a wall locker and puts it in his holster. He pulls back the side door of a van and Rudy Yid climbs in looking out through the window as the door slides shut.

The van turns out of the gate, and he gets a queasy feeling seeing a street after three days away. They go over the limestone bridge and round the railhead. Getting on the freeway they turn off into a line of traffic moving uphill toward downtown buildings. A drizzle starts and riders at bus stops put bags and newspapers up over their heads.

They come onto an overpass. He raises up off the bench seeing semi-trailers coming out below under the bridge and fancies if his hands were loose he would kick out the door, swing over the rail and drop onto the back of one of those trucks.

They arrive at the top of the hill, across the street from the courts building. Going on the light, the van dips downhill, swerving over a walk and down a ramp under a drawn steel gate. It turns to a wall and Hoje gets out, pulling back the side door.

"Let's go."

He takes him to a gate and calls in the transport number. At a buzz they go in to an elevator, taking it to the fourth floor where a Hispanic deputy sitting at a station pushes a button letting them into a holding room. Hoje points Rudy Yid to the bench. He sits down, feeling he has to urinate but doesn't think Hoje will oblige. He gazes over at the deputy, wondering if he could get any help from him. He has sleek full brown cheeks and a glossy mustache. The name on his chest plate is Perez.

Hoje goes to a door in the corner and peeks through a window into the court. Perez calls over "She's here, man. I saw her in the cafe." Hoje looks back and Perez stands up marking himself off above the knee. "Hiked up, man. She cross her legs twice around like rope. Coffee running down people's chins. She's out of high school two years. Her sister is over at Municipal."

"Everybody hitting on her?" asks Hoje.

"It's not the same, man. That Jew beard look down on those legs all day and he start to snap at young attorneys and bailiffs. You make a man sexually moody and he want to make class distinction on you. But you know who's going to get her and I hope this doesn't hurt your feelings?"

Hoje doesn't answer.

"That black guy, Townes. He's going to get her."

Hoje droops an eye.

"He's good looking, man. He's muscled up, he shines and he's getting to her."

"C'mon" says Hoje. "The guy's five-seven. She's taller than he is."

"He's not that short, man. He got those clean arms with ramheads in back and wear those tailored sleeves. The guy go to work to look good, and when he go out — that's ritual. He pump up his upper body, push back his cuticles, oil himself up and down and deck out in silk threads to show her what she never seen. They not responsible to monthly bills like you and me. A black guy put down a paycheck to look good. Stephens, Voll and you guys put on your jeans, sniff under your college jersey and take her to Round Top for *Monday Night Football* like you share American roots or something. She not like that, man. I'm telling you. She got long eyes. She want to be with a man in a dangerous place and see his dick bouncing in silk drawers."

He turns and presses the door button. A cart of dust mops is pushed in by a dapper custodian wearing bloused boots and a blue ascot. His hair glances of rose oil and he stands erect in admiration of the deputies.

"Good morning you two stiff staffs of justice."

Perez hails back. "Lee from *Hemet*. Why you grinning, man? You have sex with livestock last night?"

"You must be psycho" returns Lee. "I mean psychic."

"You bring those tree buds and apple vinegar for lunch?"

"A bag for you" winks Lee. "You can crunch through all that goodness."

"Please" Perez begs. "I got a headache."

"I keep telling you, you get up in the morning, move your bowels and get the poison out of your system. You won't get those sideknockers."

"I told you I can't go until I get to work and have a cigarette and coffee."

"You think you can't" snaps Lee. "You drop your drawers, you bear down on that stool and you don't get up until you've dropped some long torpedoes. Shit or get off the pot. That little ditty has cost more American lives than the slaughter on our highways."

He snaps out a dust mop and starts on the side where Rudy Yid sits. "Well you're sure a clean-cut looking young fella. I hope you're not in a lot of trouble."

"He knifed some old lifer downtown," says Perez, "and stuffed his balls in his mouth."

"Oh no," gasps Lee, "no respect for elders."

A bailiff peeks in through the corner window and opens the door. "You got Rudy Yitz?"

Hoje nods to the bench.

"He wants locks off; give him his folder."

Hoje makes a face and the bailiff mocks it. "Sorry, pal." He regards Perez and Lee. "You two hear about the Chinaman walking around the insane asylum with his hands in his pockets — not feeling crazy, just feeling *nuts*."

Hoje motions Rudy Yid over, and unlocks a cuff and swings out the chain. His left hand drops loose with the notion to hook it up under Hoje's chin and grab the gun. The bailiff sergeant is looking back through the door and Perez in the enclosure is turned away. Only the custodian keeps an eye on him. Hoje unlocks the other wrist, hands him the folder; and the bailiff pulls back the door. They go through a passage into a closed cubicle at the side of court. It's six feet high, three feet of glass over a base of wood panel. The two sides meet at a knobbed post, and there is a door in the corner at the wall.

The fore is busy with workers but the gallery is empty. A tall-sitting Judge smooths back a salt-and-pepper beard as he reads. In front of him three men in shirtsleeves go through stacks of folders. Three deputies are spread about. The closest to the cubicle, by a side exit, has blond Dutchboy bangs and a black semi-automatic on her hip. The next one, leaning back on the gallery rail, is an overly muscular black deputy with shoulder and rump muscles like bowling balls. A veteran deputy sits at the other wall with a newspaper in his lap. Rudy Yid looks over at the deputy city attorney, a trim little blade in a navy blue suit and bow-tie. Next to him an assistant turns in her chair, giving Rudy Yid a look. The court secretary sits by a phone pushing up her nose with a knuckle. She is a rosy-faced woman with her hair up in a bun in front, looking like she had been a Betty Grable type pin-up beauty in her day. She answers a ring and calls to the judge that the public defender is delayed. The judge stands up motioning to the bailiff sergeant in the cubicle that he wants to see him.

Hoje pulls Rudy Yid's arms back and locks his wrists. The bailiff sergeant sees it done and goes out through the holding room door. The court workers start to move about, all except the court reporter, a tanned beauty, who crosses her legs like she's going nowhere. She turns partly away. What Rudy Yid can see of her, she looks like a young model in swimsuit magazines and out of place here.

Hand on his gun, Hoje leans around him, tapping on the glass. She looks over her shoulder and smiles but doesn't turn and Hoje steps back.

The assistant prosecutor stands up and moves around patting her padded shoulders with a glossy manicure but no ring. She has green eyes and wide Magyar cheekbones but a perfect English nose. Giving Rudy Yid another look she reaches behind her with both hands to adjust the bow at the back of her dress. Putting her hands on her hips, she shimmies into a conversation with the court reporter about panty hose. Pinching up a side of her dress, she lifts back a leg looking back at the calf. The muscular black deputy chippers like a jaybird.

"*Goodness*, Sara, cover those legs. Those legs are

involuntary manslaughter."

She curls a brow. "A felony I believe."

The chestnut-haired court reporter looks straight ahead as if their quips are lost on her. Rudy Yid glances back at Hoje whose eyes are on the back of her head.

"Keep your head straight" he says for everyone to hear. "I'm not telling you again."

Rudy Yid eyes the empty gallery, thinking it's closed when an old retiree comes through the front taking a seat in a middle row. The bailiff sergeant follows him in, holding a round cookie tin. Coming up behind him, he flicks his ear, and the codger turns and chases him away with a cocked fist.

The bailiff runs to the fore giving the female deputy a peek inside the canister. She turns out of her chair, going out through the side door. Grinning at her shriek the bailiff sergeant unlocks the cubicle and goes in. The door shuts lightly, looking to Rudy Yid like the light metal doors used in trailers. It could be ripped loose with a sharp twist. He'd done it himself to abandoned trailers in Indiana Dunes.

The sergeant puts the canister up under Hoje's nose. "Look what came to chambers." He lifts the lid. Hoje's head snaps back from a plump white rat curled up, its head missing. The bailiff snaps the lid shut, shouldering around Rudy Yid and knocking on the glass until the court reporter looks back. He holds up the cookie canister, waving to her to come get one. She shakes her head like she doesn't trust him.

"I'm gonna get Perez" he tells Hoje, going to the holding room door.

It quiets down and the black deputy and the assistant prosecutor move off, leaving the court reporter staring at the back of their heads, the way Hoje is staring at hers. Rudy Yid can hear his breath two feet back.

The female deputy has not returned and the veteran deputy on the other side reads the paper. Needing to urinate Rudy Yid eases from heel to heel, glancing toward the court door, thinking there is a lobby and a side exit in a modern building like this. If he could get down the stairs and out into traffic they wouldn't catch him. Hoje warned him not to look back, but he can turn on him. If he knows anything it's that not only is the hand quicker than the eye, so is the head.

Answering the phone, the secretary presses a button. Hoje looks toward the holding room door as the jokester bailiff has a last quip for Perez before coming back. Hoje steps up and unlocks a cuff. His left hand loose Rudy Yid eases his weight that way. Feeling Hoje's fingers to the right, he glances back. His legs start to shake but he doesn't look down. He will hit him; it won't fly clear, but he has the feeling it might glance.

"I said stand straight" warns Hoje.

The lock snaps open, the cuff swinging back. Hearing the chink, Rudy Yid sees the judge sweep into the room. Feeling all he sees ride up in his eyes as if his life will be lost to him by these people in their positions he lets the folder slip from his fingers to the floor.

"Pick it up" says Hoje, his jaw out.

He can feel him squared off a foot behind him. He bends to the folder. Coiling on a knee he swings back and lets fly.

His eyes cross Hoje's as a fist clips him. Hoje blinks as though he didn't catch what just happened, still straight, when another shot hooks from the left snapping back his head. Hoje drops against the wall.

He hits the door, smacking it back on his skull. Bucking up he jumps over the gallery rail as the retiree sits up as if pierced through the heart. His ears clogged, he hears nothing until he gets out in the hall. Two men in suits at the elevator look over as he heads toward a side exit and barges into a cement stairwell. He jumps down a half flight, a leg nearly giving at the jolt. Grabbing the crossrail, he hurtles down the next two landings before hearing a door slam open above.

At the ground floor, he tries a door, looking out into a marble lobby where a line of schoolchildren stand still at the ring of an alarm. Trying the opposite door he looks down a steep iron stairwell, grabs the rail and heels down the steps to an exit. Pushing the door out aside a stone wall he recognizes the caged delivery dock and steep entry he'd come down in the van. He slips out low but a Hispanic parking attendant across the drive looks up and lets out a yell. Turning round the wall he heads up the ramp into a rain. Slipping between newsracks he goes out ahead of two cars that squeal to a stop downhill. Across the median, he ducks behind a car coming up the other way, then swings around behind a bus climbing up along the curb. Keeping alongside the rear wheel to the intersection, he crosses with it, matching the ching in the wheel stride by stride, when the bus pulls away downhill and the ground goes out from under him. Tripping headfirst he bounces on his hands and knees. He jumps up looking back toward the court building across the intersection. Deputies are coming out and he runs to the overpass, looking down at trucks emerging underneath. He told himself he would jump. Vines are thick on the wall, tempting to hang and drop, but he sees he'll break his legs. Looking back across the overpass to a switchback with curved ramps and overgrown embankments, he slips out off the curb between slowed cars into a gap to the other side. He jumps the switchback rail and slope, bouncing down the embankment between shrubs, head over when his legs whip across into the brush. Working loose he clears his head at the ramp and crosses over. Climbing the middle embankment he slides down the other side nearly into the ramp again, hooking his arm into the brush and yanking back. A half dozen cars go by with drivers staring out at him. He crosses the ramp to a narrow walk heading through a tunnel up toward the freeway. Looking back for a truck to get up on he hears a beat coming.

Under the clouds a copter swings out over the court building. Turning back to the cars coming through he gets looks, recognized as an escapee. He peers around the edge up an embankment to a high line of shrubbery. A water groove at his foot leads up alongside the wall. Seeing the copter circle out wider, he ducks around the wall and scrambles up, snapping his legs over wet slope to keep from slipping back. Near the top he grabs into shrubbery, pulling through to a wire fence. Poking through vines he sees a narrow outlet along a block of old homes then looks back down the embankment at the cars on the freeway. Over on the other side a patrol car forces its way through traffic. Taking digs in the side, he pushes along aside the fence, keeping a hand up not to be jabbed in the eye. A steel power box blocks the way and he gets low around it onto a grooved path. The shrubbery is set back here arching like a tunnel, and he runs so that his pants legs hum. Seeing the street through vines on his right he goes two blocks when the way closes at a fence. He looks down through the wire at a steep dirt embankment and the pillars of the underpass. A car passes below, another comes the other way. Climbing over he slides down the slope, leaning up and running head-on. He crosses in the open and scrambles up the other side, getting a leg over the fence and dropping aside the brush. In a narrow way again he pushes along a path until the shrubbery thins and he stops before going out in the open. Twenty feet on, the embankment tapers down, ending between the freeway and a ramp. Across on the other side the bank rises three times higher than what he stands on, up toward a line of trees at the top; but he can't cross eight lanes in daylight in the open.

Turning back he urinates into the brush feeling it run like a trance coming on. He ducks back along the vines on the fence, seeing a way behind apartment buildings on one side and woodframe homes on the other. Slapping at mites biting his face he watches the rain wash the alley, when a truck with a bed of mattresses standing on end turns out in the middle of the fall with the motor on and smoke coming out the tailpipe. Grabbing the top of the fence he swings over and drops. He cuts through the rain across a sidestreet, going on side patches of gravel when the truck starts to move. The wet pavement echoing like somebody running alongside him he chases it down the middle of the alley.

Drenched up and down he gets aside a garage, ready to go back. On the other side further down the sliding door of an old brick garage wobbles on its track. Angling across, he grabs the bottom corner and pulls it back. Twisting a shoulder in, he pries in a knee and pushes through on the stone floor.

He looks around by some light through a dusty side window. Boxes of nails and bolts are at the front. Old soda cases and stacks of newspapers are at one side and headboards and plywood lean against the back with rolled-up rugs standing in a corner behind a bike with no seat. It's a long time since a car has been there.

His ears clogged from the chill in the walls, he shivers as though plunged in water and startles at a wail. Bracing up at the door he sees a patrol car coming, driving up a fin of water. Leaning away as it comes on with two patrolmen he gets over to the other corner, watching it turn out on a sidestreet. He stands with his nose numb against the crack. He doesn't know if he got far enough but the rain is his friend now. His heart pounding against stone he steps back to shake out the cold in his knees. He takes off his top and rings it out. His pants, socks and shoes are so soaked ringing them out won't do any good.

Pulling the top back on, he steps over boxes of nails and fittings onto a bent Phillips screwdriver that he picks up and slips in his pocket. A stepladder wedged between boxes is draped with a flannel shirt that he holds up and snaps in the air. It is dusty and stuck to paint chips on the sleeves but looks big enough. He looks around for anything else when a beat comes from the distance. Getting back over to the door he looks up through the fall at a helicopter by the freeway. Circling, it comes on over the woodframe homes. Palms over roofs flap and bend while alley fronds along fences ripple like water. The garage door trembles and he holds it at the crossbar. It comes, lights flashing and he looks up at its white belly watching it go by like on a movie screen.

He turns to the side wall to urinate. Letting go a stream that courses through the boxes, he stacks some up near the corner and sits down, pressing a knee against the door to see out. Reeling now that he got away he holds still and gets an idea where he is. When he went over the switchback embankment he saw a freeway lane going north. On the way to jail the bus turned into a freeway heading south, picking up speed and getting near downtown buildings in ten minutes. Working backwards he figures if it's the same freeway he has only to cover the distance between.

The rain stops and the sky brightens and dims like an old Sylvania television picture being adjusted. He stands in the corner thinking foot patrols will come now but it stays quiet until a Vietnamese man comes on a bike with a horn and basket. Through puddles, he goes down one side and back on the other looking between garages.

His legs numb from the cold floor, he sits with the flannel shirt over his shoulders and drops like tears running from his nose. He sneezes between his hands. Closing one side of his nose, he blows out from the other the way his father used to. He looks behind him and notices an old Gallo wine bottle wedged between boards. Unscrewing the cap he takes a whiff of a little left inside. It's not sour and will do him good but he can't put it to his mouth.

As the alley begins to dry a tall Hispanic woman with shorts cut high up over the back of her legs comes out with a bag of garbage, a cold cuts package sliding around on top. The light coming through the crack is cold and the chill from the walls and floor goes up his back. Going stiff there he feels a vapor all over but won't let himself nod off. One nod, another and he snaps back up. Hearing chatter he looks out and sees schoolchildren coming with packs and books. He stares out at their little faces as they move around what's left of the puddles.

He fights the cold as the afternoon fades. It works through his stomach shaking his sides. He watches a few cars go through the alley and a driver get out and pull into a garage.

As he's up he clears an area at the wall, bringing over stacks of newspaper and making a mattress of them. Moving the bike from the corner he undoes the necktie around the rugs and rolls them out over the newspaper so that a side flaps against the wall. When it turns dark he'll get under the rugs and beat the fever building up. As long as his throat doesn't get sore he can beat a fever in a night.

Head bowed like a tunnel digger he sits until dark then feels his way back, easing down on the carpets. He pulls the top two over him holding the screwdriver and keeping his head up from the stink in the wool. The time to go will be around midnight when most of the cars are off the street. He'll wake in time. If there's one thing he can do after working three shifts in a mill for ten years it's tell time in sleep. He thinks of the wire fences he'll have to climb with scraped hands, but wants at them. His worry is to stick to the freeway and not wander out in the streets. Getting warmer he fancies that once he gets to his car, Harvey will have a place in his shack to wash up and old clothes packed away from younger days.

CHAPTER 22

He thinks he's in the steelyard with a jacket over his head. The rugs shift over him and a damp waft from underneath stinks like a scale pit. Feeling a warm rill down the small of his back, he checks his pants to see if he hasn't urinated. He slept so fast he felt nothing. His head feels clear enough to think he broke the fever but his eye is sore and half shut. Arching his back and straightening his knees, he swallows hard. He pushes the rugs off, puts on his shoes and feels his way to the corner catching a draft of air against his chest. He sees no moon. All's still. Pulling on the flannel shirt he buttons up and puts the screwdriver in his pants. Low in the corner he pries himself out into the alley. He stands and it's warmer to him here than in the garage, but his eye is blurred. It's gotten no better.

Glancing around at porch lights he stays to the side thinking he can go all night in these wet clothes. Crossing the sidestreet to the freeway fence he kicks a leg up in the wire and swings over. Scrambling up the slope he looks down at the freeway below. It's wide open with long gaps between cars. He slips down through the brush near the shoulder, looking back to the curved underpass. Two cars swing out side by side whipping by ten feet from his head. Digging in a heel he gets a grip in the weeds and leans up, looking as far into the underpass as he can. He scoots up, crossing the first lane at a swerve of wheels. A car swings out along the far wall. He bobs his head to get going and slips to the pavement. Headlights shooting ahead he bends as if in a wind tunnel. The car curves at him tipping away and he lunges, his leg jumping from the tires.

He gets a leg up over the center divider, waits out a half dozen cars, and heads across. He scrambles up to a line of trees against a fence and bumps along between, climbing a ridge until he's over the freeway lights. Darker as he goes, he comes to an old stone bridge wide enough for a single car.

The fence is over his head and rusty. He grabs on; it doesn't budge. It is twined on top like barbed wire and he leans over it and drops to the cement. Shaking the sting out of his legs he climbs an identical fence right across, dropping aside the abutment. The slope is steeper here and he pushes one leg in front of another working through wet brush into a clearing with piles of burnt wood and tin cans strewn about. Still a moment at what looks like a hobo camp he thinks he hears someone tromping through. He slips into the brush listening, but no one comes.

By glimpses of the freeway below he pushes into a thicket of young trees bent over by the rain. Easing around them underneath, he slips and slides into a ravine, into the drop. Catching into thick branches he yanks himself up to both knees and climbs back up through the growth.

Picking his way, jabbed in the middle and legs he works through the trees, coming to a cleared ridge out over a giant interchange wound around in the sky like a carnival ride. At the edge he looks down a sandstone slope at a wide ravine with a cement wash running water like a river. Letting down to his right he sees the freeway heading out under a sign for Pasadena. He's gone the wrong way but sees only three lanes. There had been four. Backing around the heel under the ridge, he looks down the back slope at a single lane veering underneath a sign pointing north and heading up to a freeway parallel to the cement wash.

Chopping the slope he bounds down and heads across a gravel yard into the shadow below the interchange. It is loud here from the rush of water and run of tires overhead. Looking up at giant stone columns and walls, he moves to the bank over the wash and follows it up toward the freeway, into the lights of cars coming around. He gets to a flat stone path between the wash down to the right and railroad tracks and freeway embankment up on his left. The freeway veers out for a depot strip along the tracks and he comes under cover running behind workbarns and warehouses. He heads to the first underpass thinking there will be a fence to climb but goes straight through into the open.

Past the depot he comes under cover of high brush getting glimpses of the freeway signs overhead, but no names he recognizes.

Doubletiming like a soldier through underpass after underpass he runs against the flow of water, passing islands as thick as jungle that have sprouted up through cement. Not knowing how far he's going he glances back at the distance he's covered.

He goes some miles his legs holding good when the reeds and brush thin. The freeway veers closer to where he can see across to the same high bluffs he'd passed on the way to jail. He'd turned out around them on the bus heading out of the

Valley. He's not far now but running out of cover.

Patches of light glance across his shoulders and face. He could run harder but holds back. Cars honk and lights click into high beam. A patrol car going by will turn to the shoulder and aim a light down at him. He would have no way then but to go into the wash and let it carry him back until he could catch into one of the islands.

His step isn't light now, the concrete jolting him back. Looking back once again he staggers at a dip underfoot. It jolts him to the shoulder blades, the sound of it hollow in his ears. He clears his head and goes on but everything soon seems rearranged. The path has flattened out; the sky ahead lower by half, even the air seems different. Then he feels headlights not hitting him but glancing off the bank. Sidling up the slope he looks back at the freeway closing in around the bluffs and heading away.

CHAPTER 23

He runs under an interchange half the size of the first and comes out on a soft dirt bank. The wash has narrowed, the sides steep here. Going alongside a cinder block wall to the next overpass, he eases down to the edge of the wash and can't see out the other end. It has gone under. Climbing back to the corner of the wall, he hooks an arm over the top and pulls up, looking out across a street corner. Swinging over he stumbles back in wet dirt. Wiping himself off he crosses a sidestreet into an alley, coming up aside a closed market with a coin laundry behind it. An old man sits inside, his back to the window and the door open. From the shadow he sees the old man telling himself a story, laughing and shaking his head at each part. His hands are over his legs with two fingers curled as though a cigarette were between them. Half into the light he calls until the old man turns his head.

"*Where's Lankershim?*"

His eyes brighten and he taps his lips together as if he has an answer. Twice he means to stand up as Rudy Yid waits for him to get a word out. Moving closer he pokes his head in and sees a sink where he can wash up and take a drink but he can't risk going inside. A clock says four-thirty, later than he thought. He turns into a dark street, going between trees and parked cars toward the lights of a convenience store ahead, thinking he'll call out to somebody and ask the way to Lankershim. He comes near and the corner flashes colors. A patrol car swerves into the store lot and another heads up the street. He sinks looking where to turn. Looking up he sees somebody looking down from a front window.

Slipping between car bumpers, he runs to the other side, back toward the wash, ready to take it underground as far as it goes, when headlights come fast. Thinking the police car turned back he heads into a sidestreet, seeing a drive between apartment houses and cuts through it into an alley. He moves through patches of light, when headlights turn in ahead. Getting up between garages he reaches over a gate and flips the latch. He moves around behind the garage, pushing up between bushes to the fence as the alley lightens. A roll of tires comes on wet gravel and a spotlight beams out on the side. He pushes back from the fence, low to the ground at the beam through the fence. Chin down, he sees the bumper of a big coupe. A driver is staring out the side window. The car moves on and he crawls to the fence, watching it go down the alley.

His chest beating to the damp ground, he wonders if it was some undercover man or local vigilante. Every undercover man ever pointed out to him in Chicago drove an old coupe. He stays where he is a minute then moves back around the garage to the alley.

Alley through alley he expects dawn to break. He slows at a wide avenue ahead coming up behind an old furniture store. He lets a car go by and angles into a sidestreet. He passes body shops and a salvage yard coming to the lot of a boarded-up discount store on one side and a row of Quonset huts on the other. Damaged cars with chalk-marked glass line the curb on the right and he moves behind them for cover when a car squeals to a stop up on the lot and he hears shouting. Looking up over a ledge he sees the lights on, two doors open, and two husky drunks the size of football players yelling face to face. They start fighting and the whacks of their fists sound like whaps on a dusted carpet until the one with the bigger mouth knocks down the other and starts kicking him. He can watch no more and sinks back.

At a railway high-line he goes up a rocky slope stepping across a track looking out over razor wire fences of an industrial zone. He goes along looking for a place to get off, thinking the only way now will be to approach a Mexican in a truck and ask for a ride. A white driver will turn him in.

The sky starting to dim he sees lunch trucks being loaded up from a warehouse door. He eases toward the wire fence to call out to one of the drivers when his eye is caught by something further, a break in the silver fence leading into a field of power lines. Footing down the rocky slope into the field he starts going double time under the lines with night fading in the distance. The wet ground giving he comes out in the open as a rim of light lifts over a line of foothills onto an old road with low whitewashed buildings that look familiar.

CHAPTER 24

Coming to the liquor store he goes around a path to the yard in back. His car is covered with dust pocked from rain. The crease has been pulled out and painted. He wipes a window looking in for the keys.

"Thought you wasn't coming back."

He turns and sees Harvey sitting on a pail between a workbench and tree. His head is bandaged under the fedora.

"What happened?"

"A customer come up behind and clobbered me."

"For what?"

"I guess he didn't want to pay. He lit out with the car."

"How much he owe?"

"Sixty dollars."

"For sixty dollars he hit you?"

He nods barely holding his head up.

"You gonna be okay?"

"I was yesterday till noon but I'm no good this mornin'."

"Harvey, I don't have any money to pay you either but I got two guns in the trunk. You could get a hundred for either one."

He helps him to the car. Harvey gets the keys out of his pants and unlocks the trunk. Rudy Yid unwraps a bundle from the wheel well and another from under the spare, showing him a short .12 gauge pump and 9mm handgun.

"Give me fifty dollars and take one."

"I was countin' on your fifty." He leaves the lid open, turning back toward the pail. "My nephew's comin' this morning. Maybe he'll want one from you."

He sits awhile longer wiping his nose and goes in. Opening a utility can, Rudy Yid loads the shotgun and snaps a clip into the 9mm. Filling his pockets he leaves the shotgun on the spare, lowers the trunk lid, wraps up the handgun and brings it over to where Harvey sat. Taking a long drink from the hose, he runs it over his sore eye.

He sits chin in hand when a white Olds comes up the path alongside the workbench. The driver is a white-haired character notched under the eyes which the Polacks on the South Side used to say is the sign of a natural.

"Where's Harvey?"

A young brunette is on the right and a burly character with sorrel hair and silver sideburns is in back. Rudy Yid gets up. "You his nephew?"

"Who're you?" says the driver.

"He worked on my car. He said his nephew might be interested in a gun. I got a short shotgun in the trunk."

He gets out of the Olds, puts a donut bag and cup of coffee on the workbench and follows Rudy Yid, who lifts the trunk lid on the shotgun. As the nephew looks it over the two riders get out to stretch their legs. The brunette looks no older than twenty-six and not like she belongs with these two. In a skirt and blouse she leans back on a heel on the grass looking past the lines toward the foothills. The nephew catches him looking at her and Rudy Yid unwraps the 9mm.

The nephew takes it, calling the burly character. "Ever see one?"

The burly character slaps it one hand to the other. "Army sidearm, officer issue. I had one like it when I was a kid. A police colonel hung it up in a chow hall at Leonard Wood."

"*You* were in the army?"

"No, I worked in the kitchen."

The nephew looks down at the license plate. "You from Illinois?" he asks Rudy Yid.

"Yea."

"I was in Illinois, five years."

"It wasn't Joliet was it?"

"Downstate." He nods, "those jail pants?"

"Yea."

"You the one escaped downtown?"

"How'd you know?"

"It was on the car radio." He nudges the burly character. "This is the one who shanked two jailbirds in their sleep then cut and run."

He clicks his tongue. "He must've got all worked up about something."

"They turtleheads?" the nephew asks.

Rudy Yid guesses at what he means. "One of 'em."

The burly character leans in. "We had a boy in

Leavenworth who was beyond a turtle. He looked like a porpoise. We called him Flipper."

The nephew looks Rudy Yid over. "You a pothead, a popper, a speeder?"

"No."

"Mind if I see your arms?"

Rudy Yid rolls up his sleeves. The nephew pulls his arms out straight, twists his wrists and lets go.

"You wanna go on a job?"

"What kind of job?"

"A stickup. You got the blood for something like that?"

Rudy Yid wraps the guns up, takes them and the utility can to the Olds then gets in back with the burly character. The nephew looks back from the wheel.

"I'm Sam Ellis. That's Jasper Dial sittin' with you and this is Sheila. That's her dancin' name. We three met at a strip joint in St. Louis and sort of gravitated to each other."

She looks over her shoulder and rolls down the window. Sam Ellis backs the car up the path, swings out in reverse on Lankershim and heads south, stopping in front of a Goodwill store. Getting ten dollars he takes a flat from the trunk and carries it across the street. She looks back at Rudy Yid.

"What size pants you wear?"

"Medium long. Could you get me a short-sleeve shirt and a pair of socks?"

"You'll take what you get."

She goes into the store and he watches her through the window as she goes through the aisles stuffing a grocery bag. She pays a woman at the counter and comes out flipping the bag in back.

Jasper leans over to her. "You don't have to snap at people. Our new man's been sittin' here not saying a word."

She doesn't answer and he tugs on her sleeve. "Y'know, Sam Ellis and I were talkin' and he said if he ever buys it, it'd be okay with him if you and me got back to the crib and got it on — and I mean *gettin'* it: legs kickin' in the air, cursin', hollerin' out the name *Jesus.* All that good shit."

"I saw what you got."

"Yea, but did you see the piledriving ass behind it?"

He nudges closer, his side to Rudy Yid. "Y'know I can be good to a woman if she'll give me half a chance. Y'see I know it's not just sex but sensuality. Sometimes it can be beautiful; sometimes it can be raw; and sometimes you just wanna lay there and touch."

"Oh I could just have a bowel movement in my pants" she says.

Sam Ellis is coming back with the tire and Jasper sits back slapping Rudy Yid on the knee. "Yes sir. I learned my lesson first time I married, I was seventeen. She looked like just Connie Stevens on *Hawaiian Eye*, blond ponytail and all."

He nudges Rudy Yid. "You know when the honeymoon's over? You're in there shavin' and she comes in, plops down and takes a shit. It's over just like that."

Sam Ellis turns the car back around and drives to a wide apartment complex. A sign on the wall offers apartments for $125 a week and $495 a month. In front the bushes have been pulled out and a line of trees stunted low.

Sheila gets out of the Olds and goes in through a side door while Jasper goes to a white Ford Galaxy parked by a wall and drives off the property. Sam Ellis pulls around to the rear. Rudy Yid takes the clothes bag, gun bundles and utility can and follows him into the building. They go up a flight and down a hall passing opposite a frail Oriental woman with splints on her wrists.

Sam Ellis opens a door to a front room with a couch, sofa chair and dinette set. A gaunt man in brown pants and a frayed white shirt stands back.

"Got a new man" says Sam Ellis. "This is Hurmon" he says to Rudy Yid.

Going into a room, Sam Ellis pulls a long grip out from

under the bed, swinging it up. He empties out two loaded army carbines and magazine clips, and looks back at Hurmon at the door. "Show him how to use one."

He goes back out to the room straight across, and Hurmon comes to Rudy Yid. One eye stands up higher than the other making him look a little cukoo. He leans forward picking up a carbine.

"You used one?"

"No."

"You weren't in the army?"

"No."

"You must be Jewish or disabled." He snaps in a magazine under the stock. "We had these in Korea. Red Chinese was comin' in waves a thousand across, pickin' up from the dead. They didn't care how many fell. If I tell you I killed three, four hundred, I'd just be roundin' off. I don't count 'em men because the Chinese army encouraged homosexuality among its ranks." He holds the carbine to Rudy Yid. "Thirty rounds on a light trigger" he says snapping in a clip underneath. "Even if the law moves in tomorrow they won't trade with us with these."

Rudy Yid puts his things down and holds the gun up closing his sore eye. Hurmon turns as Sam Ellis and Sheila come out of the next room and leave the apartment.

"What kind of job we goin' on?" asks Rudy Yid hearing the door close.

"Sam Ellis didn't say?"

"No."

"A bank." Hurmon looks on him, holding out his hand. "This is the hand of friendship. You in or you out?"

He takes the clothes bag into the bathroom and gets under the shower. Dirt runs off him like erosion and he dries off with an old towel. The mirror has been broken out of the medicine cabinet; he can't check his eye. He puts on a pair of suit pants, tightens them with a belt and puts on a long-sleeve shirt. He comes out to the table and looks outside at a light rain falling in back. Hurmon gives him the last two bread rolls from a package and a bottle of Coors. He eats the two rolls like wisps and sips the beer. His head begins to slump at Hurmon's words and Hurmon taps him on the shoulder and points to a green couch.

"Go over there."

He lies down senseless and sleeps a few hours. He wakes looking over at Hurmon in the sofa chair mumbling half words and smacking his lips. Hurmon takes his smokes from his pants, lights a cigarette and picks some tobacco from his lip.

"You want the couch?" Rudy Yid asks him.

"I sleep better in a chair. I used to sleep black as a cat but I got married. My wife and me got up four in the mornin', sittin' over coffee for two hours."

"You thinking about tomorrow?"

"Not much to think. We do or quit."

"Sam Ellis know what he's doing?"

"He oughta by now — did five years in Marion. But his mind's not on it. Some men gotta have a woman by 'em. Sleepin', eatin', a woman gotta be there. And he's one."

"She got experience?"

"She talks game but she ain't done nothin'. She started in the colleges out here. Her and her friends used to put on high skirts, slit underwear, and go see cons in San Quentin. She's the reason his brother up and left. He couldn't look at her. And that big boy Jasper. He did ten years in Missouri for armored car robbery. His own daddy turned him in."

"How much money could we get tomorrow?"

"Tomorrow's hardtack money. Biscuit money. Don't say I said but we're joinin' boys up North to take an armored car, and that'll be the last one for me. Sam Ellis can go his way; I'll go mine. I practically raised that boy. I was the eldest cousin. I used to take him and his brother off his mother's hands. We used to sleep three in a bed Saturday afternoons.

Now she's talking about getting rid of me and he's listening. Turned up her nose when she saw me. But I'll save him the trouble. I got more sense in my little finger than they got in both heads. Comes to where a man only has himself. Sleep on a hard board long it's his. I stayed with relatives the last few years. Couldn't find work and whatever I did was no good. Smokin', coughin', rollin' off too much toilet paper. Just the way I sat watching television. I'll ask my time, thank you, and they can wonder where the hell I've gone. I'll find me a little place and live out what I got left there."

Footsteps come down the hall and Rudy Yid sits up. Sam Ellis, Sheila and Jasper come in. Sam Ellis calls to Hurmon. "Let's go."

"You're not waitin' till tomorrow?"

"We're going now."

Sam Ellis motions to Rudy Yid who puts on his shoes and follows him into the room with the carbines.

"We're gonna take a bank. Most traffic is from the lot in back. You're up front. They come in, slip behind 'em and bring 'em down by the side wall. Your gun's gonna be empty. Don't lock one in unless we tell you."

Putting on sport-coats, Jasper and Sam Ellis bulge out in back like two Midwestern trucking executives going to a luncheon. Jasper puts two handguns in shoulder holsters and wraps Rudy Yid's short shotgun in butcher paper. Sam Ellis rolls up a steel wedge in a nylon satchel and ties it around with string. He fills his pocket with clips and slides an automatic under his belt line in back. Hurmon and Rudy Yid lay out car coats on the bed and slide the carbines through canvas straps sewn into the lining. Putting a few pounds of magazines in the side pockets, they lay one flap over the other, rolling up the carbines in the slack. Rudy Yid puts his 9mm and a handful of clips into his pants.

Sam Ellis and Sheila go out to the Olds in back and Jasper, Hurmon and Rudy Yid go out a side door to the white Galaxy. They follow the Olds a few miles west of Lankershim to a

Presbyterian hospital, around back to a street where cars are parked on one side. Sam Ellis takes a hookrod from the trunk and goes to a blue Bonneville, sliding the rod down the window well and pulling up the door-lock. Getting in he tears the ignition wires out from underneath the steering column and taps two together. The engine chinks and he puts the car in gear, pulling out in front of the Olds. Heading back they cross Lankershim, dipping down through a dusty underpass and up a ramp to the Golden State Freeway. Five miles ahead tall palms sway in a gray drizzle.

Turning off aside a golf course, to an underpass, she parks the Olds in the shadow of the wall then comes around front of the Bonneville to take the wheel from Sam Ellis. Jasper U-turns the Galaxy to the other wall and he, Hurmon and Rudy Yid go back across to the Bonneville. Jasper gets in front and Hurmon and Rudy Yid get in back with the wrapped carbines across their knees.

She turns back through the underpass getting on the freeway as a little sun breaks through. The next off-ramp turns out on a long grade heading up to a business area. At the top she turns onto a boulevard with a palm tree along every parking meter. The rain has stopped and customers come out to their cars. His stomach starts to quiver and he's ready to ask to stop so he can run to a toilet. They cross an intersection and she veers into the curb lane. All three in front look ahead to the right. He leans forward and sees the building, Camera City Savings and Loan, diagonal to the corner with an old mission face and cobbled patio.

A bus is at the light. It goes and she turns, moving up past the red zone and parking at a hard angle to the bank doors. Straight ahead the road dips down along the other side of the golf course toward the freeway. Jasper gets out with the wrapped shotgun, heading down the walk toward the rear. Sam Ellis goes up the patio with the rolled-up satchel.

Rudy Yid and Hurmon unravel their coats outside, pulling them on. Feeling his head reel, he comes up the patio holding his arm against the carbine, a little sunshine gaining on him. Getting to the doors, he expects a crowd inside but sees only a few customers in a roped-off lane. He steps in to the right, looking back out as if expecting somebody. In the reflection in the glass two tellers and three other employees are behind the counter. Jasper is toward the rear playing with a pen and Sam Ellis is talking to a heavyset unarmed guard. Looking out at the Bonneville, he sees Sheila staring ahead.

Hurmon comes through the back going up a stoop to a fountain. He nods to Jasper who steps away from a counter and unwraps the shotgun. He starts walking, letting the paper drop. Hearing steps the guard is about to look back when Jasper hooks an arm around his neck and pulls him down. Swinging up the shotgun he goes at the customers. *"Get low!"* A sturdy man in a red nylon jacket is slow to move and Jasper levels the shotgun at him. The man drops straight down covering up.

Sam Ellis climbs over the counter backing the tellers and others to the wall. Getting them down, he unties the satchel, takes the wedge and breaks open a cash drawer. Jasper walks back grinning to Hurmon, taking his place at the fountain while Hurmon comes to the center with the carbine, his head up as if it's going good.

Sam Ellis is at a second drawer, when an elderly couple comes in through the back and up the stoop. Jasper collars them with one arm forcing them down at the wall. Rudy Yid looks back watching the old man tremble through the seat of his trousers. A siren turns his head. A Volkswagen hot rod turning east onto the boulevard is pulled over by a patrol car. He looks out to the Bonneville and sees Sheila looking over her shoulder as a Hispanic patrolman approaches a teenager behind the wheel, while his partner steps up on the curb. Rudy Yid looks back at Hurmon whose face hasn't changed.

A young mother crosses the street heading up the patio with a towheaded boy. Getting out the carbine, he tilts back trying to will her away as she comes up with a red rashed face. She pulls the door and the boy scoots past her. She misses him with a knee, grabbing his jacket. Half in, she sees Rudy Yid up with the rifle. He leans to her and she yanks back caught between doors, letting out a yell. Catching her arm he bumps the door, the carbine clanging on the glass. Across Palm Boulevard the patrolman on the curb looks over. Gripping her as if she were sponge, he pulls her to a corner where she falls to her knees dragging the boy down with her. He gets them on their sides and looks over at Hurmon and Sam Ellis who breaks open another drawer.

Across the boulevard the hot rod speeds away. The two patrolmen go to the car and get the speaker up. Hurmon calls to Sam Ellis. "*Two cops!*" Zipping the satchel, he throws it across, climbing over. He comes up looking across the boulevard. The patrol car is sitting there.

At the curb Sheila puts the Bonneville in gear to pull around back, when straight down the way, a plain sedan swings out in front of two cars, comes up the grade and turns into the rear lot. Jasper hops down the stoop. "They're here!" He gets back with the shotgun ready.

The patrol car turns out, forcing a gap across turn lanes, swinging to the opposite curb. The two patrolmen slide out from behind the wheel with shotguns and crouch low.

Taking the satchel, Hurmon trades his coat and carbine to Sam Ellis for the handgun. Sam Ellis calls to Rudy Yid to switch sides. Emptying the magazines from the coat, he nods to load up.

Rudy Yid snaps in a magazine and gets the carbine up while behind him Hurmon has the satchel in one gaunt hand, the automatic in the other.

In back two plainclothesmen have strapped on vests and edge up along the wall with shotguns. The one in front no more than peeks around the corner when Jasper looses a shot. The glass bulges blowing in shreds across the rear.

Stepping back Sam Ellis drives out the glass in front setting off a clanging alarm. He opens up on the squad car slugging the side so it rocks against the curb. As the two patrolmen press up against the fender Hurmon runs out head down, on shattered glass. A foot slides out and he hits down. A blue Dodge, police flasher on, swerves through the intersection to the red zone behind the Bonneville. A thickset undercoverman with muttonchops and a sport cap sees Hurmon pushing up, coming with the gun and satchel and lunges to the passenger window firing a semi-automatic out the side. A shot snaps up Hurmon's head like a noose. Sam Ellis fires back on the Dodge clipping the shooter's head and whipping a ribbon of blood across the cracked windshield. Snapping in another magazine, he yells to Rudy Yid to go.

Hurmon kneels on all fours dripping on both hands. Rudy Yid comes up behind, pulls him around and hip-carries him throwing blood. Sheila is over to the passenger side. She reaches over the backrest and pushes the door out. He lifts him in face down, swinging the satchel in with him. Getting to the other side he gets the carbine up, looking into the blue Dodge ten feet back in the red zone. The undercoverman twists on his side. His thick face is spattered with an eye full of blood. Gripping the gun in both hands he calls himself by name to get up. Rudy Yid sees he's not finished. He hears Sheila yelling, "Shoot him! Let him have it!" but he can't turn the gun on him.

Sam Ellis waves to Jasper who runs to the front and barges out on the patio. He heads across the glass, picking up Hurmon's gun, coming toward the Bonneville, when the undercoverman gets an eye in the window and lunges up firing with both hands.

Jasper's ear breaks open from a shot. Wagging his head as though he didn't hear it, he falls, the shotgun clacking under him. Rudy Yid turns, firing through the Dodge window, driving the muttonchopped undercoverman man half over the seat, his jaw torn from his neck.

Down the block two patrolmen run through the backup ducking around pedestrians pressed up behind cars. Rudy Yid opens up along car tops sending chunks of metal and glass flying. Sam Ellis is ready to go when a bank customer springs up, leaping down over the stoop. Running out back he is nearly shotgunned by the two plainclothesmen. Skidding he drops straight down. The two patrolmen join the other pair aside the car, exhorting them to shoot. Rudy Yid fires away driving up the hood when the gun clicks. Grabbing into his coat, he sees Sam Ellis run out. In a second of quiet with the hood for cover the patrolmen bob up loosing shotgun blasts across the patio into the wall, ripping Sam Ellis with a wedge of pellets. The back of his neck and ear tear open and he falls flat while another blast scrapes the concrete, swiping his face. He yells out blinded.

The carbine on the car roof Rudy Yid fires back unhinging the hood and clipping one patrolman on top of the head, spilling him back behind the others. Leaning out the passenger door Sheila screams at Sam Ellis to get up. He staggers holding his feet, turning with half a face toward the bank as the plainclothesmen run up from the rear. Seeing one where he just stood, he wobbles back toward the Bonneville in a line toward Rudy Yid when a blast splits his shoulder blades like ribs broke by a butcher ax. Sam Ellis falls and Rudy Yid fires back through the bank pinning the plainclothesman aside the door, driving out the plaster along the metal jam until a round jolts back his head, dropping him at the wall.

At the click of his gun he feels a door bumping his leg. Sheila is looking up at him from behind the wheel.

"It's too late."

Pulling out the door, he pushes the carbine in aside Hurmon and leans up over a puddle of blood from his head. She swerves out before he can close the door and it slams his leg. Cars are stopped ahead in both lanes and he thinks they're trapped when she turns out across the white line and jumps the car over the curb, jolting him straight up smacking his head with Hurmon under him. Straightening the wheels along a lane of grass, she eases the accelerator down ripping ahead, chopping wet ruts like a machine. At a gap between cars she jolts back onto the street, cracking the windshield across, bouncing them again.

Swerving out clear she heads to the freeway veering through the underpass and up the opposite ramp. The traffic is heavy across and she goes along a strip of shoulder, turning down into an exit across from the golf course. To the underpass she pulls up in the shadow behind the Galaxy.

Hearing sirens he gets out in back. Reaching in to Hurmon he lifts him by the collar. He is black with blood. One eye is open, moving a little; his arms shake underneath him on the seat. He lets him back down. As he takes the satchel she is by him, handing him the keys to the Galaxy.

"Stay close" she says looking in.

She heads across to the Olds. He wipes his hands in his coat and throws it over Hurmon, leaving the carbine and shutting the door behind him. Going to the Galaxy he gets the gun out of his pants and slides it under his leg on the seat. Watching from the Olds she pulls out. He starts the car and turns in a U behind her, following her past the ramps through a narrow lane between the freeway and a stone wall. At the next corner the way is clear. Wet with sweat, he rolls down the window, letting in the drizzle, when a beat comes overhead.

Thinking it's straight over he twists around as two patrol cars turn in ahead with flashers on. Sheila pulls off, and he puts a numb foot to the brake, turning to the curb behind her to let the cars race by. She pulls out and he straightens the wheels going after her.

Getting to Lankershim, he follows her a few miles to a familiar intersection. Down the next block is the apartment house with the weekly-monthly sign on the side. He moves up behind ready to turn, when she rolls down the window, waving to keep going.

They go on nearing a city bus yard and turning into a street littered at both curbs. Slowing she leads into a drive between small apartment houses, to the back by a fence. Stopping a few feet over he puts the gun in the satchel and follows her through a laundry room and up a flight of stairs. The door at the top opens to a green-walled room with a couch and table set. There are no blinds and a sour smell draws his breath up short.

She heads into a hall to a bathroom and he goes around the table and opens a sliding glass door to a small porch that looks out at dirt lots and a cinder alley. Hearing her come out he heads back seeing her go into a room on the side. In the bathroom he clicks the switch but there is no light. A little daylight comes through a small window and he looks into a faded mirror at a damp face he can hardly recognize, like a stranger's he half resembles. He stands over the bowl, urine running.

Going back he puts a chair aside the window and shakes out the satchel. The bills fall. He gathers them up, when a patrol car rolls into the alley.

On his feet, he watches the car bump along the ruts to a side street and turn. He goes to the door aside the bathroom and looks in. She is on her side on a bare mattress, a folded-up coat under her head. A valise he hasn't seen before is next to a chair.

"A police car went through the alley."

She looks up with wet eyes. "It turn this way?"

"It went on. You think they're setting roadblocks?"

"I don't know." She eases her head back down.

"We goin' when it turns dark?"

"You'll get caught. Leave with the morning traffic."

"How about you?"

She doesn't answer.

"You goin' your own way?"

"Where I'm going they're not going to appreciate me bringing anybody along. You've got no place to go?"

"I was thinking about the border."

She leans up. "The border's red hot now. You have

anybody, a relative, somebody who knows you by another name?"

"No."

She looks over at the valise. "I have a few numbers."

"Somebody's gonna help me?"

"Yea for money until it runs out."

"They won't turn me in?"

"They don't do it just for money."

"It looks like a few thousand out there. How far would that go?"

"It can get you identification and hide you out. It won't be the Holiday Inn I can tell you that."

"What kind of place?"

"Different places. They can hide you on a farm so you can earn your keep and pass you off as transient labor."

"And after that?"

"After *that* you'd be lucky. Forget everybody you ever knew and get the knack of blending in; and if you can learn to work like they do, and grow your hair like they do, and move on like they do, you might have a chance. I won't have it any easier."

She sits up in front of him. "Why didn't you shoot when I yelled to you?"

"I couldn't do it?"

She stands and goes by him to the bathroom. He waits awhile then goes back to the window to count the money. Stacking the bills in denominations he splits the stacks in two and counts his half. Gazing out to the alley he remembers the way to California thinking he can get past San Bernardino and go into Mexico through the desert. He remembers the patrol cars on the way were one-man cars and if he's stopped, one patrolman won't take him.

The sky darkens and rain falls again. He sits thinking. He remembers Southside Jewish guys who'd been in the army in

196

Texas coming home with stories of Mexican whorehouses at a place called Eagle Pass. As he pictures a dusty town across the border, the drizzle stops and Mexican music comes up from a window below. Two men speaking Spanish go out in back wearing serapes. They light up cigarettes under a carport and one takes out a flap of leather and begins to string stitch holes with plastic. As he watches a thought comes. Picking up her part of the money he goes to the bedroom door and pushes it open. She looks up.

"I thought of something. On the way to California I picked up a hitchhiker going across the country and sleeping off to the side of the road. He and a friend were going to mountains in Mexico to live with Indians and learn how to use a loom. He said it was so high up there it was like leaving the face of the earth. He asked me a couple times if I wanted to go."

"Why didn't you?" she asks.

"I thought I had it better, but who could find you in a place like that?"

"He'd been there?"

"No, he heard from friends. One guy was up there six years and went to New Mexico and made things even Robert Redford bought."

She shakes her head as though she wishes there were a place like that.

"He didn't look like a fantasizer. He'd been hitchhiking two years. You could see he knew what he was doing. You wanna try?"

"The border is going to be strung with agents."

"What if I told you I know a place to cross?"

She grins as if it sounds farfetched.

"It's where soldiers go and we wouldn't be going with nothing. We got four thousand. For as long as it lasts we'll have enough to eat and clean rooms."

She looks as if she doesn't know what to say. He goes to the chair and sits down by the valise, putting the money down.

"Where you from?"

"Up by San Francisco."

"In a suburb?"

"No, a place its own."

"Pretty nice up there?" he asks.

"It looks that way but it's not."

"No, what's wrong?"

"It's for rich people and if you're not like them they leave you out. They don't let you join clubs and don't invite you to dances."

"Is that so bad?"

"That's okay to you?"

"If a guy's not bothering me what do I care if he doesn't wanna dance with me. He can dance with the fuckin' wall for all I care."

She gives him a look.

"You Jewish?" he asks.

"Why do you ask?" she says.

"You're Jewish. I can tell. You got a look."

"What kind of look?"

"A look. I never had it but it's a look."

"Where are you from?"

"Chicago. The South Side."

"That a tough place the South Side?"

"It wasn't bad where they could keep blacks out, but it was full of Catholics."

"They pick on Jews?"

"The parochial school guys but it stopped when they got older. I think the nuns taught 'em. They were hard-bitten over there."

"What'd they do?"

"They were across from us on 38th. They'd catch a guy or throw rocks. Y'know, they see a rock and their eyes dance. But I wasn't afraid of 'em. Not one."

"No?"

"Nah. They hit a kid once and he went into convulsions. The smaller kids on our side yelled back, 'Don't worry, Rudy Yid'll be comin' to settle up.' "

"That you?"

"Yea."

"And *you'd* go settle the score?"

"Yea, five minutes before the bell I'd run out of class, jump the fence and go across."

"Just you?"

"Yea."

"You weren't afraid they'd jump you?"

"*Jump* me." This time his tone is sarcastic. "They were lucky they could walk home. They wobbled. The nuns and women janitors ran out and hit me on back of the head with brooms. They had to call grown men. My mother used to beg me to stop but it was in me. I could feel it in my hands from the time I was small. My father was about as low as they come. He used to tell me I'd come to this."

"Your father was no good?"

"Good for shit."

"He picked on you?"

"Nah. He couldn't do nothin' with me from the time I was twelve, but he begrudged my mother every bite of food and every breath she took. She was heavy and she'd eat a little soup and it would stick in her throat; and her own father brought him to her. She's sitting home and he brings her an old bachelor. It'd been better if she wasn't born. She used to sit in the dark on a Saturday afternoon and say to herself, '*Tateh*, what did you do to me?' But she never hated him for it."

He clamps his hands over his ears and looks down at his shoes. "It's better she's gone. She couldn't have lived through this. Her heart would have split."

She puts her head back to the pillow.

"What do you think?" he asks. "You wanna try?"

199

She looks away, turning her head.

He knows why she won't go. She was through with this business. He could see it in her eyes. Nobody saw her in the car and she didn't go into the bank. She is going to get away and see if she gets identified to this. Even if she is she can say she was misled by two ex-convicts.

He sits in the dark thinking he won't be able to get up, that it will take all his strength. From the second he saw her he could hardly turn his eyes.

The drizzle has stopped and he sits by the glass door thinking five weeks back to the glistening day he'd left Chicago, the gray dappled road downstate and those beaters driven up from Arkansas filled with junk. He knew where those hillbillies were going with a slip of paper in the shirt pocket: Wilson Avenue in hope of getting a garage or a few rooms and hiring on for a Chicago paycheck. How lucky he'd felt it wasn't him, but he would trade places now.

As it turns dark he takes the clips from his pockets and puts them next to the couch. He sticks the gun between the cushion and armrest, takes off his shoes and lies down with his head on his arm. Cold air chills his spine and he begins shivering so hard he thinks he'll pop a joint. He gets up and slides the window shut but the sour cat smell forms up again. When he was small he carried grocery bags full of cans for a cat woman who had fifty slinking around on old furniture and counters. He'd hold his breath in the kitchen as she dug out a quarter. He'd never touched a cat. He could kiss a dog on the lips but he could never touch a cat.

CHAPTER 25

He sleeps jammed up against the armrest bucking his head like an animal trying to push out of a pen. He wakes a half dozen times, his throat sorer on each one. He sits up shivering and looks out the open window. His head is numb and a sharp sneeze brings a stitch in his chest. He wants to sleep once more to clear his head but the damp draft swirls the cat stink from the carpet and he pushes up.

He sits on a cold commode, then washes his face and hands and takes a drink from the spigot. Going back to the couch he tucks in his shirt and folds a handful of twenties. He puts the gun in the satchel with his share, the clips and twenties in his pockets, pulls on his shoes and looks around.

Downstairs he heads out through the laundry room. Wiping the Galaxy's windows, he gets in putting the satchel on the floor. He tries the radio getting static. Opening the glove compartment, he finds a road map of Western states. Without enough room to open it up behind the wheel he takes it out to a light over the laundry room door. Finding Los Angeles he moves a finger east seeing a way through the desert under San Bernardino across Arizona, New Mexico into Texas at El Paso. At the craggy Texas border it's there on the map: *Eagle Pass*.

Back in, he gets a roar from the engine and turns on the heat. The fuel gauge needle comes up to half. Backing up he turns toward the front.

Going two blocks to Lankershim he turns at an open service station and donut shop. At the bus yard, headlights flash along the fence, swinging his eyes left to right. He comes to the overpass he got off on five weeks ago, heading into the opposite ramp, descending over vehicles skimming through the underpass.

The freeway runs up into foothills, splits along a natural pass and starts a climb. Feeling a strong thrum from the engine he passes a San Bernardino sign over two lanes that split away. They wind around a downward slope out along a ridge where cars ahead start coming together. Thinking it's a roadblock, he eases out to the shoulder. To an exit downhill he swerves round a steep curve into an outskirts area.

At a wall with signs for scrap he starts across at a corner, seeing a small gas station downhill to the right. Turning fast he feels something skin up alongside. Wrenching away he clips the curb, bouncing back. Over his shoulder a white sedan is in the middle of the intersection with its lights off and blinkers on. A driver with short white hair, a face as grim as a bat's stares back at him. He leans to the satchel, getting a hand in, when the sedan hits out into the dark.

Slipping his foot from the brake, he straightens the car and eases down the slope into the station. A young clerk is stripping the sides of cigarette cartons, stacking up the packs behind him. Leaving the engine on, he no sooner gets out than the clerk steps into a pantry closing the door behind him. "*Hey!*" He knocks on the glass.

Getting a bad feeling in the dim light he gets back in. Turning out, he goes to the base of the slope along a row of fenced structures like block houses on cemeteries. Crossing a steep drive from an embankment he comes to an inlet with a wire gate and trespassing signs. Looking over his shoulder he rolls back to the steep drive and pulls up the slope into an area of old homes on wide lots.

He goes from corner to corner coming to a closed end. Afraid he'll be stopped for prowling he winds his way back, turning into a gravel lane leading into the dark. Heading out the back way behind the houses the gravel ends at a dirt path alongside a wire fence. Driving to the corner of a field he pulls out across a ditch to a road straight over.

Picking up speed he looks for lights. The way takes on a stripe coming up on an old signboard advertising San Bernardino ahead as a truck transport center. Seeing he's lucked along he pictures pulling into a Union truck stop, getting directions to Interstate 10 from a couple of truckers, then heading into the desert.

He drives without passing another vehicle, coming through a junction with rows of route signs on a crossbeam overhead. None of the plates reads 10 but he senses he missed something and turns back.

Pulling off he brings the map out to the headlights and compares the numbers overhead to red route lines, matching 74 with a route bearing south into 10 not far from Arizona. Along a thin silver horizon into a valley stubbled with brush, the light of day no more than gets over his head, when he begins sneezing so hard his ears ring.

Through two junctions the road becomes blacktop and he eases on the pedal, coming up on a town. Slowing at the sign he goes up the thoroughfare along cars parked head to curb. Four men wearing western boots come up the sidewalk like women in high heels. More townsmen stand around in front of a hall as though there is a breakfast meeting in town. Going by a diner billboard his eyes swing back at a patrolman beside his car talking to a local. They watch the Galaxy go by, looking at the plate. Feeling a leg shake he passes the plots at the end of town, looking back in the mirror.

As the sun lifts, a ring of sweat builds around his collar. Rolling down the window he starts spitting up phlegm like a machine squirting oil. He passes a gas sign, coming to a junction. Turning across a rough alternate he pulls into a trading post. Indian attendants twice as dark as Mexicans stand at a shaded pump by a government Chevrolet. The driver who looks Indian sits half in and half out with a revolver on his hip.

He sees the gun and holster and starts to turn back, when a Texaco signboard for auto repair points him down a road. Turning out he drives a mile farther to an old station ringed by trees and house trailers. He pulls up to the pumps, behind a motorhome with Canadian plates. As he gets out with the satchel, wind flaps his shirt in back like a shimmy cloth. He goes up behind a couple chatting it up with the attendant while young Indians with hair glancing like crows work on tires and cars.

Paying the attendant to fill it up, he goes around back to an old restroom with a stall and sink. He wets some paper, wipes off a spattered seat and sits down to rest as the wind whistles through vents and cracks.

Telling time by the shadow of trees he thinks it's not yet ten when he crosses into Arizona. A low sun in his eyes he comes into a cactus valley grooved with streambeds. As all seems well the car starts to miss, the temperature gauge needle near red. Trying to ride it out he rolls up the window, turns on the heat and drives slower with hot air hitting his face and legs. A squeal under the hood grows like a whistle from a teapot until he pulls off, rolling over dirt to the shade of a cactus tree.

Steam comes up from around the radiator cap. He'd let the car cool before he tightens it but a patrolman would stop and ask if there is a problem. Looking around he sees tracks toward another cactus tree back off the road.

He bumps along easing the car down to a streambed. The shade on the bank is littered by bottles and food containers. Lifting the hood, he gets back in rolling up the window and stretching out. An arm across his face blocks fleas that got in. His empty stomach twists from heat but he's not thirsty, thinking only for the car to cool to go on.

The shade moves off the car and up the bank. His shadow straight over his head, he walks down the streambed sitting down on a sand bench and covering his face and ears from fleas.

Sneezing again, he gets up and goes back to the car, picking up a food package cover and using it as a pad to twist the radiator cap tight. Closing the hood he gets back in, starts up and pulls out. The way clear he struggles with himself to keep a light foot on the gas.

In the next hours he passes two Indian reservations. The gas gauge is under a quarter tank when he pulls off 10 at a junction, into an adobe station run by an Indian family. Giving a teenager twenty for gas he steps into the store, buys a cheese sandwich and bottle of Coors and goes out to some shade on the side. While he eats, two children watch from a worn-out step, and he thinks he sees in their dark eyes that they know he's being hunted.

Keeping the map open he nears Phoenix thinking spotters are set up on the way in. Turning off he checks the map, seeing a way around underneath. He turns onto a two-lane stretch that runs out at an old cavalry road. For the next twenty miles he rumbles over gravel, fearing a tire will rip open. Through dust swirls under a sky bluing darker he gets onto paved road along an Indian reservation, veering back south to 10.

Glinting in his blurred eye the way nears Tucson and he pulls off to check the map again. There's a pass through a mountain area and another Indian reservation but the road marks are so faint he thinks twice. He pulls back on under a lowering sky and gets behind a semi-trailer leading in. Seeing most of Tucson to one side he stays behind the truck feeling its pull. He passes a patrol car with flashers on over on the other side, then another by a ramp on his side before he gets in the clear.

The sun colors like a red yolk. The ground changes, saltpans to boulders, one atop the other like acrobats. The way darkens and his eyes slump at these configurations eery in his lights.

Into a headwind he turns on the heat and picks up a little music through static on the radio. His head sagging at the long open stretch, he feels himself drifting, looks up, sees he's across the line with headlights coming and nearly twists off the road.

Looking to turn off he comes up behind semi-trailer trucks, slipping around one in behind another signaling right for a rest stop ahead. Turning with it he moves around a line of semi-trailers down to a row of cars and motorhomes, taking a space at the curb near stone benches and shade stands.

Getting out stiff with the desert chill through his shirt he buttons up. Passing travelers in jackets and sweaters sitting at tables with snacks and drinks, he holds the satchel in one hand and rubs his forehead with the other, not letting them get a look at him. He urinates into a metal commode and rinses his hands with cold water. There is no soap and he steps outside, picks up a smooth stone and rolls it in his hands under the tap.

Back in the car he gets off his shoes, puts the gun between his legs and stretches out to the passenger side with his head on the satchel. Closing his eyes he feels himself swaying back.

CHAPTER 26

A whirl of dust whips through the benches. A newspaper page flaps against the windshield. He wakes and can't see out, thinking they have him. Grabbing the gun, he shoves open the door and scrambles out on his knees. Nothing is moving but the wind. Down the walk the tables are empty and cleared. Back in he sits shivering. He doesn't know how long he slept but decides it's enough. He puts his shoes on and heads up the walk to the restroom.

Getting back behind the wheel he gets the heat on and heads out along the semi-trailers.

He drives three hours in pitch dark out-distancing the rock formations and stopping at a small Shamrock station opening for the day. Looking around at shrubland he sees he's out of the desert. He pays a young attendant to fill it up. Inside he gets a carton of milk and a package of wafers from a machine. Back out he opens the map and sees he's not faced with the entire width of New Mexico, only half before crossing into Texas near El Paso. It looks like two hours to get there but he'll have to go through El Paso to find 90 which goes down along the border.

Under a dim sky cattle graze on shrub behind wire. He

nears the Texas line passing old signs of barbecue restaurants and souvenir shops. The shrubland has stopped, and he moves up a long grade, seeing another desert south. On new road, he sees all of El Paso nestled against a curl of mountains. Easing into morning traffic, he is side to side with drivers who take no notice of him. They're going to work but he doesn't know the day. He could think back but it would be of no use.

The road turns toward the middle of the city. Two lanes split away and the wind picks up. He veers out without signaling, crossing a solid white line. A black patrol car draws up even, the trooper, a young crewcut Hispanic or Indian with an eye on him and the other up ahead on a heavy green Olds changing lanes. He trades looks with him and gets over to the right. The patrol car swings in behind. It was going to happen now after all this way. Tilting he pulls the satchel up to him. An eye on the Olds zigzagging ahead he feels for the gun, and suddenly loses place. Looking up fast his eyes swivel as the patrol car clears the mirror, crossing the line.

CHAPTER 27

He gets around El Paso. The road is set along the base of a mountain range. He's gone two hours when a rattle starts in and the steering wheel trembles in his hands. He pulls off scraping up a trail of dust. He feared a flat all along but he's lucky he got this far. He gets out the spare, an old jack and iron. Prying off a wheel cover he loosens the lugs, works the housing up under the back bumper and starts pumping the handle. The jack is loose and for every three teeth it works up, it slips two numbing his hands. The stalk sways. Steadying the side of the car he pulls the flat off, gets on the spare and lugs and starts to lower the car when the jack rips down over the teeth, bouncing the car and snapping out the stalk. He jumps or gets a leg cracked in two. Standing back a minute, he wipes his face and bends back down to tighten a lug, when he sees a car coming with a wide grill and double antennas. Fast enough to pass, it swerves onto the shoulder behind him.

A trooper gets out looking at the Missouri plate. He stays down on a knee, his good ear to the trooper.

"What's the problem?"

"A tire went flat" he calls, his breath whistling out.

"Looks like you struggled with it."

"The jack's no good."

The trooper nudges the jack with the point of his boot then picks it up, clicking it like a toy. His revolver is short-barreled with an ivory grip the shade of an old man's teeth. The lattice holster points back over the hip so that the handle is out several inches. He sets the jack back down and stands there as though he's tired of driving.

"You get lots of flats out here?" Rudy Yid asks tightening a second lug.

"Flats ain't the problem. I got 'em comin' down here with old radiators and alternators. I spend half the time doing emergency repair. I get offered tens and twenties like water. My wife says, 'Hell, get your toolbox, go make some real money.' "

Rudy Yid sees the possibilities. "Yea, if you got ten, fifteen cars a day you'd do okay."

"No I wouldn't. The day I put on overalls and come out here I'd never see nobody. Some people find their own dinner and some can't, and it hasn't much to do with you all-round."

Rudy Yid catches on. "Isn't that the truth?"

"Which are you?" asks the trooper.

Rudy Yid grins. "So far I have to say I haven't been able to find my own."

"What kind of work you do?"

"Meatcutting."

"You work for a chain?"

"No, independent."

"I worked in a packing house in Abilene before I got into

the law. Started as a strikebreaker."

"No kiddin'? Doing what?"

"I was a penboy. We got old bulls. We'd get behind 'em, push 'em through a gate into a headlock, and a steel block would come down and bust their head and neck in one shot."

Rudy Yid winces.

"You didn't know they killed 'em like that?"

"I heard but I never knew."

"You don't wanna know, huh? You can stand at the block, break a hindquarter saw and bone, and take yourself home a nice cut but you don't have the stomach for the doin'."

"Nah" admits Rudy Yid. "I used to go to the pens and sneak in and play with the calves right before they went into the room and got hung upside down. I saw it once, like a pail of blood tipping over. My mother used to bring home a piece of veal; I said not for me."

The trooper nods. "I see a lot of hypocrite in that. A man's gonna eat meat he oughta be able to kill it. Reminds me of people who keep a dog and the day comes don't have the decency to shoot it, but leave it out here and let it suffer thirst and hunger before coyotes tear it to pieces. I saw one old boy about eighty let a dog out and sit back on his tailgate, drink a beer before he left."

Rudy Yid tightens the last lug and the trooper looks down at the plate again. "Where you from in Missouri?"

"St. Louis."

"My wife's family's in Granite City across the line. We went through last year. Stopped at the Memorial and had a lunch there on a barge on the river under the arch."

"On a *barge*, they put 'em anywhere now" says Rudy Yid.

"Put what anywhere?"

"The arch."

The trooper's eyes cross. "I'm talkin' about the Gateway to the West."

"Yea" nods Rudy Yid. "They're getting more prestige every year."

Getting up he stoops to the flat, swings it into the trunk, then looks over at the jack at the trooper's feet. Scratching his ear, he walks over, picks the jack up off the ground and takes it to the trunk. He closes the lid, nodding good-bye.

"You got business this way?" asks the trooper.

"I thought I'd see the Old — " stops Rudy Yid at a catch in his throat.

"Usually people go to Arizona for that. They got towns set up. You been sleepin' in your car?"

"Just last night at a stop."

"You bring any luggage? I don't see none."

"I have a satchel. I thought I'd buy what I need."

The trooper nods. "You brought identification, didn't you?"

He sees he made a mistake on closing the trunk. He should have shifted over to the passenger side where the satchel is on the floor. He nods to the car.

He waits for the next word but it's not coming. His heels turn in the dirt. Pulling the door open he gets in and lifts the satchel up next to him. He feels the trooper's eyes as he slips his hand down his pants for the keys and can't reach them. His fingers slip twice before he pulls them out. He gets the key in the ignition, looks in the mirror and sees the trooper still there. A truck roars by and he pulls out in its wind.

At dusk, he stops across a dirt road from a cantina and gets out with the satchel. Leaving the keys and the window down he heads out across a field.

CHAPTER 28

A breeze swathes a coastal Mexican town. An elderly couple sit on a bench in the shade. The woman eats an orange while the man peers through glasses at a newspage printed in

English for tourists. The year at the top is *1988*.
The paper has been read and lies next to the old man's leg.
The woman puts the last section of orange in her mouth, rubs
her fingers with a tissue and gets up with her husband to go.
One takes their place. He wears brown pants and a white shirt
rolled up at the sleeves. He's swarthy enough and his features
are the usually smooth Mexican issue of nose, cheekbone and
mandible, but the gaze of the eyes is somewhere other than
here. He picks up the newspage and looks it over. Turning to
the back he sees:

Vietnam Veterans. We Need Know-how. 134
Revolucion, Guadalajara, Jalisco. See Long:
Freelancers.

The next day he walks an old street, carrying a small
wrinkled bag. Up a flight of stairs he comes to a door with a
Freelancers card taped to it.
He knocks several times and the door is opened by a stout
man, bald except for red stubble on the sides.
"I came about the ad."
"You're American?" he asks in a British accent.
"Yea."
"I told them to cut the ad. When did you see it?"
"Yesterday in the paper. You Long?"
He doesn't deny it. "We have the men we need."
"What was the job about?"
He looks the caller up from the shoes. "Don't matter, does
it?" He starts to close the door, when he notices something
aside the caller's head. His eyes go off center. The door holds
still.
"You were in Vietnam?"
"Yea."
"You look local," he says eyeing the bag. "You live near?"
"I came on the bus."

211

"How far?"

"A hundred miles." The caller looks past him into a dim room with a few boxes on the floor.

Long steps back. "Come in."

Holding the bag against his leg he goes to a chair in front of a desk. A military rifle stands against the back wall.

Long opens a connecting door and looks in at a silver-haired man in a side parlor. The words between them are soft-spoken leaving the visitor straining to hear. Long looks back.

"What's your name?"

"Ted Telez" says the visitor.

Long repeats the name to the silver-haired man and shuts the door halfway, coming beside the desk, in reach of the gun.

"What's the job about?" the visitor asks again.

"We're sending combat veterans to Africa."

"Africa?"

"What did you expect?"

"I thought somebody needed help around here."

"You can hire all the Mexicans you want round here. Mexicans are a dime a dozen."

The silver-haired man comes out, his hand to the caller. "I'm Ted, too" he says in a Scottish lilt.

The caller shakes hands with him, and the little Scotsman's eyes circle his face. "You're American?"

"Fooled me" says Long. "I thought he was one Mexican bugger down here."

"A very handsome Mexican" corrects the Scotsman. "Sit down" he says pulling a chair up close for himself. "You're American of Mexican descent? That what you are?"

"Yes."

"You were in Vietnam?"

"On the Cambodian border."

"They were all on the Cambodian border" smirks Long.

The older Ted ignores the remark. "You met the enemy?"

"Yea. They wrote about us in *Time* magazine."

Ted tugs on his ear and points to the visitor's. "That?" he asks.

"That's something else."

The Scotsman grins as if he'd like to make a joke. "In this business we say there are two soldiers. Those who look where they shoot and those who don't. Which were you?"

"I looked."

"You've seen men fall?"

"Yea."

He taps his temple. "Has it stayed with you?"

"I'm okay."

The Scotsman seems impressed. "A hardened man with a burned-over heart, are ya? Where in the States are you from?"

"The Midwest."

"And you've drifted here?"

"Yea."

"What kind of work have you been doing?"

"Well, that's the problem. They don't let you work. They're nice people but if they see you digging a ditch they get around you until you get out. They don't have enough for themselves."

"So how have you been living?"

"I came with money and when it ran out I tried everything. I tried boxing awhile. Then I started taking care of an old Irish guy from the First War. A good man, a bayonet fighter in the Argonne Forest. I used to get him up in the morning, get his legs going, fix him breakfast and take him to the park and sit with him."

"And you got by?"

"He gave me money and had a cot for me to sleep, but he passed on."

"What have you done?"

213

The visitor nods as if it's a good question. "It was hard awhile but I started helping another old guy. I need work if you have anything."

"Did Long say we have the men we need?"

"Yea, what was the job about?"

"It's a Central African republic with a new strongman. To show he's pro-West he wants a small American cadre. The job is partly to train troops and partly just a presence of Western swagger. It's still a thing there in the Third World, that Vietnam episode. Would it be something for you?"

"I'd go" nods the visitor.

"Before you're disappointed, the pay is not what you might think. Eight hundred a month on a thirteen-month go and if you're imagining lush green land what you'll see mostly is bad patch."

"You found enough men here?" asks the visitor.

"We have twelve billeted near the airport to go tomorrow."

"That's all?"

"That was our number. We get good commission on that."

"You don't go to the U.S. for this?"

"No. Stateside men . . . Let me put it this way. This is a spare life for thirteen months and stateside men tend to get feverish and susceptible to nervous ticks and exaggerations. We've found that men on the drift in their odd about way have the stability for this work."

"Are you the officers?" the visitor asks.

"Oh no. That's past. We're jobbers now. We send you off, then it's back home."

"Will you be coming back?"

The older Ted leans across to the younger. "Ted, is this work you want to do or are you just wantin' to put in some time somewhere?"

"I want to work and go places."

"Then let me come out as to the nature of this business. I'm not a biased man myself. I've seen all things in all men, but those who hire us have battled rebels taught by the Cuban, and to these men, the Cuban, Central American, the Latin in general are of one face. The market on our side is generally for white mercenaries. If you were white we could in a last-minute expedience take you along."

"I am white" says Ted. "I'm not Mexican."

"You're not Mexican."

"No, I'm dark from sun and put oil in my hair and mustache. I could shave it off."

"You're not of Spanish descent?"

"No, I'm from Polish-Russian people."

Ted sits back. "Why did you say you're Mexican?"

"It's an identity to live down here."

Ted glances at Long. "That's one on us and we thought we had it all figured out by now." He smiles. "And Vietnam? Is that true?"

He nods.

"Are you fit? Do you do anything?"

"A lot of walking. Ten, fifteen miles a day."

The older man regards him with warm eyes. "You look to me a respectful young man and in this business one often makes decisions on another man by his look, and I haven't been wrong often. As I said we have the quota and we're just about to close up here, but if you want to come along we can arrange for you to spend the night with the men in case one changes his mind. I can't promise anything but it happens."

"I'd go," says the visitor, "but I have things in León to take care of. I could be back tomorrow."

"I'd hate to have you come for nothing. This way you'll meet the men and have a meal for your troubles."

"It wouldn't be trouble" says the visitor.

"How far is León?" asks Ted.

"Four hours on the bus with the stops."

"Could you call and make arrangements?"

"There's no phone, but a bus leaves at four in the morning. I'll be back before eight tomorrow."

"I could hire a taxi," suggests Long, "and bring him back."

The visitor is surprised by the offer. "I better go myself. I have to say goodbye to the old man and make arrangements for him with the neighbors. I don't want to keep anybody waiting."

"Farewells, eh" sighs Ted. "Tell you what then. If you're willing to come back, one of us will be here until nine tomorrow and then we're off."

He takes a pencil and business card and reaches to the visitor. "In case circumstances change put your moniker and address there so we'll know, if we're back again."

The visitor takes the pen and card. "What happens after thirteen months there?" he asks.

"They may ask you to stay."

"And if I want to go would they stop me?"

"They could but it's usually not done even if there are questions. It would blight their name in the mercenary community. The others you've thrown in with would stand behind you."

"And if I don't want to come back to Mexico?"

The older man knows what he's getting at. "Would you like to start over?"

"I would" he says giving back the card.

"There are ex-nationals along the Gold Coast, men like you see in American films, who know how to make up papers."

The Scotsman gets to his feet holding his hand out to the visitor. "Put all you can in one suitcase. Don't pack a weapon."

"You'll be searched" adds Long eyeing the paper bag. "You have a gun there, do you?"

If the Scotsman had asked he would be truthful, but he regards Long a moment.

"It's my lunch."

"Or *mine*, eh?"

He gets off the bus and goes up a cobbled street to the side of a house. An old man on a metal frame bed listens to the key in the door and begins to weep. "I thought they had you" he gasps as the younger man comes in. "This time I thought they had you."

He sits the old man up and his tears soak through his shirt. "I'm here. It's okay."

"They weren't police?" he gasps.

"No. Two English men." He goes into the kitchen, puts the bag down, mashes a banana for the old man and takes it to him. He washes a mango for himself, cuts it along the stone and sits down at a table a few feet from the bed.

"Who were·they?" asks the old man his tears running.

"Two English guys, I said." A slice of mango slides in his cheek. "They're looking for American soldiers to go to a country starting up in Africa."

"*Africa!* Kiss my ass with their Africa. Did they follow you to the bus?"

"Nobody followed. I told them León. I was looking back." He finishes the mango, takes the old man's plate to the sink and moves a chair over. Turning him back on his side, he sits down.

The old man pinches his lips. "What kind of chances are you taking? What did you expect telling them you were a soldier? You were going to fool them?"

"They're not fighting over there. It's a new boss and he wants American soldiers around. They pay eight hundred a month and they give you a passport when you're finished."

The old man's head raises from the pillow. "And you would go to Africa?"

"They said to come back and there might be a place."

"No, you're not going."

"No, I am going."

"Where are you going? You have one good eye."

"I told you they're not fighting."

"You would leave me here?"

"For a year that's all. You just have to hold out for a year. Esperanza and her sister stop in every day for a little something to do. Pay them twenty dollars a week to clean up and do the buying. They'll cook the rice and meat and set out the pills. Juan at the bank will bring a check for rent and what you need."

The old man's eyes tear over. "What are you doing to me? They took my leg off."

"Your leg was full of stone. The blood wasn't going through."

"No. In Israel they would have saved it. Here they have one way. I gave up everything to come here."

The younger man stands up. "Who asked you to come? I get a lousy message to you that I need a few hundred dollars and what do I get, who shows up? What good did you do me? What did you come for, to weigh me down? I see a way to save myself and I got you on my hands."

"You couldn't have existed without me. You would have starved."

"I wouldn't have starved. I'd have eaten mangos from the trees. I should have never asked. Did I ever get anything from you that I didn't pay for ten times over? You couldn't have dropped two hundred in the mail; you had to come to hinder me."

"They were watching. They came to me four times. Americans in suits with Israelis. The whores at the bank watched me. The whore postentrager had eyes for everything I gave him. I had to disappear from the ground. I went back to Chicago to a cold room. But I knew what to do. Little Mexican Tommy who used to deliver orders for us. I saw him at

Armour a grown man with a stomach, and for five hundred dollars he took me. I went out at three in the morning in January to his truck with money in a belt. I thought he would kill me on the way. We drove like fire twenty hours and he took me across. And without sleep I came on a bus. Another father would do this? I came and stopped walking. Now you want to leave me?"

"You left your own mother and father to the Nazis and ran away. You knew what would happen."

"I could have taken two old people? I didn't have enough to eat myself."

"You could have stayed. Your brother stayed. You were a butcher, a tough guy. The Polacks were scared of you. You could have cut a few throats in your own stinkin' way. Where were you — hiding in the woods in Russia and shittin' behind the trees?"

The old man looks at him as one does at a foolish son. "And where would you be now? You wouldn't be."

"If I was meant to be, I'd have been."

"You wouldn't have known your mother. You wouldn't have known your father."

"Yea I'd have missed a lot with you. Once in my life I ask. You got a kitchen. You have two girls like Esperanza. Old men come here and buy themselves a little television and live. You like the music on the radio. You don't know what you're listening to but you like it. Keep some beer and Ramon and his grandson will come and play a domka with you. You could make a year if you wanted to."

"You want to go, go but you'll never see me again."

"What if you go back to Israel and get your pension back?"

"No, Liba can't take care of me anymore. She doesn't have enough strength for herself. And they would make me tell them where you are."

"They wouldn't do that."

He wags a finger. "You don't know those whores but I do.

219

I can only go to an old home and give them my pension. They take every penny. I wouldn't have a dollar to send."

"What do you want me to do?" the younger man asks.

"Give me an idea. You say you're smart. How long can I keep doing nothing? I know every hole in the street. The women laugh at the way I walk. How much longer before the money runs out?"

The old man's eyes widen. "We'll go to Russia. They have to take me back. They can forget about you in Smolensk. They can kiss us both a full ass in Smolensk. They'll give us a flat and you'll work and find a girl. How many girls look in Russia for a boy like you. We'll pay a taxi to take us to the embassy in Mexico City."

"No, I don't trust them. They'll get what they can out of us and throw us out. And what kind of work could I do there? They'll put me in a plant and I won't even know what they're saying."

"Not Russia, where?" asks the old man.

"I told you, Australia. I could make something out of my life. I talked to an English priest in the park by the port. He said the country was built by thieves and it's not good form to ask personal questions. Those were his words. He said foreigners come with new ideas and do good. The whole inside of the country is meat business. He said it's like America fifty years ago. I should have gone there when I got out of high school. That was the place for me. I'd have a chance to go with ten thousand saved up. I'd start a business and bring you over. You'd still have something to do in your life. You want to go live in a cold flat and count a few rubles for bread?"

His father nods that he wants up and he sits him up, gets his arm around his neck, brings him to the toilet, and stands outside. Standing him up he gets his arm back around his neck and brings him back. The flattened muscles on his heavy bones are so rubbery he slips through his grip. There was never anything about him that wasn't difficult. He lays him on the bed, straightens his leg and pulls the spread up over it.

Turning off the light he sits thinking that if he stays in the chair and doesn't lie down, he'll wake in time to go out and catch the bus, and once he is on the way, everything will take care of itself. His father would last thirteen months. A whore sees to himself.

He looks down at the closed slanted eyes, hollow cheeks, white hair and pajama leg flat on the mattress. *No, not this time.* He would die in his waste right there, even with Esperanza and her sister coming in to help. He remembers thirty years back their store on Kedzie. He played in front of the counter with a cup or toy while his father stood behind the block with a thick neck and whiskers like wire, a murderer's face, angry he had a wife and child to support. A customer named Shulstein, a penny-pincher who came in once a month for a chicken, used to wait until he went in back and say about him that if he'd stayed in Russia he'd have gotten ten years for his face alone.

He remembers dark summer afternoons when it poured rain. Between pours he would go stand out at the curb to watch a stream of black water as high as a man's knee. The women going out of the store would yell, "Gai avek, siz shmitzig," but he used to stand there and study that black water. A weariness comes over him until he feels he'll have to lie down. He goes over to his side, takes off his shoes and stretches out. Looking down over the mattress his dazzled eyes begin to see that water again. He lowers his arm to let it run over his hand and sees a face form underneath, a hard parched face like a European's fifty years back in the war, the eyes up as if they know him.

"Are *you* Rudy Yid?"

The question isn't friendly and he doesn't have to answer; what profit is there in this playing now, but he humors him nodding back with a weak grin.

"Yea . . . *Southside* Rudy Yid."